NEIGHBORHOOD WATCH

Also by Cammie McGovern

The Art of Seeing

Eye Contact

NEIGHBORHOOD
WATCH

A Novel

Cammie McGovern

VIKING

VIKING
Published by the Penguin Group
Penguin Group (USA) Inc., 375 Hudson Street, New York, New York 10014, U.S.A.
Penguin Group (Canada), 90 Eglinton Avenue East, Suite 700, Toronto, Ontario,
Canada M4P 2Y3 (a division of Pearson Penguin Canada Inc.)
Penguin Books Ltd, 80 Strand, London WC2R 0RL, England
Penguin Ireland, 25 St. Stephen's Green, Dublin 2, Ireland (a division of Penguin Books Ltd)
Penguin Books Australia Ltd, 250 Camberwell Road, Camberwell, Victoria 3124,
Australia (a division of Pearson Australia Group Pty Ltd)
Penguin Books India Pvt Ltd, 11 Community Centre, Panchsheel Park, New Delhi–110 017, India
Penguin Group (NZ), 67 Apollo Drive, Rosedale, North Shore 0632,
New Zealand (a division of Pearson New Zealand Ltd)
Penguin Books (South Africa) (Pty) Ltd, 24 Sturdee Avenue,
Rosebank, Johannesburg 2196, South Africa

Penguin Books Ltd, Registered Offices: 80 Strand, London WC2R 0RL, England

First published in 2010 by Viking Penguin, a member of Penguin Group (USA) Inc.

1   3   5   7   9   10   8   6   4   2

Copyright © Cammie McGovern, 2010
All rights reserved

LIBRARY OF CONGRESS CATALOGING IN PUBLICATION DATA
McGovern, Cammie.
Neighborhood watch : a novel / Cammie McGovern.
p. cm.
ISBN 978-0-670-02203-8
1. Women ex-convicts—Fiction. 2. False imprisonment—Fiction. 3. Self-actualization (Psychology) in
women—Fiction. 4. Psychological fiction. I. Title.
PS3613.C49N45 2010
813'.6—dc22   2009047210

Printed in the United States of America
Set in ITC Galliard
Designed by Amy Hill

For Mikie—

whom I love more with every year

NEIGHBORHOOD WATCH

Violence in the suburbs is not accompanied by the sounds we associate it within cities. No screams or gunfire or sirens. In our case, one ambulance, one fire truck, and five police cars moved onto our street and did their work without a sound. We had only a blanket of silence and the frozen images we gathered, standing at our picture windows watching uniformed men, too many to count, go inside and emerge an hour later with a body, tagged and covered. Though the lips of the ambulance drivers moved as they bore their grim weight into the car, we heard none of the words they spoke. Cocooned in our living rooms, we armed ourselves with telephones and called one another with nothing to say except that we couldn't believe what we were all seeing.

It's been twelve years since I lived on Juniper Lane and we watched one another's lives through windows that opened up like TV screens onto the street. I suspect the houses are no longer identical. Additions have been built. Exteriors painted alternate earth tones. I expect it's no longer possible to park in the driveway of the wrong house and believe you are home.

When we first moved onto the block, we stood taller than the trees planted on our front lawns. From the highway, our street looked like an oval of Monopoly houses dropped down in a cornfield. We moved here imagining strollers and children's toys littering the driveway. We pictured sprinklers going, muddy footprints and messes we would one day yell about. We bought these houses assuming the unsettling newness would give way to something else, something more. That was the point, we thought. What we would bring to the identical beige our houses were painted. Life. Mess. Children. But then nothing transpired as anyone planned. For a while it was better than we imagined. And then it was worse.

I was the one who'd insisted on this house. From the first time we saw it, I wanted it more than I could even explain. "Please," I told Paul, who looked a little pale at the prospect of a mortgage a thousand dollars a month more than we could afford. "We won't spend money for ten years after this," I promised, imagining this community would feel like a safety net, a family of some kind, assurance that we wouldn't be alone.

Then we moved in. The first neighbor I met was Kim, a Korean mother of three. She came over, dictionary in hand, to apologize for what she'd done to our toilet. "It's a terrible tragedy," she said, flipping through the pages of her Korean/English dictionary.

"A tragedy?" I said.

"I flush diapers and everything gets backed up. I didn't know."

We learned soon enough, when we found a stranger's tampon floating in our toilet bowl, that the problem—clogged pipes—was endemic and not easy to resolve.

"Isn't it awful?" asked Barbara, the second neighbor I met. She told me she used a strainer to fish the stuff out before anyone else saw it. "I'm a little tired of hearing my husband point out all our problems."

It was unsettling, to say the least.

"Yours might be better!" she said, walking away. "Don't listen to me!"

I try to remember things as clearly as I can, living as I do now in close quarters with women who know nothing of suburbia beyond what they've seen on TV. I tell them it wasn't all perfect. Some days it felt as if we hovered expectantly, our collective breath held for some new piece of bad news. I tell them nothing was exactly how it looked. Some days it seemed as if the drama we'd moved there hoping to avoid was, in some way we couldn't explain, what we were all waiting for.

One thing that's easier about living in prison: The worst has already happened.

CHAPTER 1

In the twelve years I've lived in the Connecticut Correctional Institute for Women, I've tried in vain to forget about the past and focus instead on the here and now, on contributions I can make to improve the quality of life for everyone in here. I am different than most of the other inmates, who've grown up in either juvenile detention centers or trailer parks they shared with rats that were, for some, more pleasant than their stepfathers. Scratch a female inmate, I've discovered, and you'll usually find a girl whose mother had terrible taste in men. I've also learned this much: I'm not better than any of these women, nor—for all my education and degrees—am I smarter. We've made the same mistakes, misjudged other people and ourselves.

Officially I am the prison librarian, a job for which I get paid thirty-five cents an hour. I solicit donations from publishers and local libraries, and in twelve years have transformed a bookshelf of thirty tattered paperbacks into a library of more than six hundred titles, some delivered straight from the publisher. Books with pages so sharp and clean the girls have gotten paper cuts turning them.

For the last six years I've also served as an inmate representative on the prison welfare committee. There I won Wanda her right to keep more than one nail polish in her cell so she could re-create her old days as New Haven's most popular manicurist, the life she had before she shot and killed the husband who'd been beating her for fourteen years. Wanda is my best friend here, and I believe her when she says she felt like she had no other choice. *What's done is done,* she says, *and I'd like to get back to work.*

To a certain extent, she can. Not for money, of course, but she can ply her trade, as can I. Once upon a time I was at the top of my class in the UConn Library Science Program. I was the first hired and the fastest-rising assistant to the head librarian the Milford Town Library had ever seen. Readership, circulation, and interlibrary loans all increased under my stewardship right up until the day I was arrested, after which, of course, I have no more figures. We were on the cusp of numbers that would win us more state funding. I wouldn't mind knowing what became of that, but I don't.

The media dubbed me "the Librarian Murderess." One newspaper described me as a "Victorian Volcano," as if being a librarian might still be a reflection of one's sexual mores, which of course is ridiculous and archaic thinking. We librarians like books. We also enjoy research. Above all, we like serving people, which is what defines librarians, not our myopia or our sexless hair buns. We believe that when books are present and learning is possible, all people benefit. In my time here I've watched a twenty-three-year-old woman learn to read to keep up with her daughter in the first grade on the outside. I've watched another go from reading only the worst of our most popular titles—the blood-soaked crime novels the women here have a bottomless appetite for—to other genres: a collection of short stories, a biography of a tennis pro. Small satisfactions, but real ones nevertheless. Sometimes I believe I've made a larger difference here than I could have at my old job, where—let's be honest—the illiterate didn't often walk through the door.

But a recent flurry of attention surrounding my life here has been a little unnerving. Some years ago, following a *Phil Donohue Show* featuring inmates freed after new DNA testing proved them innocent, I had twenty women stop by my library looking for stationery and ball-point pens. I'll admit that I got caught up by the episode, too. The shaggy-haired blond man looked in the camera, one prominent front tooth missing, and said, "Freedom is the sweetest drink I've ever tasted." He'd served twenty-six years in prison for a rape he didn't commit against a woman he'd never met. For the women who came in, I started an impromptu seminar on formal letter writing: "Don't end every sentence with an exclamation point!" I told them. "Don't dot your *i*'s with little hearts!" For me, the pleasure was watching women who'd written nothing for years pick up a pen and compose sentences on paper. *Yes,* I thought, my heart filled with the warmth of purpose, *here it is, the reason I'm here.* None of us knew there would be a two- to three-year wait for new DNA testing. That it would require petitions, judges' orders, and exorbitant costs. Or that the tests were often too inconclusive to warrant a new trial or verdict reversal. I learned this only over time, doing my own research. I tried to tell my writing group not to get their hopes up. "There's a backlog of requests since that show," I said. "Hundreds, probably." More like thousands, but I didn't want anyone to get too discouraged.

After a few months, the group whittled down to a handful of the most single-minded women, who, unfortunately, also seemed the most guilty. Rayanne, in for stabbing her landlord, a crime witnessed by eight other people, has continued writing letters steadily for four years, pleading for her case to be reopened. She was being threatened at the time of her crime, she argues. She was high on drugs. The place was dark. She heard a gun. What she means is, *Yes, I did it. But it wasn't my fault.*

I wrote letters, too. As an example for the others, and thinking of the blond man imprisoned for twenty-six years. I loved his story, the footage they showed of his handwritten note. For a year, I received nothing beyond the standard form letter, cautioning patience and explaining the inundation of requests. Then, about three years ago, I got a letter which I thought at first was from a lawyer. Inside the envelope, typed on a plain white sheet of paper, was a single sentence: *Think about the cat.*

I assumed it was meaningless, sent by one of those mysterious people who write anonymous letters to inmates. I almost threw it away, but something about it struck me, and for a few days I used it, folded up, as a bookmark.

Every time I opened my book to read, I touched it and thought, *What cat?* We'd never had one. Paul loved animals but was allergic to so many things we never dared venture into adopting pets, not even as a replacement for the children we didn't have. I thought of my older sister, Claire, who worked at an animal rescue center and talked about animals in a way that sometimes seemed dangerously eccentric. I wondered if she was trying to say that my plight was nothing next to some cats she knew. It occurred to me only later, doing sit-ups with my cell mate: *Linda Sue had a cat.*

Or there was a cat in her house the day she died, anyway. I never heard her talk about it. But I saw it once in her upstairs bathroom peeking out from a cabinet underneath the sink. I could picture it perfectly— the yellow-green eyes in the dark, how I bent down to pet it and saw something else. I meant to say something to Linda Sue, but in the blur that followed I didn't. I couldn't.

So what happened to it?

There was no mention of any cat at my trial, no inventory of bowls or litter boxes in the files of discovery from the police. After Linda Sue died, no one once mentioned a cat that would need to be adopted. Apparently no one else knew she had one.

What happened to that cat, hiding coyly in that bathroom cabinet eight hours before her owner was murdered? It probably disappeared at some point while a team of strangers wearing gloves and surgical booties swarmed into the house, leaving doors open in their wake. A cat witness to a murder would offer even less than a dog, who might have barked at an outsider or the sight of its master bleeding to death at the bottom of the stairs. A cat would offer fewer clues. Except this one: Someone else saw it, too. Whoever wrote this letter was there that night. And after twelve years of silence that person was getting in touch with me.

With no return address and no readable postmark there was no way to trace the writer of this note. But it activated me again. I got the address of a new Innocence Action office that had opened up in our state. I wrote them a letter saying I had recently received new information regarding my case and would appreciate an opportunity to talk to a lawyer about some overlooked avenues for defense at my trial.

Four months later, Jeremy Bernstein came to see me. The first time we met he looked so young and handsome, even with his tortoiseshell glasses and terrible razor rash. It had been years since a man had tried to shake one of my manacled hands, and I felt a little breathless just sitting across from him. He took all of thirty seconds with the cat letter before folding it up and sticking it back in the envelope. I feared the interview might be over before it began.

But no. He told me he didn't know what to make of this cat business, but he'd been reading my file. Did I realize a hair had been found in the blood beside the body? Maybe he was nervous, too. He did a lot of paper shuffling. "And skin cells from under the victim's fingernails. Did you know all this?"

Yes, I said, laughing. *Of course I did.* They were never tested because our defense strategy—that I was a parasomniac, sleepwalking when I committed the crime—didn't require it. I never argued that I wasn't at the scene of the crime. I said I wasn't conscious when I did it. Jeremy leaned forward. "I've applied to have them tested," he whispered, as if this should be a secret between us. "I've been looking over every-thing—the fingerprints, the weapon—and I think it's possible you weren't even *there.*"

He was studying my face, measuring my reaction. On record I have psychologists supporting my claim that I don't remember what hap-pened that night. For three days after Linda Sue's death, I watched in disbelief as the murder of our neighbor got played out nightly on the local news. I responded as any neighbor would, making phone calls as the story spread like a virus around the state—*Yes, that's right,* we had to tell people. *That's our town, our Juniper Lane. Our dead neighbor.* I moved between the library and home in a frightened daze with a grow-ing sense of unease I couldn't place until the night I found my night-gown at the bottom of my laundry hamper, stained with a great Frisbee-sized circle of blood.

I washed it, assuming the blood was my own.

Only later did I see that the stain was on the front, spread across the chest, an unlikely placement for a menstrual stain. Realizing this, I moved as if following someone else's orders. I folded my nightgown, the stain a faint pinkish brown, placed it in a bag, drove first to the library where I worked and then, a few hours after that, to the police station, where I told them I needed to talk to someone. Eight hours later, with a detailed description of my past parasomniac episodes—most, but not all, dating back to my childhood and college days—I signed a confession. While I had no memory of the night, I believed that in all likelihood I was responsible for the murder.

Jeremy has said the whole sleepwalking defense was a ridiculous gamble no right-minded lawyer should have taken. My defense should have pointed out the almost entirely circumstantial evidence against me. Yes, my fingerprints were in Linda Sue's bedroom, but I had been in her house on the afternoon of her murder. She had given me a tour of the upstairs, taken me into her bedroom. Other than the bloody nightgown stain (untestable because I had washed it so quickly), no physical evidence except the fingerprints directly connected me to the crime.

The weapon had been washed ("with such care for a sleepwalker," the prosecutor at my trial enjoyed pointing out). I'd also left no footprints anywhere in the blood, showing more foresight than O.J. had, they said. What clinched my innocence in Jeremy's mind were the photographs of the nightgown and the solid, oval stain of blood. There were no spatter marks at all, which, given the manner of death (head bludgeoned three times), would have been impossible. "How do you bludgeon someone and get a stain like that? I don't understand what they were *thinking,* frankly. There was spatter on the floor and on the walls and none on your nightgown? It's ridiculous."

Jeremy is a sweet man, not young enough to be my son, though now that seems to be the tenor of our relationship. In the three years since he began working on my behalf, he has gotten married and fathered a child. I've seen baby pictures, one including his wife, Laura, looking ashen and weary, propped up in bed, a blanketed baby at her side. Beyond that one picture (which, I have to admit, I have a hard time forgetting), I can't imagine what his home life is like. I don't know if he's a hands-on father who changes diapers or a distracted one who eats quick dinners and returns to work. Judging by the amount of time he's devoted to my case, I'd have to guess the latter.

In the beginning the careful attention Jeremy paid to the details of my trial embarrassed me enough to wish I'd been more present at it. If I'd paid better attention, would things have gone differently? Jeremy has called Franklin Mayhew, my first lawyer, an idiot and has cited incompetent representation as the basis for my habeas corpus appeal. I certainly see his point, but at the time, we honestly thought we had the best lawyer money could buy. My husband, Paul's, boss had recommended him, saying he'd gotten his son off a third DUI arrest. "Miracle worker," he said. We dialed the number because we needed a miracle. We liked Franklin's small and unpretentious office—and the fact that he rode his bike to work. If the helmet sitting on his desk seemed odd, we chalked it up to absentmindedness for unimportant details. That he worked on his own, with an answering machine for a receptionist, might have been a red flag, but he waved away any doubt by saying, "Low overhead is my secret. I take no case just for money."

Though he took a lot of our money, almost all of it in fact, we still stood by him. After the verdict was announced, I squeezed his hand and told him not to feel bad, he'd done his best.

By that point Paul had developed an edge I hadn't. It was through thin lips and a stiff handshake that he thanked Franklin, just before I was led away in handcuffs.

As I've reminded Jeremy, it wasn't entirely Franklin's fault: I confessed, after all. Any defense lawyer would have had a steep hill to climb clearing me. "Who confesses to a murder they didn't commit?" the handsome DA asked. The jury nodded in unison like a dozen marionettes, woodenly agreeing with their puppeteer. "You'd have to be either crazy or guilty. And since we've established the defendant wasn't the former, that leaves only one possibility."

After I started working with Jeremy, I understood that there are lots of reasons innocent people make confessions. Developmentally disabled people are more inclined to confess once they understand what the interrogator wants to hear. Juveniles and people with mental illness, ditto. I don't include myself in these groups, but I can relate to them. I know how it feels to sit alone in a room with detectives who insist on one version of events. In my case, one of the detectives, an older man named Don Fenlon, spoke gently, saying he wanted only to help me. He had a sister named with my name—Betsy—and no children either. I believed him when he said that most people in my situation agree to some part of the charge. "Here's the trick," he whispered. "Start showing remorse right away. That always helps. Play your cards right, you might get away with involuntary manslaughter. I can't promise anything, but I have a feeling these guys like you."

I *was* an innocent back then, a child when it came to the judicial system. I thought he meant *like* in the social sense. I didn't know *like* also meant: *They're pretty sure you did this crime.* I thought being liked would help, that telling the truth—I didn't know what happened, didn't remember the night—wouldn't be a mistake. According to the transcript, I asked twice about speaking with a lawyer and was told both times that it was "a little early for that." Once, someone said, presumably as a joke, "Do you have any idea what those guys charge?"

Was I naïve to believe for so long that the detectives meant me no harm? That we were all working together to get to the bottom of what happened? Yes, I told them, Linda Sue and I were acquaintances who had been spending more time together. She'd invited me into her house, where she admitted some surprising things to me.

"Like what?" Detective Weaver asked. He was the younger detective and unattractive in the extreme, digging for earwax one minute and propping his dirty shoes up on the table the next. "Sexual stuff? Was that it?"

"*No*," I said. He stared at me and waited. "She had recently developed a new friendship with one of our male neighbors. We talked about that."

He looked down at his notes. "This is Geoff you're talking about, right?" He folded a piece of paper and used it to dig some dirt out from under his fingernails.

"Geoffrey, that's right." No one called him Geoff.

"Friend of yours, too?"

"An old friend of my husband's. They grew up together." To my everlasting regret, I kept going when he rolled his hand in a gesture I interpreted as encouragement. "We all like Geoffrey. He's an author, quite a successful one. Not that his book was still a best seller, but I suppose just writing one seems glamorous."

He sat up and lowered his filthy shoes to the floor. "To you, you mean."

Now I understand that those detectives had written their story before they asked me a single question. I was a lovelorn librarian, crazed with jealousy over my neighbor's good luck. "*Everyone* loved Geoffrey," I insisted, a quote that got repeated at the trial more times than I can count.

In recent years, the most famous false confessions came from the Harlem Five—the teenagers convicted of the Central Park Jogger assault who served thirteen years in prison until another man confessed to the crime. After DNA confirmed their innocence, all five were exonerated and released from jail along with their sad stories: one had an IQ of 87, and another, 73. None could read above a second-grade level. Though we don't share these numbers, we share the same mistakes and believed the same lies. We've sat across from police officers and told them exactly what they wanted to hear. Without getting my hopes up, I've started reading a little more about exonerees freed since that *Phil*

Donohue Show. Most of them have been black men, victimized by a mistaken eyewitness, their crime nothing more than walking down the wrong street wearing the same gray sweatshirt or blue baseball cap a victim described to police a few hours earlier. Overeager police have a hard time letting go of wardrobe coincidences, I've learned. If anything, these men are more innocent than I. Most were nowhere near the crime, never knew the victim, and had no idea why they were brought to a police station for questioning.

I knew the victim. I had become an unreliable confidante and repository of her secrets. I participated in "neighborly" efforts to help Linda Sue that I see now only isolated her further and sealed her fate. If I didn't leave my hair in a pool of blood beside her body, I am not without some culpability. Though I still don't remember what happened that night, I remember all too well what happened in the weeks and days before Linda Sue's death. And what I *can* remember from that night—what we talked about in her living room, what I saw upstairs—made me wish her, if not dead, then eradicated somehow. Gone from our lives. No, whatever the DNA tests show, I'm not wholly innocent.

I suspect none of us is.

Three weeks ago, Jeremy got the results of the test on the hair found in the blood beside the body. It wasn't mine or the victim's. Traditional DNA testing on hair is a fallible science—hair is not composed of living material and therefore has no genetic markers. But as luck would have it, the follicle, still attached, contained enough markers for three out of four experts to conclude it wasn't mine. Enough evidence for a sympathetic judge to rule in my favor, a judge who is on record as having opposed the death penalty and mandatory sentencing. For once in this whole process I got lucky. The judge wanted to make an example of the flaws in the judicial system he'll be retiring from soon. "Everyone wants to leave a mark," Jeremy told me. "You're his."

I've tried to keep this a secret, but I'm not sure it's worked. I've learned that women in prison can be extraordinarily generous, especially in hard times. I've watched my fellow inmates nurse one another through sickness and spend their last commissary dollar on Christmas presents they hand out wrapped in toilet paper. I've also seen the wall of silence that goes up around anyone who gets special treatment. I fear it's already started. At lunch, when I asked Taneesha to pass the salt, she said I was a bitch if I thought I could get whatever I wanted around here. Everyone's been prickly, even Wanda, who says she doesn't want to know when I get the news. She's not around when the guard finds me in the library and tells me my lawyer is here.

I walk into the small, beige-colored conference room, where we're allowed to sit, unshackled, alone with our lawyers, and I already know what he's going to say. Jeremy can't control his facial expressions or his body. He's a foot tapper, a finger drummer. His body talks for him. This time, though, there's none of that. He simply leans forward beaming like a child. "There's no match!" he whispers. "We're getting you out of here!"

CHAPTER 2

Whmen I first came to CCI, I spent four days being asked so repeatedly about my feelings for events I didn't remember that I started giving the answers they seemed to want. *What difference did it make,* I thought. *My trial is over, my fate decided.* "Yes, I probably did love Geoffrey Steadman," I said, sighing. "Everyone did. He was that kind of man."

The intake therapist looked at me. "Manipulative?"

"Charming. Smart. Funny in those unexpected ways." I smiled and held her eye. She had short gray hair and looked maybe sixty, but I thought she recognized what I was saying. Did I sound crazy? Like those poor Manson girls with their tattooed foreheads and unwashed hair? Surely not. Surely people could recognize what I would still—even then, in spite of everything—characterize as a relatively normal, married person's crush.

By the time I got my cell block assignment, I was already something of a celebrity. Not that people welcomed my arrival, just that they were aware of it. They assumed I was crazy and rich, and for a while I let them believe both things. With so few ways to differentiate ourselves, I took advantage of silly ones. I used expensive tea bags and washed my underthings every night. I medicated myself into a stupor by doubling the doses of the Elavil I'd been prescribed by the psychologist, who didn't know I had two other prescriptions in my bag. For months I moved through my new world in a gray fog I couldn't taste or feel. I slept fourteen hours a night and shuffled through days, exhausted and yawning. I have very few memories of the time before Wanda arrived and became my first cell mate to ask if I knew what the rules were about nail polish in here. "Someone told me you can have one color only, someone else said three."

I lifted my head off the pillow and grunted. I knew she was in for murder, a long-termer like me, looking at thirty years, and she was thinking about nail polish? "It's not me I'm worried about, it's everyone else," she said. "I like to offer choices."

Within a week she'd begun an exercise program of sit-ups and weight lifting using cinder blocks she found outside in the yard. She tacked up a daily activity schedule including time for work, self-improvement, and isometric exercises. She asked me for advice on the self-improvement portion, and then, after I threw her a book from my side of the cell, she said that what she really wanted to do in here was meet some men. I wondered if she was taking the opposite drugs I was. Uppers of some kind. "In a women's prison?"

She pointed out the window at the medium-security men's prison across the way and flicked her hair. "There's Riverside over there."

We were about the same age I guessed, in our mid-thirties. She had thick, long brown hair, skin the color of honey, and cheekbones you could roll a marble around in. She walked over to the window as if she might catch a lineup of prospects along the fence. "You see them sometimes, right?"

"I guess," I said. We had a maintenance crew of inmates from the men's prison that came through occasionally to fix a toilet or a broken light. I knew girls who put on makeup and changed their clothes before they came. "If you're interested in that type."

"What?" Wanda laughed. It was her second week and already she was laughing, full-throated and deep. "Like we're better than them?"

I let myself get swept up in Wanda's campaigns for longer exercise times, more nail polish, and eventually a real library. She was the one who pointed to the shelf of water-damaged books and said, "I bet you could do better." She got me going again, thinking about the rest of my life. "Look," she said one night after lights-out. We were lying in our beds, like two girls at camp. "I spent seventeen years coming home every night to a terrible man. Being here, it's like I'm free."

I think of Wanda as the best friend I've ever had, which might be a surprise to my old neighbor, Marianne, who has made a duty out of visiting me twice a month for the last five years. Though nothing is official—we're awaiting judge's orders, which means paperwork and bureaucracy—she's heard the news from Jeremy. "I just can't believe it," she says, beaming and shaking her head. "You're coming to stay with me when you get out. That's all arranged."

I'm surprised by this and also grateful because I don't have too many other options. Or, if I'm being honest, any.

"Jeremy's a little worried about you moving back on the block where everything happened." She means the murder, of course. "But I told him it's all new people now. Everyone you knew has moved away. Really, Bets. I think it'll be fine."

Her face tells me she's less sure. I know that visiting has been one thing, but living together might be different. I reach a hand across the table and squeeze hers.

In the last two years, we haven't been required to wear handcuffs for these visits, which means that before every visiting day, Wanda paints our fingernails and we sit in this room doing everything we can think of with our hands: waving broadly, gesturing like mimes. Though full body hugs are allowed only at the end of a visit (and Marianne and I generally pass on this), I've come to appreciate the simple pleasure of a hand squeeze. "Thank you," I say.

I give Marianne credit for her loyalty over the years. On Christmas, she brings me chocolate and on my birthday, a present, though I do sometimes wonder if she's wrapped something she found around the house. Last year she gave me a clear plastic desk organizer. "For paper clips and staples," she said. I didn't know what to say. It's been twelve years since I've seen a staple.

I appreciate her good intentions, even if our visits can be awkward. We pick our subjects carefully. She asks very little about my life inside, and we no longer mention her daughter, Trish, or her husband, Roland. I don't know what he thinks about my staying in their house or if he's even still there to offer his opinion. It's possible he's left and Marianne has never mentioned it to me, because I know how her mind works. She believes my life is hard enough and I shouldn't have to hear bad news. When I've asked about Trish, she's said only that "she chooses not to share her life with us," which I now realize means they don't talk at all. She doesn't know where her daughter lives, or what she does. I know Marianne visits me in part to fill in the holes she doesn't like to think about too much. At one time she helped me adapt to our neighborhood life of surfaces and veneers, and now—as unlikely as it sounds from my spot here in prison—I help her maintain it.

When we first moved onto the block, Paul and I were twenty-five-year-old newlyweds who'd never cared for a houseplant, much less a house with a garden in front. We were beginners at everything, our ignorance on display every weekend as we stooped over chores we'd never done before—sealing a driveway, edging a flower bed, cleaning the gutters. Marianne and Roland were older than we were and experienced in these matters. They talked us through the basics of replacing storm windows and laying new grass seed over a half-dead lawn. She was patient and nonjudgmental, a maternal figure, though she was only ten years older. I imagined our life might look like theirs down the line, with two bookish children and oddball interests, like the solar panels they'd stretched across their roof.

Now with only twenty minutes left, Marianne pulls her hand free and remembers something she brought in her purse. I'm allowed to accept nothing from visitors except the quarters that must be used in the vending machines before the hour is over. Even a magazine article is contraband, as Marianne must know because she shouts at the guard as she pulls it out, "I'm just *showing* her something, for God's sake."

I'm grateful she doesn't scream, *Plus she's innocent,* to add to my problems.

"Wait'll you see this," she says, unfolding the article. "It's about Geoffrey."

We've tried to make Geoffrey a joke between us. He lives in Los Angeles and writes for television now, a crime show so stupid Marianne has declared it unwatchable, though she has, at least a few times. "Be glad you didn't see Geoffrey's show last week," she'll say. "A serial killer into dismemberment. That was nice." I've never seen Geoffrey's show because in here, guards control the remotes and we watch the same lineup every day: *Oprah,* then *Ellen,* then the reality shows that we talk about afterward as if we knew these people personally. The article is from *Finer Homes Digest.*

"Turn the page," Marianne says. I gasp. It's the first time I've seen a picture of him in twelve years. The caption below reads, "Geoffrey Steadman and his wife, Renata, chop vegetables on their Ashfield stone countertop." From Marianne's updates, I know that he has two daughters—six and four—both adopted from China. In the picture, the two adults face the camera. The girls are seated at the counter opposite them, two tiny heads with straight black hair, shoulder length. I do the math and figure out this means they probably spent at least four years battling infertility, which makes me feel both sorry for them and grateful. He knows now what it's like, month after endless month, to discover you are once again empty-handed.

CHAPTER 3

The first time I met Geoffrey was at my wedding, where he came as Paul's childhood friend, not yet a published writer, not yet famous, with his mother as his date. Both Paul and I were nervous and ridiculously uncomfortable. During the ceremony we recited our vows so softly we had trouble hearing each other. When Geoffrey stood up to offer a toast at the reception, obviously drunk but still so good-looking and at ease, we breathed a sigh of relief to have the spotlight of attention momentarily off us. He raised a glass, first to Paul for being so unafraid to take this leap, and then to me for making it with him. We felt grateful, caught up by something wondrous and larger than ourselves.

Four years passed before we heard from Geoffrey again, and by then his life had changed so radically we were surprised, frankly, to get his phone call. He'd published a book of short stories that had been not only a best seller but nominated for a major book award. He'd been photographed in *Vanity Fair*. At the library we had a hard time keeping our three copies of his book on the shelf. He was famous by then, or at least in our world he seemed so. He was also married, though we hadn't been invited to the wedding, which took place in Jamaica and was, we were told, family only.

His voice on the answering machine sounded more subdued than I remembered, as if his new fame had become an embarrassment perhaps. In truth I wondered about this. I liked his writing, but I had to admit that the level of attention he received seemed mystifying to me, unless, as some people suggested, it had to do with the author photo. The picture was arresting, taken from above in an outdoor setting. He looked as if he'd been caught by surprise, playing in some leaves. One review called him "the Marlboro Man of Letters," and his thick head of wavy hair got its own mention in the *New York Times,* which called him the most accurate male chronicler of the female experience since Dreiser wrote *Sister Carrie,* but added, rather petulantly, that it was hard to say if this reflected sensitivity or came as a result of a studied attention to his own hair and looks. By the time he called us, most of the hoopla had died away. He hadn't won the prize, nor had he come out with the much-anticipated follow-up novel.

He wanted to see us as soon as possible, he said in his message. The last we'd heard, he was living in Florida with his new wife, Corinne, a biology professor. He told us he was coming to New York and wanted to drive up. Would Friday night be okay?

Of course, was the answer, and right away we started overplanning the visit. We hired cleaners to do the carpet, and bought too much beer and wine, only to start the evening with Corinne's face-inflaming allergic reaction to the carpet-cleaning chemicals and Geoffrey's announcement that he'd quit drinking two years ago. Awkwardly, we moved everything out to the patio while Paul hunted for seltzer.

To me, Geoffrey's sobriety was the biggest surprise, but I'd never seen him with anything besides a scotch in his hand. Paul had, of course. He had countless memories from their predrinking days as children when Geoffrey was the spirited boundary tester of their group, the driving force behind the neighborhood golf course fire, the point man on dumping fifty boxes of green Jell-O into the community pool. That night, though, I could tell there would be no reminiscing over childhood pranks, because the real surprise of the evening came early, while Corinne's face was still a throbbing, angry red that didn't match her expression, which was demure and sweet. She wasn't, technically speaking, a beautiful woman, though she had all the trappings to be mistaken for one: long blond hair that fell below her shoulders, low-cut jeans, and the flat chest of a dancer, which I later learned she had been.

"I'll tell you why we're here," Geoffrey said. "We're looking for a place to buy a house. I've been doing some research and this neighborhood fits most of our criteria."

We didn't answer right away. "We've got to get out of Florida," he added. "Pretty quickly. I thought of this place and you guys."

We were surprised, of course. For all the practical rationale we told ourselves when buying this house *(Brand-new everything! No home repairs for years!)*, we also understood the aesthetically depressing reality of our street. These were cookie cutter designs with symmetrical driveways lining a street of identical homes. In the beginning, I loved the identical layouts in such close proximity to one another. I'd wanted the borrowed cups of sugar and the shared lives, but after four years living here, I understood that the idea of having neighbors was nicer sometimes than the reality. So why would someone like Geoffrey *choose* it?

"We need to disappear for a while," he said, as if to answer my unspoken question. "Or I do. I need to eliminate my distractions. Figure out how to concentrate again and—well, you know." He took a drink of water. "Finish my novel." Corinne said nothing.

Because we had no response, he kept going. "I want something like I had as a kid, but I can't deal with home, you know what I'm saying?"

Of course we did.

"You guys are friends. You know me. The *real* me." He meant Paul, naturally, though he kindly included me, gesturing with his hand. I worried about Corinne, so silent on all this, but we were flattered. We were better friends than we thought! So close, our life was something Geoffrey wanted to emulate!

Of course there was more to it than that. While the Steadmans were in the process of putting in two offers and finally buying the house next door to ours, I learned that Geoffrey had had some trouble with the law. Something to do with a hunting accident where a Texas Blue Horn, a bird recently put on the endangered species list, had been accidentally shot and killed in a spray of pink feathers he described as "the most beautiful and tragic sight I've ever witnessed." He'd turned himself in because he didn't have much choice—there were fourteen witnesses—and then balked at the fine they tried to impose. Fifty thousand dollars. "For a bird," he said, shaking his head. "Think about it. A *bird*."

Paul and I had our own complications that hovered over our lives, the miscarriages we never mentioned in front of other people, the babies I thought of every time I saw the brownish black stain while changing our sheets. If Geoffrey had his reasons for moving to this neighborhood, I had my own for staying where I was.

CHAPTER 4

The reality of my situation can't be denied. Twelve years ago, I owned a house filled with furniture and belongings that were long ago sold off to pay exorbitant legal expenses. I am being released with no money, no job, no place to live, no clothes, and no car. The working world requires computer skills I don't have. Everyone will mean well and no one will hire me, knowing where I've been and the people I've lived with. Jeremy has also made it clear that, though I am not guilty in the state's eyes, I am also not entirely innocent until my crime is resolved. Only when the real killer is found do I stand a chance of getting any restitution from the state for the years I've lost.

Jeremy has advised me to take advantage of the opportunity I'll have following my release. "You've got to get going right away. The police may reopen your case, but they won't spend any time or money drawing attention to their ineptitude twelve years ago." He's been going through the files of discovery and reminding me of the facts he believes are most significant. There was no sign of forced entry into Linda Sue's house, and no fingerprints on the front door, meaning she opened her door to the assailant, who arrived at approximately ten-thirty P.M. Inside her house they found four sets of fingerprints. They were able to identify three of them as the victim's, Geoffrey's, and mine. The fourth, with prints throughout the house—in the bathroom, the spare bedroom, upstairs, and downstairs—is unknown. I know food was found on the counter, but there are other details I haven't heard about before: a tea kettle on the stove still warm when the police arrived, two mugs with tea bags waiting beside it. The murderer was someone she liked well enough to invite in and offer tea to at that hour. No neighbors saw a car drive down the street after ten o'clock, no unknown tire prints were found in the muddy puddle on her driveway. Whoever it was had arrived on foot.

"In all probability it was someone from the neighborhood," Jeremy says. "But that doesn't mean the job is going to be easier. People have moved and they aren't going to be easy to find." He hesitates before he says the next thing. "I think Paul will be a good resource. He's kept his own files, I know, and done some of his own investigation."

I nod because he's right. Good old Paul, who, in the face of finding himself the spouse of an accused murderess, grew a new personality and became obsessed with my defense. If Franklin missed details, it's hard to imagine that Paul did. He got copies of everything, paid for experts to weigh in on the evidence—the blood spatter pattern, the police collection procedure—and became so fixated that for three years after my conviction he still couldn't stop talking about it.

"What else?" I say to Jeremy as he shuffles his papers. I can tell there's more.

There is. Some evidence that someone else might have been living in Linda Sue's house. Two toothbrushes. A pair of men's shoes.

That could be only one person.

"*Living* there?" I say. My voice sounds unnatural, dry and thin.

"Evidence of an ongoing presence. Maybe not living there but visiting often enough to have left personal items behind."

I know who it is of course, but does this mean Geoffrey was there *that night*? Did *he* write me the cat letter because he is finally ready to talk about what happened?

I suspect Jeremy had a hand in arranging the media waiting outside on the day of my release. I am only the second female exoneree in the last twenty years and the first with no drug history or prior arrest record. I am an example for one of Jeremy's favorite arguments: This could happen to anyone. In truth, I don't know if I'm a good candidate for this role. I look nervous and tongue-tied on camera. My glasses reflect the spotlight, making the headline that will roll beneath footage of my release—LIBRARIAN FOUND INNOCENT OF CRIME AFTER TWELVE YEARS IN PRISON—superfluous, I fear. I'm wearing an outfit Jeremy chose from my boxes of old clothes. A peach-colored sweater with a lace collar of the sort Viola, my old boss and the head librarian, favored.

"There's also your hair," Wanda pointed out last night. For two weeks, she avoided any mention of my release by focusing on her exercise regimen and the letters she writes to various men across the highway. For Wanda, who lived too long in a prison of monogamy, juggling three beaux at a time is not unusual. I hadn't known how this night would go—if we would ignore the box I'd packed in the corner, or if we'd say a proper good-bye to each other.

"What about my hair?" I said.

"Well, you can't see it." She didn't mean it unkindly, only as a fact: We have no mirrors in prison. Some women put up tinfoil, others used windows after dark. Later that night, Wanda got permission to use a pair of scissors and give me the first real haircut I'd had in a decade. She cut away all the frizzy gray and left me with a cap of silver white. I could tell from my reflection in the window that I looked much better, like a sprightly Peter Pan.

This morning when I walked down our corridor for the last time, carrying my box, everyone whistled when they saw my hair. "Better than the braids! 'Member those?" Justine called out. She'd been in twice as long as I had and she was right. For a few years in the beginning, I grew my hair very long and wore it in braids. "You go and have a good life for all of us," she said, and laughed, her eyes watering a little.

"You're a bitch if you think you deserve this," Taneesha snapped from the corner.

"Let her go, Taneesha," Wanda called, standing beside me. "You go on."

That was all we said for a good-bye.

Stepping outside the prison fence for the first time in twelve years, Jeremy at my side, is dizzying in a way I didn't expect. We walk silently up to the gate and to a crowd of reporters waiting just beyond. We need my picture in the morning paper, Jeremy has said, making no comment about my new look except to say, "Betsy, my God, your hair," which I take to mean this isn't the style he would have chosen for me.

The reporters ask if I'm angry that the state has offered me no restitution for the years I spent wrongfully incarcerated. Jeremy and I have gone over my answers. I'm supposed to sound grateful that a justice system capable of such errors is also capable of correcting its mistakes. I'm supposed to say, *Yes, I will fight for restitution,* without sounding too angry. The best exonerees are the ones who talk about their imprisonment as a spiritual awakening. "My body has been in prison, but not my heart!" the last one screamed into the microphone at his press conference, one fist raised in the air. His name was Bruce Whitman and he was white, too, imprisoned sixteen years ago for the murder of a girlfriend when he was nineteen years old. Now he's a bespectacled, balding thirty-five-year-old who has spent his adult life in a jail cell writing poetry that recently found a publisher. I heard that his picture was in *Time* magazine, and that on the day of his release, seventy people gathered and cheered for so long the reporters had to cut short their questions about charges still pending.

The crowd waiting for me is smaller. Mostly reporters—about fifteen—plus a TV crew and a few people from Jeremy's office. I recognize only a few faces personally, which isn't a surprise. I don't have the extended family Bruce had. The weeping aunts, the cousins, the army of relatives who never gave up hope. The only person I have is Marianne, in her arms, standing alone, a bouquet of flowers.

"How does it feel to be out?" one reporter calls as flashes go off.

I smile for the cameras. *Great,* I mouth.

"What's the first thing you want to do when you get home?"

They don't realize that no one who's been in prison for twelve years still has a home. "Sleep late and drink some good coffee in the morning." I've prepared this line and practiced it with Jeremy, who smiles beside me.

"Do you think you'll get your old job back?"

It's been more than ten years since I've heard from anyone I worked with at the library. "I don't have any firm plans yet. I'll need a job, of course." Jeremy has urged me to say this in the hope that it might produce an offer.

Though I wrote my statement, Jeremy has revised it a little. Last night, he explained: "The main point here is that you're grateful to be given your life back. That you're looking forward to simple pleasures—pizza, movies, watching the sunset. Yes, you'll be suing the state if they don't come up with a reasonable offer soon, but that's not the most important thing on your mind right now. Much better if you don't seem too angry at this point."

I deliver my words with Jeremy's instructions in my mind: *Be aware of the TV camera but don't look into it.* "Twelve years ago, I left behind family and friends to enter this prison on what we now understand was a false conviction for a crime I had no part in. I am neither bitter nor broken by this experience. I have learned much about the fortitude of the human spirit and I believe I have survived with my own intact. I also understand the hard work has just begun. Reclaiming my old life won't be easy. Part of my new job will be fighting for justice in our system. I am one of countless men and women still sit behind bars, innocent of the crimes they are serving time for."

Cameras flash as my halting voice limps to the end of this statement that I deliver without any of the emotion it needs to pack a punch.

The crowd has grown slightly. For a second I look up and think I see Paul standing in the back, looking up at me hopefully. It's hard to be sure because the flashes leave spots dancing in front of me. When my eyes clear, the shadow no longer looks like Paul but like Leo, which I know is impossible. And then whoever it is disappears again. My brain is playing tricks on me, imagining that I'm not standing here alone, facing my future with no one beside me.

CHAPTER 5

Getting into Marianne's car, I feel a little like a refugee from some natural disaster. I have one battered cardboard box containing the handmade presents I've received over the years: a paper towel roll kaleidoscope, a collage of shirtless men that Wanda made to cheer us up when we hadn't seen a real one in a while. I have these things but no purse, no wallet, no money, no ID except the inmate tag I've worn around my neck for a decade.

"One thing at a time," Jeremy told me when I pointed out that my driver's license expired ten years ago. "You don't need a license until you've got a car." It's overwhelming to contemplate. If I ever land a job interview how will I get to it? "First things first," he said. "You know what you need to do."

I do. In the car I ask Marianne if she remembers Linda Sue having a cat. She startles for a moment. "A *cat*," she says. "Why do you ask that?"

"I thought I saw one that day when I was in her house, looking around." I don't need to clarify this—*the day Linda Sue died.* With Marianne I seem to leave as much unsaid as possible. I've always wondered if Marianne knows more about that night than she's told me. If she's visited me in prison out of some complicated sense of guilt. Not that she knows who killed Linda Sue, but I've wondered if she knows something. Once, in the buildup to my trial, Paul remembered a detail I'd almost forgotten: The day after Linda Sue's murder, Marianne and Roland weren't around at all. Several of us tried calling, but hung up, unsure of what sort of message to leave. When they finally heard the news, they seemed genuinely shocked and then preoccupied by other matters the rest of us knew nothing about. They'd always been like that—a family with secrets the neighbors didn't pry into.

Sitting in her car now, headed to her house to live with the husband she may or may not be separated from, it occurs to me how little I know about this woman. For many years she never worked beyond projects like me and Neighborhood Watch. Recently, she's parlayed her old safety obsession into a part-time business of selling personal security devices out of her home. We used to joke about this before Linda Sue was murdered. Then, of course, we stopped and wondered how prescient she was.

For now, Marianne says she doesn't recall any cat. "Of course I was never inside her house, though. You remember how funny she was about that. She wouldn't let anyone in. I *tried,*" she says, as if even after twelve years she were still a little hurt by it.

I was inside Linda Sue's house twice and it looked just the way we imagined it might from our glimpses through her window. Empty. It's hard to guess what she was afraid we'd see. "She probably felt a little self-conscious. She didn't have much furniture."

Marianne looks at me. "What was I, Martha Stewart? Did I go around telling people they had to buy sofa sets and matching curtains?"

"No."

"She thought I didn't like her. I *did,* though. I was interested in her. We were *all* interested in her."

Marianne is right. We were all interested in Linda Sue. We drive for a little while in silence. "So, no, she never mentioned a cat to me."

She's already told me there's a party waiting for me back at her house. "Just a few of your old friends," Marianne says, which makes me more nervous the closer we get. Which of the many friends who never wrote or visited me in prison will be there? Which of my coworkers whose testimony helped to convict me? The potential for awkwardness is so rife I turn and stare at the draining light of day. In twelve years, I've ridden only in the back of a Corrections Department van, ankles shackled, going to and from the courthouse. Now I'm surprised by odd things. The cars on the highway seem bigger than I remember. Twice, we pass people talking on the telephone as they drive, which I've never seen before. It's dark by the time we get to Juniper Lane and I can't see much on the block except that the trees are taller than I'd even imagined.

Inside about half of the twenty people gathered shout "SURPRISE!" when we walk in; the rest look confused and surprised themselves. Jeremy warned me to expect this because the news coverage of my case still runs twelve-year-old photos. "Some people won't recognize you. They think hair dye might have been available in prison."

Before I left CCI, I used a staff bathroom and saw myself in a full-length mirror for the first time in more than a decade. I examined the ways I'd aged—the lines around my eyes, my new hair so short and white I almost look blond. But the biggest change was in my body. I am thinner now, with muscles in my arms and legs. Even the features on my face look more pronounced, my eyes bigger, my jawline sharper. For twelve years I've exercised two hours a day because Wanda insisted it would stop the suicidal thoughts, and to some extent she was right. She taught me the art of exercising in a tight space, calf raises and iso-metric pulls. Even as we bent over and coughed for strip searches we made ourselves stronger, and here is the proof: I look like a different person. "You'll dye your hair tomorrow," Wanda whispered last night, after my haircut. "And buy some makeup." It was her only acknowledg-ment that I was going somewhere, with such possibilities.

My old boss, Viola, is the first person I recognize, though she looks thirty years older, her shoulders stooped, her head hanging forward as if the thin bun of white hair on top of her head were weighted some-how. She puts a papery, cool hand in mine and squeezes. "It's good to see you, dear."

"You look well. Very fit."

Behind her, I see Kathy from our AV department, the only person from the library who wrote to me in prison to say she was sorry the others hadn't been in touch, but no one knew what to say. She smiles now and gives me a hug. "You look wonderful, Betsy. Maybe we should all go on a prison diet." She means this as a joke, but now I remember how awkward Kathy could be, how no one ever wanted to take their lunch break with her.

In the corner, I see Paul standing with an older woman who seems to be making an argument by stabbing the air with her hands. In the old days, Paul always got caught in conversations like this. He isn't striking like Geoffrey. He's smaller, softer, his hair and skin paler, but I always thought he was handsome and I'm happy about how he still looks like his old self. He peeks up at me and waves with the tips of his fingers. I wave back.

I met Paul in my senior year in college, three months before our graduation at an annual party called SOMF—Send Off the Month of February—which culminated in a fraternity tradition of creating snow sculptures and watching while fraternity members urinated on them. "I don't get it," Paul said, standing beside me as we watched.

"It's symbolic," I explained. "They're going to the bathroom on winter."

Neither of us was even a little drunk. We smiled at each other and shook our heads, adults in the presence of children. Later we sat down on a stone wall and he told me he hadn't been to too many parties. I'd spent four years of college going to all of them, afraid that if I didn't I might miss something. When I asked what he'd been doing instead, he answered seriously, "Going to the library mostly. And labs. I've taken a lot of labs. They eat up the afternoons so I have to study at night." We started dating after that, at a different speed than I'd ever gone before. He was sweet and gentle and hesitant in ways I'd never seen a boy be before. We went out on coffee dates, then lunches, then finally a movie date I ended by asking if he ever thought about kissing me. "I mean, sure," he stammered. "I've thought about it."

Eventually I had to tell him that, yes, boys occasionally slept over in the suite I shared with five girls. In fact they slept over *most* nights, I wanted to say, but didn't for fear of shocking him. I loved him for knowing less about the ways of the world than I did, and for being the first boyfriend I didn't feel panicky around. When I was with him, a calm settled over me and, for the first time in my life, I took charge of things. We decided we'd stay in the area for grad school, live together to save money, and get married the following year, all before we'd known each other six months.

When I asked him for a divorce two years after my conviction—two years of visits spent going over the mistakes we'd made in my trial—I said it was for him. I wanted to give him a chance to have a real life, by which I suppose I meant to have children with someone else, but I was thinking of myself, too. I wanted to leave the past behind. When he resisted, as I knew he would, I told him I was tired of focusing on my case. "Don't you see I won't have a life if I do that?"

He stared at me. "You *want* a life in there?"

It broke my heart, all that we weren't saying. "Yes, Paul. I want a life."

Though he wrote a few letters, he didn't come again after that. Seeing him now, I feel a strange mixture of sadness and relief. We have so many touchstones in common. He knows the details of my case better than I do, and the way our life before the murder might have looked fine from the outside but wasn't always. He knows the secrets we tried to keep. The ones we're probably both thinking of now. When he finally comes over, it's nice to hug him. "It's good to see you, Bets. You look great."

"So do you," I say.

I ask if he's held on to the old documents and transcripts from the trial. "Oh, sure," he says. "Why? What's up?"

"Do you remember anything in there about Linda Sue's cat?"

He narrows his eyes slightly. It's as if we're picking up on our conversation exactly where we'd left off ten years ago. *Here's another detail we shouldn't forget, another possibility.* "There was a cat in her house that day. I saw it when I went over. About three years ago, I got a letter from someone who knew about it."

"Maybe they meant the stray? The gray calico with the fluffy tail— you remember that one?"

Now that he's said it, I do remember that cat. For about six months, he became a fixture on our block. He'd appear around dusk and follow someone home or pick a porch to sit on. Some of us fed him, some didn't, but I don't think he went a night without a house to sleep in and never the same one twice in a row. In the evening he was very affectionate, winding himself around legs and purring, and then in the morning he'd slip out the door and disappear the first chance he got. Barbara once said he reminded her of a few old boyfriends she'd had in college.

I ask Paul if he ever saw it after Linda Sue died. He considers for a minute and shakes his head. The more I think about this, the more significant it seems. Not the cat but the fact of this letter, the directive tone, the circumscribed admission, as if someone were weary of sitting on his guilty secret and now wanted to get it out in the open. *Think about the cat, you nitwit.* I had for years and still couldn't say what it meant. Did the cat walk through the blood and carry off some vital piece of evidence?

"Do you think Geoffrey might have written it?" I ask tentatively.

"No." I've always wondered what Geoffrey was doing in the lead-up to my trial. He'd left the neighborhood but had still, in mysterious ways, made his presence felt. I know he called people, told them certain things. "No," Paul says again. "Geoffrey didn't know anything about the cat."

This seems odd. A minute ago, Paul didn't either. "You talked to him about it?"

He leans toward me to explain. "It was in the files of discovery. There was a cat food dish and litter pan."

"So you *did* know about it?"

"Yes."

"Why didn't you tell me?"

"Because I didn't think it meant anything. I thought it meant, you know, she had a cat. But I asked Geoffrey about it once and he said no, she hated cats."

So he's thought about this, too, and puzzled over it. Maybe he doesn't want to get caught up in a small matter the way we did before my trial when we dwelled obsessively on inconsistencies that took up all our time and got us nowhere. A muddy footprint on her porch; a phone call Linda Sue made that morning to a lawyer in Hartford. Every revelation felt like a breakthrough until it wasn't: The footprint belonged to a carpenter who'd worked on her roof the week before; the lawyer didn't recognize her name. Whatever she was calling him about remained as mysterious as the message she didn't leave. "I never knew what to think," Paul says. "Except maybe she was cat-sitting."

Marianne pulls me away from Paul to introduce me to a couple of Court TV fans who apparently have been following my case from the beginning. They tell me they saw the problem with my nightgown right away and they never liked the DA's explanation for the sandwich. It's disorienting to have people know so much about me and nothing really. When we finally exhaust the topic of my trial, there is nothing left to say.

Marianne steers me from one group to another, people who all smile and ask if it feels good to be out. "Oh, yes," I say, wishing it were possible to tell the truth: *It's a funny mix of feelings.* The only new people I like arrive toward the end, a gay couple living in Geoffrey's old house who seem to appreciate the oddity of the situation. They look about ten years younger than I am and tease each other like new lovers.

"Bill wants the sordid details of your prison life," Finn says, smiling at his boyfriend.

"I do *not*," Bill says, blushing. "Oh, all right, sure. I'm *curious,* but only because I went to a boarding school that always felt like prison and I wondered if that's true."

I smile and wrinkle my nose to suggest that I can recognize a joke. "Probably not," I say. "Did you have a rule against caffeinated coffee?" He shakes his head. "There you go, then. Prison was probably a little worse."

Finn tells me he's a fact checker and researcher for magazines, the sort of job reference librarians wish they had when they get tired of dealing with the crazy public all day. When I tell Finn this, he says, "I actually wanted to be a librarian. I'm one of those people who overromanticize that job."

"People do," I say.

Before they leave, Finn surprises me with a question no one else has asked. "Is there anything you'll miss about prison?" Every article I've read about myself assumes this has been a decade-long nightmare, that all of this time has been stolen from what should have been my rightful life on this block alongside these neighbors. I've never admitted the more complicated truth: that my stolen years came earlier and my real life, in many ways, began only recently. I know this much: Disguises are a kind of a prison, as is the pretense of being something you're not. In prison I found a life that was full and rich with people who depended on me, real friendships, real lives I made a difference in. Here that was less true. So yes is the answer, though I don't say all this. "The mashed potatoes," I say, and everyone laughs.

Before he leaves, Finn tells me he works at home during the day and I'm welcome to stop over anytime I'd like. He leans closer so he's not overheard. "You know, if being here starts to feel a little weird."

"Thank you," I say, wondering if he can tell it's already feeling a little weird.

After everyone leaves, Marianne's nervous energy seems only to intensify. I sit on the sofa watching her straighten two piles of magazines. "I don't know why I invited Jean," she says. "She's never been a very sensitive person and she certainly proved *that* today." Was Jean the woman who asked if prison had made me an angrier person? I don't remember.

"I liked Bill and Finn," I tell her.

"Did you?" She looks up hopefully. "Yes, they're very sweet."

I can see that her pale cheeks are flush, her forehead damp, evidence of the effort this day has been for her. Roland never appeared at the party, which I assume means they're separated and he's no longer around. By the time I left, Roland spent the bulk of his days and nights in the basement, where he kept a workshop filled with design plans for solar-powered water heaters and fuel cells that never seemed to work as well as they should. At least according to Marianne, who rolled her eyes about his work and pointed to the sky. "Solar's always going to have problems. Like how it's not always sunny."

We also knew—for all of her attempts to dismiss his work—that it wasn't insignificant. Roland worked for an alternative energy company and sometimes groups of people came to his house for meetings, most of them well dressed and driving tiny cars that looked as if they'd been tooled by hand from thin sheets of steel. Through Roland, we learned that green energy development wasn't just for hippies and counterculture aesthetes. There was money in those minicars lined up along the street, money in the layers of peasant clothes they wore. Once I saw a man in cowboy boots and a bolo tie clasped with a fist-sized disk of turquoise step out of a limousine and walk around the house to Roland's basement door. We assumed they would explain it sooner or later—*he's from Texas, an investor, a crazy old coot*—but Marianne never mentioned it and neither did Roland.

It's been a year since the last time Marianne mentioned Roland's name, and I haven't got the heart to ask where he lives now. For all her buoyant enthusiasm over my release—the balloons, the cake, the WELCOME HOME banner hand-painted and strung on one wall of the living room—there is a sadness about Marianne that isn't hard to see.

"What's happened to the old neighbors?" I ask, trying to make the question sound casual. I need to find these people and talk to them, the sooner the better.

"Well, the Baker-Harrisons moved to New Jersey. But a nice part.

Montclair, I think. I don't know if Helen still has that faux-finishing business. And Wendy Stubbins died from something. Brain cancer, I think."

Wendy Stubbins was one of the young mothers on the block. Once I saw her walk up the street carrying a trike in one hand and her toddler by his overall straps in the other. "You're not listening," she hissed as she walked past, her child's limbs pinwheeling through the air. I remember so many snapshots like that, so many times I wondered: *Would I do that?* It was easy to believe I would have made a firm but fair mother, one who could discipline with one throat-clearing sound and a narrowing of the eyes. "Wendy's *dead*?" I say in disbelief. Her son couldn't be more than fourteen now. I always feel a pang when I hear about motherless children. As if there should be a way to match us up, a dating service of some kind.

"I don't know if Jim ever remarried. He was a little bit of an alcoholic even before she died. I don't know what happened with that."

He was? For the umpteenth time I wonder how much I witnessed and failed to see in those days of watching so much on our street.

After we've cleaned up, Marianne leads me to Trish's old bedroom, apologizing along the way for the state it's in. "I haven't done much with it," she says, which might be an understatement. Apparently, in twelve years she's done nothing at all because it still looks like a little girl's room. In one corner there's an empty hamster cage, in another a dollhouse with one door hanging loose. The twin beds are covered with throw pillows and stuffed animals.

Trish's brother, John, was the one most people noticed first. The smartest boy at the middle school and probably the oddest. He could solve a Rubik's Cube in under a minute but couldn't, when pressed, clip his own fingernails. He had a nervous personality and a habit of licking his lips and then spitting when he spoke. I know Marianne worried about John for most of his childhood. She got him out of PE classes, and had the mandatory swim test required for graduation waived so that the valedictorian of the class could get a diploma. He never learned to drive a car or ride a bike. Once I saw him struggle for ten minutes to open a bag of potato chips.

Marianne tells me that these days he works as a software designer and lives in Alabama. She sees him twice a year and says he's become a churchgoer. "Apparently he's always wanted some type of community. I never realized that. I've asked him does it really have to be a *church* and he says, 'Yes, Mother, it does.'"

Trish, though, I never hear about. No old stories about her childhood. No verbalized regrets. It's as if Trish has died and there is no need to keep repeating the fact. I'll also say this, though: There were times—not every visit, but often enough—when Marianne would lose her train of thought midstory and her stare would grow vacant, whatever she'd been about to say gone. I thought of Trish then, and assumed she was part of whatever it was Marianne hadn't said.

It made me sad because I remember Trish well as such a bookish and appealing girl. In my early days, when I worked in the children's room of the library, Marianne brought her often and let her check out ten books, the maximum number allowed per card. They were always returned before their due date, and I could tell by the way Trish fingered their spines that she'd read every one. She was a little odd, like her brother. When she was eight she joined a project I organized making shoe box dioramas of famous places in literature. I left the choice up to the children, and we received some wonderful ones: Pooh's Corner; Wilbur's barnyard pen; the Borrowers' home, with thread-spool tables and matchbox beds. Then Trish showed up with the most elaborate diorama of all, what looked like mounded Play-Doh hills dotted with flowers and a small dollhouse hospital bed in the corner. "It's Yr," Marianne whispered after I'd studied it for a while without a guess. "From *I Never Promised You a Rose Garden*."

I looked at her, confused. Trish had read a book about the imaginary world of a schizophrenic seventeen-year-old living in a mental institution? I assumed Marianne was joking. She smiled sheepishly. "Sometimes they let her check out from the adult room. I don't know if it's a bad idea. I don't know how much she understands."

Trish smiled as she slid her diorama onto the table beside Laura Ingalls Wilder's log cabin home. She seemed delighted with her project, grinning fiercely as she straightened the title card out. I looked back at Marianne, who studied her daughter. I could almost read her hopeful thought—*Maybe it's fine.*

I didn't stay in the children's room for long after that. Though I never made the request and nothing was ever directly said (to me, anyway), after my third miscarriage it was understood that I'd be better placed elsewhere. After that, I saw Trish at the library only occasionally, and I was usually shy, as I was with all the children, never quite sure if they would remember me. Trish surprised me, though, starting a conversation herself. Once she asked if my hand got tired stamping books. Another time, what the best part of being a librarian was. The question surprised me. Who'd ever heard of a child asking an adult a question about her life? I asked her, "Do you want to be a librarian?"

She beamed. "Not at all," she whispered. "I want to be a writer."

I thought about Trish in prison sometimes, when my mind wandered to children I'd known and liked in the past, but I asked Marianne about her only once, enough to know I shouldn't again. "She's gone from our lives," Marianne said. "Cut herself off from us." It was clear enough that the choice was Trish's and not her parents'.

Now I look at Trish's bookshelves filled with ceramic animals and, behind them, her childhood books—some predictable, many not. I recognize a few fantasy titles, some sci-fi, the vampire books that were just coming out when I left.

At one end of the shelf I see *Middlemarch* by George Eliot. My favorite book in college, and more than five hundred pages long. Was it possible Trish had read *this* as a teenager? Was she *that* precocious? I pull it out and then my breath catches at the inscription I find on the first page:

> *To Trish—*
> *I loved this when I was your age.*
> *Friends Always (I hope),*
> > *Geoffrey Steadman*

CHAPTER 6

I can still remember the first time I saw Geoffrey at my library: He came in and stood by our "Hot Books" shelf, seven-day loans on popular fiction. I was working in the back office, out of view, but I watched carefully as he looked around, as if he'd come in not for books but for something else. I could have gone out there on any excuse. I waited five minutes, then ten, to see what he would do. After fifteen minutes, he left.

Two days later, he returned while I was shelving an overflowing return cart, struggling with a rolling ladder that hadn't been working for a while. "Let me get that," he said, taking the book from my hand, tall enough to reach the shelf without help.

"You know Dewey!" I said too loud, after he'd placed it properly. I tried to laugh as if I'd made a joke because Dewey is so often the punch line of librarian jokes. We all have more mugs with "Librarians Dewey it in the Stacks" than we know what to do with.

"Yes," he said, grabbing a book and reaching up again, so close I could smell his musk deodorant. He told me he was here to do some research. "I'm trying to write something from a teenage girl's point of view, except now I realize I know almost nothing about teenage girls."

His eyes were so blue and clear it was hard to look at them for long. I told him I knew a little bit about teenage girls—or what they read, anyway. "And of course I was one once," I added. Was that too flirtatious? It's true that I wouldn't have said it standing at the front desk with my colleagues around, sorting through request slips, listening to everything. "I was a bookish girl. Not very popular," I admitted. "Mostly I sat around watching people who had more friends than I did."

He smiled. "That's *exactly* what I need. A girl who's an observer, a watcher of everything. Can you remember your life at age fourteen?"

All too well, unfortunately, but I didn't tell him that. Nor did I admit that *bookish* and *unpopular* would have been kind adjectives to describe me at that age. I was also surly and difficult, given to wearing layers of black and writing bleak, angry poetry.

"I'm happy to give you the books I read at that age," I told him, thinking I'd amend the list and leave off *Go Ask Alice*. I composed a cheery list of Judy Blumes and classics: *Jane Eyre, To Kill a Mockingbird, Little Women, Gone With the Wind*. The same books, I realize now, that are sitting on Trish's shelf. This makes no sense. Was he using me to befriend her? She was twelve when he moved in, fifteen by the time we all left. What kind of friendship could they have possibly had?

"This is great," Geoffrey said that first day, checking out five of my recommendations and reading them all inside of a week. I started thinking of more, reading a few myself, storing up anecdotes to tell him on the days when he came in. Eventually I told him the truth about my adolescence: "I don't think I was invited to a single party until I got to college and forced myself to do a personality makeover. I found an article in a magazine that walked me through it."

He clapped his hands and laughed. "A *personality* makeover. I love it. Does Paul know about this?"

I stopped short for a second. Paul *didn't* know all of it, or not in any detail. I'd never told him about my sleepwalking episodes because the episodes seemed to be behind me. I told myself it was a temporary matter, more connected to the stress of school than to any deep-seated psychosis.

I got called away before I could answer. "Look," Geoffrey said later, resting his books on my desk. "I'd like to hear more of your story if I could. All the re-creating yourself fits right in with what I'm doing."

I smiled and mouthed, *How about later?* pointing to the line behind him. For the rest of the day, I reconstructed my old stories. I made up funny details and forgot what was true and what wasn't because that seemed less important than getting in his book.

Eventually he started finding his own books. "What do you think of this one, Bets?" he'd say, assuming I'd read everything, though, like many librarians, I'd become someone who talked about books more than I read them. I could tell you which writers had the longest wait lists. I could recommend books I'd never read based on the request slips I'd processed. Geoffrey changed all that, reminding me of the books I loved as a girl. When he asked me what my favorite book of all time was and I told him *Middlemarch,* he included it in that day's stack of books. That night I opened my copy for the first time in years, reread a few passages, and wondered why I'd named this book so quickly, and if it wasn't all just a little depressing: Dorothea with all her do-gooder sincerity and her terrible marriage to Casaubon, the phony writer and academic. Now I wonder what Geoffrey had thought when he read it. Did he see pieces of himself in that character? Apparently not if he passed the book on to Trish, but why would he have done that?

I remember how nervous I was to discuss the book with him. In college I'd wept over it, how Dorothea with her good intentions ended up with so little, and in the end, dead. Rereading it, it seemed more frightening than sad: a childless woman filling the emptiness at the center of her life with gossamer plans and projects to help the poor. What would Geoffrey know about me and my delusions of importance—my dream that what I did at the library mattered to people, mattered to *anyone*—after he read it? I felt embarrassed about the whole thing until the day I looked up from my desk at work and saw him standing there with tears in his eyes. "Oh, Bets, what a book," he said. "I cried at the end and I never do that."

After that, we tried to have something we were both reading at the same time. His favorite book was *Sometimes a Great Notion* by Ken Kesey, and I did what you never see a librarian do: I sat at the front desk with a book open, reading it. I wanted to love it—he'd loved my suggestions—and in the end I did, or pretended I did, anyway. Geoffrey said reading books with me took him back to the time before they'd become a complicated pleasure. Reading new ones now meant he knew the writer or the writer's agent, and inevitably those threads of connection made him uneasy; not with jealousy, I didn't think, but with a self-consciousness I could hardly believe the first time I saw it.

"Sometimes I wonder if I'm just a copier," he said. He didn't say any more and I didn't ask what he meant, though now, of course, I understand.

At the trial, witnesses reported seeing him at the library as often as three times a week. His library records put it closer to once a week, though naturally there were days he came in without checking books out. Gretchen, another assistant librarian, bitter about my promotion over her, described Geoffrey as almost constantly standing at my desk or walking beside my shelving cart. This was a dig, too, as any librarian will tell you. Shelving should have been my lowest priority, a job easily relegated to students or volunteers.

"What did you think, overhearing their conversations?" the DA asked Gretchen.

"I felt embarrassed mostly," Gretchen said. "They were a little sophomoric, the way they went on about books. I wondered how much she was trying to impress him."

"Can you define *sophomoric*?" The DA sounded annoyed. First rule for witnesses: Don't talk above the jury's heads.

"When someone tries to sound smarter than they are."

I don't think Gretchen hated me all those years we worked side by side before Geoffrey came along to interrupt the quiet and skew the balance. I think she hated her life, which included a husband she didn't seem to like and a live-in mother-in-law. Geoffrey represented a pleasure most of us had long ago stopped imagining. A man stopping by to say hello, to lean across our beige desk and make a joke. Of course I sounded sophomoric at times. Who wouldn't? Now I wonder who else he was manipulating, giving up portions of his writing day to.

"Did it ever sound like flirting?" the same lawyer asked Viola.

"In my mind, any conversation that goes on longer than it technically needs to while working is a flirtation. So, yes." Viola sounded so unlike herself saying this, I wondered if she'd written it down somewhere and memorized her line.

"Did it seem *sexual* to you?"

"Oh, no." Her eye flicked over for a second to mine. "I never saw that."

In the end, my coworkers did me far more harm than good, though I don't blame them. They were librarians, keen observers with sharp memories. During the trial, I'll admit, I liked hearing their stories—the validation, after everything, that my friendship with Geoffrey hadn't all been in my head.

It surprised me that no one ever mentioned how we started eating lunch in the garden behind the library. We never planned our meetings, we just wandered outside and found each other. We'd eat and talk as if we were in the middle of a longer story we could never finish. "So where were we?" Geoffrey might say when I sat down. "Oh, right. Tenth-grade English. Your first lesbian teacher."

He told his own stories, full of teen-boy pranks where he was the ringleader and Paul was a background player. Neither of them had been good athletes, which meant they never joined Little League or Pee Wee football. The afternoons of their youth were free for trolling through the woods at the end of their street. "We built teepees and stored food and berries to live off of if we ever had to."

I loved hearing his stories. The ones Paul told were mostly from high school, after Geoffrey had already become a star writer for the newspaper with a column titled "In Steadman's Stead." "All the school jokes came from his columns," Paul told me. "The principal quoted them, the teachers, everyone." Alone with me, Geoffrey told stories that predated the discovery of his writing talent. Maybe for obvious reasons. His career was stalled; he faced an uncertain future. But sometimes I wondered if there might be more to it, if for some reason every reminder of his writing life was painful to him.

I remember the lunch hour when I told Geoffrey the truth about my father's illness, how he'd had bleak patches on and off throughout my childhood, and then, at the age of forty-four, drove himself to the hospital in the middle of the night and told them he hadn't slept in fourteen days. He stayed there a month and came home a changed man: heavier, paler, with hands that trembled too much to open the vials of pills he'd returned with. We didn't know what to say to the stranger he'd become. For months, his only conversation was about nurses and fellow patients from the hospital. "Eventually we got used to it," I told Geoffrey, looking not at him but at a spray of orange daylilies. "He never went back to work after that. Never drove. Never left the house really, except to go out in the yard a bit. He loved to garden. That's what he did when he met my mother."

I'd rarely spoken about my father the way I did with Geoffrey that day, revealing facts that are unimaginable for people who haven't lived with mental illness. *He never worked again. Never left the house.* "Sometimes I think he was criminally overmedicated in that hospital and never had the courage to wean himself." Geoffrey nodded. Part of me felt insecure at having spoken so candidly, part of me wondered, *If I offer more details, will he use them?* "He stopped drinking alcohol because of the meds and instead put cough syrup into his tea. At night if his hands were shaking too much, I did it for him."

"Hmm," he said, closing his eyes and nodding.

I hoped he was thinking: *Good detail. Usable.* "You have an incredible memory," he once said, which kept me talking. The irony is that I *did* have an unusual memory. I could recall the names of old teachers, of classmates I hardly knew, details about what the popular girls said as they lined up the apples slices and cottage cheese they ate for lunch.

I remembered everything except for the episodes I forgot completely.

Eventually I told him the truth about my parasomnia episodes, though I framed it as a thing of the distant past. "I used to be quite a sleepwalker," I said.

"*Really?* What was that like?"

"Usually I'd wake up and be in my sister's room, trying to take her things."

"You'd steal in your sleep! I love it!"

"She'd yell at me and that would be that."

He laughed and clapped like an audience waiting for an encore. This was how we'd portrayed ourselves to each other, as smart and flawed people, perpetual outsiders trying to fit in. "Eventually it got a little creepier than that," I admitted. "Food started disappearing in the middle of the night and I wouldn't remember anything, but I'd know that I'd eaten it."

His smile faded a fraction into concern. "What kind of food?"

"Bulky things. Half a loaf of bread. A stack of crackers. In the morning I'd wake up covered in crumbs." I wanted to strike the right note, get him to laugh again.

He didn't. "Wow. Did your parents know?"

"Not really. They thought we had a terrible problem with mice." This was initially true. Then they assumed my father was to blame. "I'm pretty sure it stopped when I was in high school, but about halfway through college it started again." I wasn't sure why I was telling him this when I'd never told anyone before. "I was living in a suite with five other girls. We had a mini-fridge. I remember moving in and seeing all that food and thinking, *I wonder if this is going to be a problem?*"

I tried to make it a funny story, though I knew it wasn't. I didn't know the other girls well. I was coming off the loneliest year of my life. Geoffrey's smile said it was fine, he was ready to laugh, so I kept going: "Sure enough, the first week a package of hot dogs disappeared in the middle of the night. There was a wrapper in the garbage and no sign that any of them had been cooked. Another morning I woke up and discovered I'd eaten a stick of butter."

I tried to blame the boys' suite across the hall. We talked about putting an alarm on the fridge. But I had enough evidence—greasy smudges on my sheets, vile stomachaches all day—to know that I was the culprit we were trying to catch, and that if it came out, it would be no laughing matter. It was unheard of and disturbing, a window to the possibility that I didn't just grow up in the disturbing presence of my father's unhappiness but contained the possibility for it somewhere inside of me.

I kept going because Geoffrey was laughing hard by then. "I had developed a thing for greasy raw meat, apparently. It was like I had the opposite of anorexia. I begged the school doctor for prescription sleeping pills and that seemed to do the trick. I'm the only person who's ever lost five pounds in a month by staying in bed."

Now I study the book that I've just pulled down from Trish's shelf. As if it were not disturbing enough that Geoffrey was pretending to have read this as a teenager, I remember him inscribing a copy of his favorite Ken Kesey book to me with the exact same closing: *Friends Always (I hope)*. I was thrilled with the sentiment, the vulnerability I read into the parenthetical add-on.

I try to imagine what this means. I don't remember ever seeing Geoffrey and Trish together or hearing him mention her. I tell myself, *If he was writing about a teenage girl, it wasn't preposterous for him to befriend one*. I dig through Trish's desk drawers crammed with notes and old school papers to see if I can find any more evidence of his presence in her life. At the bottom of the deepest one, I find a dog-eared blue spiral notebook with *DIARY KEEP OUT! PRIVATE!* written across the front.

It's so old I can't imagine finding any real secrets in here. She couldn't have been more than thirteen when she was keeping this diary, full of complaints about her brother, John, and a surprising number of mentions about our neighbors. On the second page I find Helen Baker-Harrison's name, with a story about her dog. And then one about Barbara Baylor, who apparently offered to buy some of Trish's "specially written poetry." There's even a mention of me, whom she'd seen that day at the library. Mysteriously, it says: "She seems better these days, which is nice."

It worries me to read this, but it also reminds me of the Trish I knew. The perky, happy girl. The friendly teenager, waving from the bus stop and starting conversations. "I like the new bush you planted, Mrs. Treading! I told your husband!" she'd say. What other teenager offered such comments unsolicited? I had no children for her to babysit, no money to pay her for chores, yet she seemed eager to talk, and noticed the little things you assume teenagers don't. Once I passed her as I walked to work wearing a new winter coat and she clapped her hands and said, "Oh, it's nice, Mrs. Treading. A lot better than that old one!" I could hardly believe it. It *was* better than my old one. In fact, I'd spent an hour in the store trying it on. I fell in love and spent too much. "I'll wear it for the next fifteen years," I promised Paul when he saw the price. Money had become a point of contention between us after we figured out that our mortgage payments took more than half of our paychecks. Hearing her say this made me think it was all worth it.

Trish wasn't perfect, of course. I saw her once smoking a cigarette at the bus stop, and thought: *She's a girl with secrets.* She smiled and waved, folding her cigarette into the palm of her hand. "Hi, Mrs. Treading! How's the library? Anything new?"

"Fine," I said, crossing my arms over my chest. "You know, the usual." Did she want to hear that I'd been put temporarily in charge of the mystery/suspense section? Did she pretend to care so she could laugh at me later with her friends? Sometimes she was impossible to figure out.

"I was thinking about coming down there for a book."

What else could I say? "Oh, good! What book?"

"I don't know yet."

Should I tell her I could see the lit cigarette inside her cupped hand? That it wasn't so long ago that I'd done a little smoking myself? She looked at me that way sometimes: as if she wanted to be my friend.

Now it breaks my heart to remember how much I liked Trish and how I tried not to let that show, limiting our conversations, ending them before anyone saw us. How did such a girl fall out so grievously with her parents? In her diary, the closest I can find to a clue is this: *Mom is making more rules about who I'm allowed to invite home. No one from school, no one from the neighborhood. She says they need to be home anytime someone from outside the family is here.*

In my own family, I was the one who cut us off from the prying eyes of the outside world. By the time I got to junior high I lived in fear of anything that might draw attention to my home life, the silent dinners we ate, the ubiquitous TV. By ninth grade, there was evidence of my father's strange temper—holes kicked in the walls, covered with LOVE! posters that made our house look like it was wearing Band-Aids. I thought it was imperative to keep people away.

As I keep reading her diary, I give Trish credit for having the bravery I didn't in the face of odd parents. By December, she's turned thirteen and smoked pot with Alan, who rides on her bus. By February she's gone home with Tommy, a greasy-haired viola player who asked her if she would mind taking off her shirt.

I waited until my freshman year in college to embarrass myself in such stupid, self-destructive ways. I arrived an innocent eighteen-year-old, and within three months I was passing out regularly in lounges and dorm rooms I didn't recognize. I put on the performance of a wild girl for seven months, dancing on coffee tables, inviting boys I'd just met back to my dorm room because its sterile plainness was a thrill— *Look around, go ahead! There's nothing to see!* In March of that year, I sobered up quickly when I discovered I was pregnant and had no idea who the father was. At the time I thought of it as a humiliating wake-up call. The school doctor knew, but no one else had to, I decided. I told him I'd be fine going into Stamford alone for the procedure. I took a bus and brought a backpack full of textbooks. Afterward, I lay on the gurney and read my Japanese history book. In the years that followed, whenever I thought about those first months away from home, I felt a wash of embarrassment and, frankly, relief that I hadn't paid a steeper price. I didn't know, of course—it never occurred to me—that there might still be a price to pay.

Trish's worst year started with her suspension for a cafeteria incident that she never describes. I flip ahead in the diary to see how much more I can bear:

> Guess what! We have new neighbors across the street.
> The woman is a professor (really pretty!) and the man is a
> published writer. So far I've only talked to him. She's not
> around that much. Today at the bus stop he introduced
> himself. He told me he wanted to talk to me about what books
> I read and what I like to do. He said he's writing about a
> teenage girl and needs to do some research. I didn't tell
> him I want to be a writer, too. Maybe I won't tell him at all.
> I'll just write my book and when it's done, I'll show him.

She must have been fourteen by this point, the same age I was when my father checked himself into the hospital and I spent the next year wondering what our future would be like. It was a lonely, heightened period in my life, the last year when I remember everything that happened with perfect clarity. After that, small holes began opening up, things I either tried not to remember or simply couldn't.

CHAPTER 7

The next morning I walk into the kitchen to find a bowl of batter and a waffle iron on the counter. "Roland," Marianne says, shaking her head. "He usually eats downstairs but every Sunday he comes up here, makes a mess with his waffles, and goes back downstairs."

I try to keep the shock out of my voice. "Roland still *lives* here?" He made no appearance at the party yesterday, there's no car in the driveway, no visible sign of him.

"Oh, sure." She waves her hand. "Where else would he be?"

"Why didn't he come up last night?"

She shrugs. "Roland's never liked my parties. He thinks people ask about his work and then don't care about the answer. You know Roland," she says, which makes me blush self-consciously. I wonder if she suspects that I *did* know him once, better than most people realized.

I can see that Marianne doesn't want to dwell on the subject of her husband.

Last night, Jeremy only stayed at the party for about a half hour, but before he left, he took me aside and said that while I was here I should poke around and see what I could find. "This is the house where those meetings were, right? Where Linda Sue made her scenes?" I nodded and wondered what he thought I might find. "Maybe Marianne has a list of people who attended. It would be nice to find out who might have been there and gotten angry at Linda Sue."

Marianne pours us coffee and I ask her what became of the Neighborhood Watch group after I left. "I tried to keep it going, but it didn't work. People wouldn't even put out their signs." She shakes her head as if this has been the whole problem: people refusing to acknowledge danger. She thinks she has a list, she says, and an hour later she miraculously produces it. A yellow sheet torn neatly from a legal pad, covered in signatures. I stare at it and wonder if modern science can draw DNA from pen ink or the ancient cells deposited from the hands that brushed over this page.

"Wow," I say. There are seventeen names on the list, though in my memory more people were there that last night. When I point this out, Marianne says, "Some people didn't sign in. Linda Sue never would." She sighs as if, even in death, Linda Sue's arbitrary stances could be annoying.

I read down the list of names and see ones I don't recognize and others I've so long ago forgotten, I can't put a face to them. At the bottom Trish Rashke is printed out in bubbly teen-girl handwriting. "Trish was there?" I say. "I don't remember that."

Marianne looks over, reading with her bifocals. "I suppose she was. Those were the days when I tried to include her in things so she wouldn't sit in her room, listening to music that made her want to kill herself."

This is as close as Marianne has ever come to mentioning Trish's problems. I don't know if she doesn't talk about it, period, or if she keeps her silence on this subject with me in particular, sensing my old feelings, that I was more interested in Trish than I probably should have been. I wonder aloud about contacting some of the people on this list. "I don't have any phone numbers for them. It's not like anyone kept in touch." Marianne seems to have a point she's trying to make. *This was hard on everyone, not just you.*

Except for Paul, there was no one from the old neighborhood at the party last night. But surely they haven't all moved *that* far away. If strangers have been following my story, I have to assume my neighbors have, too. So why wouldn't Marianne have called them up? When I press the issue, she finally admits, "I tried a few. They all said they were sorry but it would just be too painful to come back."

I served twelve years in prison for a murder I didn't commit, and coming back here would be too painful for *them*? Marianne waves away whatever she's just implied. "Everyone just feels terrible that they didn't do more for you back then. They don't know what to say."

Maybe they feel guilty because one of them *is*.

Later that morning, after Marianne's gone out to the grocery store, I poke around the house, though I don't go near her office. If she's using this outing as a test, she'll know if I go through her papers, and I can't risk that just yet. I notice a tray of mail by the front door and something odd in it—an envelope addressed to Alocin Bell at C.L.E.E.R. Enterprises in Alabama. It's hand-typed with this address. It must have something to do with John, who lives in Alabama. I don't move it or touch it (amazing how aware of fingerprints one can be after leaving too many at a crime scene). Instead I go through the kitchen through a doorway that matches one I remember in our old house. There's a dark wooden set of stairs and no light so I hold fast to a splintering rail on

one side and make my way slowly. At the bottom, there's a cement land-
ing, and somewhere straight ahead a door to the finished apartment.
"Hello?" I call, and then louder, "HELLO?"

The door opens a crack and light spills in a line across the floor.
"Yes?" I hear a low voice, disembodied and male.

"Roland, it's Betsy. I wanted to say hello."

Is this strange that I've been here for a day without saying hello, or
stranger that he hasn't come up himself? The door opens wider, and
there he is. After all these years, my breath catches for a moment in
surprise, but of course time hasn't stopped for him, either. His thick
hair is mostly gray, his narrow face lined. The glasses are the same, as is
the slight stoop of his shoulders and the gentle smile. "Betsy. My God.
Look at you."

"It's nice to see you again, Roland."

In truth, this isn't the first time I've been down here to visit Roland.
The first time I came innocently enough to ask about his work because
I was interested in solar panel heating for our house. I'd had three miscarriages at that point and was looking for explanations: The heat when
it first came on in the fall smelled funny to me, full of chemicals. I'd
gotten pregnant in the late summer twice, and both times lost my babies
after the first freeze. Our ducts were full of toxins, I decided. Our furnace
was a laboratory of poisonous chemicals. "I don't want to go another
year with this heating system," I said to Paul, who looked aghast and
asked if I realized how much solar heating cost.

In prison, when I told Wanda some of these stories, she always
laughed. "Shit, honey, I used to know ladies like you. High maintenance, we call them." I always defended myself. "It wasn't *me* I was
thinking about, it was the babies, my *children*." I don't know if she believed me but it was true. I didn't want material goods, I wanted a
house full of children and their distractions. Wanda had three children,

grown by the time she came to prison. "You don't know what it's like to never have one," I told her.

It was January when I first knocked on Roland's basement door. It was cold and I was surprised to find him in sweatpants and a T-shirt, as if I'd just woken him up. "Oh, wow," he'd said, running his hands through his hair. "Sure, yeah. Come on in."

I'd never been in his basement workshop before, but it was just as I'd imagined: crowded with bookshelves and worktables cluttered with rolled-up drawings and designs, notebooks propped open, covered in illegible handwritten notes—data, I assumed, and diagrams that looked a little bit like the electrolytic converter I'd once made for my ninth-grade science fair.

"So what are you thinking about?" He looked around sheepishly at the mess. Shoes and socks on the floor, a comforter balled up at one end of the sofa. For the first time, I wondered if he slept down there.

"Well, solar, of course," I said. "I was thinking about the panels you have on your roof. Maybe we could start with something like that."

He was surprised by my interest and a little stumped, too. As it turned out, Paul was right—it *was* a costly investment and, even Roland had to admit, a little unpredictable. "You still need your backups. We go weeks without sun here." His panels heated water and not much else. "Solar works better in Florida, to be honest. Here, winter is tough."

"Isn't this what you do, though, Roland? You work for this company, right?" I held up the catalog he'd given me from Sunburst Enterprises.

"Right. Sort of. I'm a consultant on some research and design projects they have. I'm not a great authority on what's happening right now. Our system, for instance, doesn't work that great. We get maybe ten gallons of hot water a week. If that."

He stood in front of me, barefoot and handsome, with a five o'clock shadow. It was hard to imagine him doing a worse sales pitch. "There's a lot of kinks to get worked out with solar. The longer I look at it, the more I think these panels are inefficient, the recovery problematic. Sure, it's renewable, but waste gets created. No one wants to talk about the panel disposal problem."

"Roland."

"What?"

"Are you saying I shouldn't look into it *at all*?"

He leaned closer, weighing his words, as if he were not sure he should say them. "There are other things out there," he finally said, staring hard. "If you're interested."

I didn't look away. "Like what?"

"I'd have to lay it all out if you want to hear more."

"Yes," I whispered, a little breathless. "What is it exactly?"

He smiled and wiggled his eyebrows at me. I'd never seen him flirt like this before. "Cutting-edge stuff. The energy future. Just this last year there's been some breakthroughs—I shouldn't say too much." I tried to imagine what he was implying. "It could be life-changing, though."

Life-changing?

He wouldn't say any more than that. He couldn't, he said.

There'd been a rumor around the neighborhood that Roland was applying for a patent. In the last few months there had been more cars in their driveway and delivery trucks. The week before I'd seen him, barefoot on the lawn, arguing with an older man beside a Lincoln Continental parked in the driveway. We could tell something was happening, but we knew enough not to ask.

"I have some information that I'm not supposed to tell anyone," he said. I noticed his eyes, brown with green flecks, almost hazel. "But I trust you. You and Paul."

He said no more. He asked me not to mention it to anyone besides

Paul. "It's still experimental." He held up his hands, like two stop signs. "If too many people know, it could blow up in our face."

"Okay," I whispered.

I didn't tell Paul. I liked the secretive aspect of it all and for days I tried to imagine what he'd discovered. I even did research at work so I could ask Roland smart questions when I finally got the courage to stop by his basement again. I thought maybe I'd stumbled onto what he was talking about when I read about plans in the works for whole communities structured around net-zero free-energy models, where they produced all the energy they used with geothermal heating and solar photovoltaic cells. There were models already in existence and vision-ary future ones, incorporating an electric car in the purchase price of every house. The very idea amazed me. People coming together in the service of a larger good, not by real estate happenstance, but joined on a mission. Then I ran into Marianne in the grocery store and told her I'd been talking to Roland a bit about his work. "It sounds exciting," I said.

She rolled her eyes and reached out for a box of crackers. "Roland always thinks he's just invented the new lightbulb," she said, studying the ingredient list on the side of the box through her bifocals.

I knew they'd met when they were both at Texas A&M, that they'd been in the same department. I figured that she must have had at least some idea about his research. "It sounds like something completely new."

She looked at me over her glasses. "Is that what he told you?"

Was I saying too much? Had he shared information with me that he hadn't even told his wife yet? "I mean, that's all he said. He didn't get very specific."

"No. Roland never does." She shook her head and smiled, a little weary, like the mother of a younger child who was precocious and ex-hausting at the same time. "Get specific, I mean."

I couldn't understand what she was saying. What about the FedEx trucks driving up to their house? Or the oversized cars parked in their driveway?

"I'm afraid Roland has gotten in over his head with a few investors who want their money back," she said, still studying her cracker box.

By the way she spoke I understood this was part of something larger that she couldn't talk about here. That if we occasionally imagined Roland surprising us with a patent that won him money and fame, it wasn't likely to happen anytime soon. If he wasn't crazy exactly, he also wasn't someone I should take very seriously. He was Marianne's burden to bear. I felt embarrassed by my own gullibility and the time I'd spent researching at the library.

A week passed, then two. When I saw Roland again, it was from across the street, our lawns and sidewalks stretched out between us. He was bent over his hose spigot. I was guiding a wheelbarrow of fertilizer toward another dead patch that had recently opened up on our lawn. Our eyes caught each other's and stayed. For a moment, I couldn't move. *Well?* his face seemed to say. I tried to put on an expression that said, *I've talked to Marianne. I understand a little better now.* I didn't want him to feel bad, but I also didn't want to get caught up in a conversation that would embarrass us both. I pointed down to the wheelbarrow as if it contained some urgent business I had to get back to. It was weeks before I approached him again, and by that point I'd planned what to say: *I've talked to Paul and he wants to stay with what we have for now.*

In the end, it was easier than I expected. "That's perfectly fine," Roland said when I told him. "I understand."

Now we stand for a long time, me in the dark, him in the light. Both of our hands, I imagine, equally damp. Once, in prison, I saw a movie with an actor who looked so much like Roland, I thought for a moment it actually was. He played an awkward high school friend visiting the movie heroine, whose gay brother calls him "possibly the saddest person on earth." Roland only looks like that actor. He isn't sad, nor is he particularly awkward, given the fact that he lives like a hermit here, underground.

"Welcome back," he says, smiling shyly and stepping aside for me to come in. The apartment looks unchanged from my last visit. "I wanted to come up and say hello. Then I heard the stream of visitors and I didn't think you needed all that plus me."

He is exactly how I remember him, honest and sweet. "I would have rather seen you, Roland. Your first day out of prison is an odd time for making new friends."

He smiles at my joke but doesn't laugh. "Can I make you some tea?"

He made tea, I remember, the last time I came here. A fruit tea, I think. Peach. "That sounds nice."

He moves between his sink and his hot plate filling a chipped blue copper tea kettle, then sets out cups and stringed bags of tea. As crowded and unkempt as the space seems, his notebooks have a tidy order to them. Note cards are pasted across pages as if he were getting ready to write a research paper. As he pours water for tea, I read one: *On cells L3 and L4, we note a chemical reaction involving Pd that would correspond to about 3.5kJ of heat. This is to be compared with the 3M—1,000 times greater—of "excess heat" observed, so such excess could not possibly be of chemical origin.*

"It was Marianne's idea to invite you back here. I didn't even suggest it." He's got a playful smile on his face, as if together we'd pulled something off. He's always been this way with me—so warm and cordial, I never understood why he didn't come out more and charm the rest of the world. "I said, 'Of course, Marianne. You do what you want.' She said it felt a little funny to have you in Trish's room—"

My breath catches for a second. Did she guess the fantasy I used to have—that Trish was mine? "I'm grateful to you both. I didn't have too many options."

"Really? You're such a—" He looks around, searching for the right word. "Well, a celebrity now. I'd have thought everyone wanted you."

"No. Surprise, surprise. But no."

We stand across from each other, the silence between us filled with everything we might say and don't. Finally, he says, "How has this all been? Getting out and all that?"

"A little overwhelming, I have to admit. Everything's different now. There's so many gadgets—everyone uses cell phones. I'm not used to all that."

"Me neither." He smiles. In his own way, perhaps, he's as locked up as I've been.

"Betsy," Roland says, holding out his hand as if he wants to take mine. He's remembering the other time I came down here. What precipitated it all—how I opened myself up once and, doing so, couldn't stop. I can't tell him what I'm thinking now. I can't look at him or return the gesture.

Just standing here makes me think about everything I've been working so hard trying to forget.

CHAPTER 8

In prison, where sex is far more prevalent than most people realize, I was the only teetotaler I knew. Mostly for obvious reasons. I was older than the others. I didn't cut necklines out of my state-issue clothes or roll my pants down to where my underwear showed. I considered myself a role model and tried to act accordingly. I watched the other women get caught up in their dramas dating men from the prison across the highway. I'd roll my eyes and listen to their stories about the inmates who came to fix toilets and shovel sidewalks after it snowed. Though the men weren't allowed to talk while they worked, looks got exchanged, as did surprisingly long and florid letters. I admit, I sometimes felt jealous. *Dear Beautiful,* one of Wanda's read. *I think about you all the time and can't wait to see you again. Next time the flakes fly, look for me.*

Twice a year, our facility hosted a Family Days picnic using the men's yard, which meant, for a few hours at least, they were allowed to join us. For some of my fellow inmates, it was a wrenching conundrum—whether to be with their children, who they never saw enough of, or the men they'd been waving at through windows for the last three months. Usually they gave their mealtime to the children and their afternoons to the men.

Except for the early years when Paul came, I never had any visitors on Family Days. I usually spent the time on a blanket in a shady spot watching the games and imagined the brood I kept alive in my mind playing water balloons and soccer. By that time, I'd given each of them a name and a personality. Shy Benjamin was my oldest, sweet-hearted but unathletic. Shannon came next, a tomboy who could hit farther and run faster than her brothers. Peter, the middle one, was the funniest and maybe even my favorite. How could I not have a special spot in my heart for the only baby I'd held, the one who'd come the closest to being real? I kept Charlotte and Henry, my youngest two, on a blanket beside me. They were lap snugglers and hand holders, the ones who answered other adults by moving behind my legs, whispering into the folds of my clothes.

Though it might have looked otherwise, for me Family Days weren't sad or uneventful. Only once did I feel unsettled by the reminder that I was spending it, by all appearances, by myself. That was the time Leo came over and asked to share my blanket. I looked up at him and blinked, the sun so bright I could hardly see his face, though I recognized him as a member of the maintenance crew. His hair was sprinkled gray and very short. He wore glasses, which was unusual. "Every year I see you sitting here by yourself and every year I say I'm going to talk to you and then . . . I don't know." He dropped one hand around the back of his neck and shook his head. "I chicken out."

I shrugged and slid over. I'd started loosening up more, having some of these exchanges for the sole purpose of laughing about them later when the girls back on the block sat around and made fun of the men. "Sure," I said. "Sit."

He had the build of a carpenter and the soft, gentle face of an office worker or accountant. Because this was a medium-security facility, I knew that plenty of white-collar criminals were shuffling through their time for tax evasion. I assumed he was one of them. "So you're the librarian," he said.

There were five hundred men living in this facility and seventy-five women in ours. It was easier for them to keep track of us than it was for us to remember them. "That's right," I said, and then, because we were smiling at each other, I added, "Why? Are you looking for a book?"

"Maybe," he said, laughing. "Do you have any recommendations?"

"What do you like?" It made no sense, the way we were grinning at each other.

"Guess."

"True crime? Ann Rule?"

He shook his head.

I raised my eyebrows. "Danielle Steel?"

He laughed and I did, too. I didn't sound like myself. I sounded like Wanda, who flirted with everyone and tried to get a marriage proposal by the end of every Family Days picnic. "Nah, probably not," Leo said. "I just finished something called *The Mill on the Floss*. Interesting book. I liked it a lot." I turned and looked at him square in the eye. A man spending his prison time reading George Eliot? "Have you ever read that one? I had a few problems with Tom Tulliver, of course." He caught my eye and smiled. "Any man would. I'm thinking about trying Virginia Woolf next. What book of hers do you recommend starting with?"

Was he serious? I stared at him for a while. "Who *are* you?"

"Leo Rankin." He held out his hand. "I was an English teacher before I came here. I'm trying to use this time to fill in my reading gaps. In college, I'm afraid I slid by on CliffsNotes and smart girlfriends. Somehow I never read any Woolf."

As the afternoon wore on, he told me he'd graduated from Brown with a double major in English and psychology. He didn't start teaching right away. Instead, he went into advertising, which he hated, though the girlfriend he was obsessed with at the time begged him to stay with it. "She wanted us to be one of those glamorous married New York City couples." He laughed and shook his head.

"So what happened?"

"We got married and I stayed in advertising. I guess it worked out until I developed a little drinking problem. The truth is, I don't remember a lot of that time."

It was all a little disconcerting: a man who read George Eliot with a history of memory lapses? He told me more: His marriage dissolved, which gave him the freedom to do what he'd always wanted to do— teach high school English. All a dream come true except for the alcoholism. "Certainly wish now I'd left that behind with the wife." The more he talked, the longer I let myself look at him—his kind face, the way his eyes crinkled in the corners.

"And what brought you here?" I asked, because it seemed as if we could joke about anything now, even our crimes. Too late, I remembered Wanda once saying you should never ask a male inmate this question, that it made them defensive and a little crazy. I worried that I'd ruined the nice time we'd just had.

"Manslaughter," he said softly. "Vehicular homicide. Two kids and their mom."

What could I say? If he knew that I was the librarian, he also knew my crime. I didn't need to tell him, *I know how you feel. I have blood on my hands, too.* Guilt like ours was dark and private.

"I should go," I said. They were packing the vans that would take us back across the highway.

"Yep." He stared down between his knees and held a flat hand up. "Sure thing."

"It was nice talking to you."

"Uh-huh."

"No, really. It was."

"You'll probably make fun of me back on the block." He looked up at me and smiled. "Right? Isn't that what today is all about? You ladies come over, prance around our yard, get us acting like fools, and then you go back home and laugh about it?"

Though I hated to say it, the answer was yes. "How about this?" I said, leaning close enough to smell the sweat coming off his T-shirt. "I promise I won't do that."

"Aw." He smiled, and for a second I thought he might touch me. "That's nice. Then what will you talk about tonight?"

"I'll do what I always do. Roll my eyes at everyone else."

Why was I leaving, I suddenly wondered, *when we still had forty minutes before we had to be back?* Sitting so close to him for so long—almost two hours when I looked down at my watch—had scared me. It reminded me of Wanda's strategies for the day, how she liked to target certain men, spend the morning flirting, then by the afternoon be in the bushes with them. What if he was this type, I thought, with a timetable in his head and a goal for the day?

Then he surprised me. Three days later, I got a letter from him, delivered by Sasha, who worked in the laundry facility we shared with the men. She was a regular conduit of mail and got paid in favors for her work; luckily for me, she was also one of the girls I'd tutored to pass her GED.

She liked me enough to pass this on:

> *Dear Lovely Lady* [We couldn't risk using names. If the
> letter was found, we'd both get in trouble],
> *I just wanted to say that I enjoyed our conversation at the*
> *picnic very much. In a bleak time of very few memorable*
> *highlights, for me that has been one. I shall remember it for*
> *some time even as I also remember the skeptical way you*
> *regarded me through most of it. I will also remember the thrill*
> *it was making you laugh, how you looked like a teenager when*
> *you did. And then, when you walked away from me—too*
> *soon, I'm afraid, earlier than you had to—how the sun*
> *glanced off your hair and your arms and I honestly thought*
> *you looked like an angel. To me, you are that beautiful. And*
> *now I wonder if I might have permission to write to you and*
> *if you'll indulge me a little and write a line or two back?*
> *I've never done this before so I'm not sure exactly what the*
> *protocol is.*
>
> Love,
Your Book Buddy

I felt like I was in high school. I showed it to Wanda, who memorized enough of it to recite lines aloud to half of our cell block. When I
wrote him back, I tried to preserve some semblance of distance even as
I drafted the thing four times:

> *Hello Book Worm,*
> *Technically, to be classified as a book lover, you have to start*
> *reading the unabridged editions of the American classics.*
> *Those are the ones without pictures or questions at the end*

of every chapter. I suspect you know what I'm talking about. This is just to say that yes, I very much enjoyed talking to you as well, and believe it or not, I liked your letter even more. You're welcome to write me whenever you'd like and I will do my best to respond, within the confines of my busy social calendar, of course.

Best,

LL

P.S. The word around here is that not one but two of my fellow residents have noticed you in the past and think you're "cute." Though I won't share names, of course, you'd be well advised to examine all your options before settling on this— how else can I put it?—more experienced member of the crowd. Up to you.

I'd included the P.S. because it was true and because I didn't feel particularly threatened by my competition—two younger women, both former heroin addicts who'd lost most of their teeth. I liked the way it made me sound casual but might also elicit a protestation of some sort. I wasn't disappointed.

His next letter read,

Please, my dear,

I didn't look across the highway from this place with the hope of shopping for a girlfriend. Give me some credit, I beg of you. Not that your suite mates aren't a lively bunch, I'm sure, but I've had my head bent down for so long that it startled me to look up and notice you. And when I did, I sensed something right away: that we are both locked in these places for reasons

that have as much to do with our innate decency as they do
with our failures. I suspect we have both lived lives that
appeared to have serene surfaces and were, for both of us,
hollow and impossible to sustain. I am here because I was too
cowardly to find another way to escape the life I never wanted
in the first place. I don't know if it felt that way for you.
Maybe I'm wrong. But something tells me I'm not.
Something tells me this crush I have on you feels different
than anything I've had in years because it is different.
Because neither one of us belongs in here and both of us felt so
guilty about our old failures that we stupidly, tragically, got
ourselves put here. Am I right about this? You tell me.

After that, the letters got heady and overlong. His started filling four or five pages of yellow lined legal-size paper, drawing distinctions between a point he'd just made or clarifying an old one, full of literary references or philosophical musings about the nature of love and the balance that must be struck in any new relationship. *I just want to be honest,* he said in one, worrying me a little. Hadn't we always been? *Even if it's difficult, I still want you to be honest with me.*

I considered a few confessions I might make: (1) I seem to be infertile though no one knows why; (2) I don't think I was ever in love with my husband; (3) I've suffered from memory lapses and a childhood I don't remember much about; (4) sometimes I'm afraid there is something unspeakably wrong with me.

I didn't, of course. Even in the blush of his lavish attentions, I knew all love had its limits.

After a while, I started watching Leo work through the steel-reinforced window outside the library—the curve of his back as he bent over the hoe, the damp patches on his T-shirt. I loved watching his body as he worked under the broiling sun. I imagined touching his wrist, his hands, the back of his neck. I could tell he wasn't accustomed to the muscles he'd developed in the last year. I gave in to my obsession and stood in the hallway outside the library, wasting hours waiting for him to look up and see me, so I could arrange my face in an expression of surprise as if I'd only just walked up. For months, those vigils were worth it—he'd mouth some joke and I'd cup my hand behind my ear, an exaggerated *What?*

We'd both laugh and make *I'll call you* gestures, as if we were teenagers. We had other signals. A pen scribbling across a flat hand meant *Did you get my note?* Once, he staggered back, a flat hand on his chest, and I thought he was having a heart attack until I understood what he meant: *I got it. I loved it.* I blew him a kiss and clapped my own hand to my heart.

For two months I became a person I didn't recognize. I ironed my jeans and put on makeup to stand by the window and wait for him to look up. I wrote to him every night, and in between I read the books he'd mentioned in his letters to me. I once stood at a window for an hour waiting to show him I'd found a copy of *Slaughterhouse-Five* by Kurt Vonnegut. *I still don't like it much,* I tried to mouth, though he couldn't understand through the window frosted with dirt. He held up his fingers in an *L* on his chest, a sign we'd developed to say "I love you."

Ridiculous, of course, when we'd only ever had the one conversation.

CHAPTER 9

Standing in Roland's basement reminds me of how feelings, once awoken, can't be so easily set aside. I leave with a flurry of excuses about the work I need to get to, phone calls I must make. In a wave of embarrassment, I retreat to Trish's bedroom, which has no phone, only the copy of *Middlemarch* lying on the desk with Geoffrey's inscription. What *was* their relationship all those years ago? Did Geoffrey flirt with Trish the way he flirted with all of us—with his friendship and his confessions? Nothing he would get blamed for later, but insidious all the same. Was poor Trish, at age fifteen, in love with him back then?

Was I?

That was the question everyone asked during my trial, and I saw the answer written on their faces: *Yes, poor Betsy, she pined like a schoolgirl.* But it was never as simple as that. Yes, I thought about him a lot. I saw our life through his eyes. After they moved onto our block, I started gardening more. I looked in the mirror before I walked up the driveway to check the mail. Was that a crime? I had a crush on him, as Paul did, as we all did, graced by a presence that seemed to make our life look more like a happy choice, not an accident. I noticed the distance in Geoffrey's marriage, the things he and Corinne didn't know about each other. "Wait, what class are you teaching again?" Geoffrey would ask her at a dinner party midway through the semester. She was teaching in Princeton at that point, a four-hour commute, which meant she stayed there four days a week. They had separate lives, weekends that had nothing to do with the weekdays Geoffrey spent with us, the housewives on the block.

I also remember this: I was there the first time Geoffrey met Linda Sue. She'd moved in only a month earlier. Newly divorced from a husband none of us had ever met, she bought the house kitty-corner to ours that had been empty for six months, whose previous owners hadn't bothered keeping things up. We all wondered if it would ever sell looking the way it did, with peeling paint and a yard gone to weeds. According to Helen, who knew the real estate agent, Linda Sue had looked it over once, smoked a cigarette on the porch, and nodded when the agent apologized for the dandelions. "It's fine," Linda Sue said, grinding out her cigarette. "I like it the way it is."

We hardly noticed the day she moved in because no truck was necessary to carry in what little furniture she had: a few canvas folding chairs and a lumpy futon. Within a week, everyone had their own story to tell of meeting our new neighbor.

"Where do you come from?" Marianne had asked her, holding a rhubarb cake, the same kind she'd made to welcome us five years earlier.

"Nowhere," Linda Sue had said, eyeing the cake. "Seriously. Nowhere."

With me, she was a little more forthcoming. When I told her I worked as a librarian, she asked if people ever returned books with personal items left inside. "As a matter of fact, yes!" I said. Only a few months earlier, I'd placed a cardboard box beneath the front desk to preserve the "bookmarks" we'd found: the snapshots, the personal letters. Once, I found a five-dollar bill folded in such a way I had to assume someone had done it intentionally. I was interested in our "finds" and wondered if we might collect enough to make a temporary display called "Place Holders" in the glass case of our lobby. Viola called the idea a little "out there," but said I could go ahead with it when I'd collected enough. I started to tell Linda Sue but stopped when I saw she wasn't listening. She had another question she wanted to ask: "Do you have that problem where crazy people come in and masturbate on your books?"

We never knew where she was from, though Helen Baker-Harrison thought she'd heard of the town, somewhere in upstate Connecticut. Helen waved her hand in a way that we interpreted as west of the river, the side that was both more Bohemian and richer. For a while we wondered if Linda Sue was an artist, based not on anything she said but on the clothes she wore: diaphanous skirts washed to a pale flesh color; men's undershirts and vests decoupaged with what looked like the contents of a drawer bottom—loose buttons, chipped mirror pieces, and china plate bits.

"Did you make your vest?" I heard Marianne once ask her nervously, eyeing the dried glue.

"Yeah, I took a class," Linda Sue said, running a hand over its bumpy terrain. "It was kind of a joke."

Eventually we learned that Linda Sue had lots of opinions and that it didn't take much prodding to elicit them. She hated public swimming pools and the Baker-Harrisons' dog, who barked at clouds. When she hadn't made any move to mow her overgrown yard a month after she moved in, and a couple of husbands had offered to stop by with their mowers, we learned that she liked it the way it was. "It just grows back, right?" she said, as if she were not completely sure. "I guess I don't see the point. You just end up mowing—what? Every weekend?"

The men were dumbstruck. "Right."

"So you'd just have to come back. No, thanks."

Once I saw her in the grocery store, staring at an onion in her hand as if she were trying to remember what it was. I pushed my cart over toward her, thinking, *I shouldn't walk away just because she's odd.* "Hello, Linda Sue!" I called. "Have you got a recipe?"

We all pretended to be avid cooks in those days. We had cookie exchanges at Christmas and potlucks we came to with recipes written out on index cards. In truth, none of us was very good. Linda Sue threw the onion back in the bin. "Oh, God no," she said. "I never cook. I didn't even bring my pots and pans with me. I keep thinking I should buy a can opener and then I don't." *Was she joking?* I wondered, and laughed hopefully. "Mostly I eat cereal," she said, nodding down at her cart filled with boxes. "But I was trying to remember how you make onion soup. Do you know?"

Paul didn't eat onions so I never bothered.

"I'm guessing onions, right? But then what?"

Had she lived in a foreign country? Been isolated in some way? "Broth, I guess. Beef, maybe."

"Right. That makes sense."

I started to push my cart away but stopped. "Do you need any help, Linda Sue? Setting up your house? Getting situated?" As far as any of us could tell, she still had no curtains or furniture beyond the three canvas director's chairs she'd arrived with. She had no TV or stereo. From the glimpses we'd gotten, she made an evening's entertainment out of flicking her lighter and smoking cigarettes. Was all this a cry for help?

"Getting situated?" she said.

"I can help you measure for curtains if you need it. We just got new ones ourselves. It's a terrible chore, I know."

She blinked at me. "Why do people buy curtains?"

"Well." I looked around, wondering if I was on *Candid Camera*. "Privacy, I guess."

"Yeah—I don't care about that."

"Window treatments can really pull a room together, I find. You'd be surprised."

"Yeah, I don't care about that, either."

As we came to understand, she didn't care about much. The yard, her trash, what anyone thought of her. All the rules that I'd assumed for so long were sacrosanct.

A month after Linda Sue moved in, Marianne started passing out flyers for a Neighborhood Watch group she wanted to form, not in response to any burglaries reported, she said, but to a "feeling" she had of "menace" in the air. Until Marianne brought it up, none of us had thought much about being robbed. We left our garages open with our dust-covered bikes there for the taking. For Paul and me, it wasn't unusual to come home and find our door unlocked with nobody home. Sometimes I sat in my car, a four-step walk from rectifying the problem, and thought, *Why bother?* and drove away. We had so few belongings of value, why would any burglar waste his time with us? And then I thought of something strange: the stain on our mattress, from the night our longest-lasting baby left us after five and a half months of growing what were already tiny hands and feet. It was the closest thing

I had to a picture of his face, a brown outline shaped like a swan on our mattress. My heart seized at the thought of someone stealing that.

"All right," I told Marianne. "I'll be there."

At our first meeting, the speaker was a female police officer with ebony hair broken in front by a small stripe of white. She looked like Susan Sontag dressed in a police uniform. "A property crime occurs somewhere in this country every three seconds," she said. "Every day I see people lose everything they have."

Earlier, Geoffrey and I had made jokes about this meeting and rolled our eyes, though we both said we would go. The woman up front continued, "You should all know that a hollow core door is a burglary waiting to happen and a solid door is only as good as its lock. Anything less than a double cylinder with a six-inch throw is like leaving your house open. You might as well stick some bubble gum in there." She opened a briefcase and pulled out the only dead bolt guaranteed to stop a burglar. It took two hands to hold and looked like a tire jack.

As she passed around order forms for purchasing one of her dead bolts, I turned around and saw Geoffrey sitting in the back, wearing a black turtleneck that so flattered him, I once embarrassed myself by saying so. Geoffrey widened his eyes as if to say, *Is this woman serious?*

Ever since he moved onto our block, I'd worried that the inanity of our lives might be too much for him, that at some point he'd announce the truth: He'd lived here as a research experiment and now he couldn't take it anymore. I smiled and turned to face front, now so aware of myself in his sight line, I couldn't listen to anything until Linda Sue, sitting next to me, raised her hand. "I have a question."

"Yes?"

"You say we should call in if we see a suspicious person driving down our block, but how are we defining *suspicious person*?"

"That depends. Someone you don't know driving slowly. Someone who's dressed badly, or driving an unmarked car. People talk about white vans and there's truth to that rumor. Some criminals do drive unmarked white vans."

"I don't think that's what you really mean, though, is it?"

"I beg your pardon?"

"I think you mean we should call the police if we see a black or Hispanic man driving down the street."

A silence settled over the room.

"Oh, Linda Sue." Marianne stood up. "Let's not get into all that right now." I could hear Marianne's impatience, as if she hadn't even wanted to invite Linda Sue, which was possible. When I'd run into Linda Sue that morning and asked if she was going, she said she hadn't heard anything about it.

"All *what,* Marianne?" she asked, her voice full of innocence.

Marianne crossed her arms over her chest. "All this defensiveness and posturing. I'm sorry, but I'd rather make a mistake and regret it later than get raped at knifepoint."

Oh, dear, I thought, wishing I were closer to Geoffrey so I could whisper, *I'm sure Marianne doesn't mean to sound so ugly.*

"This is exactly our point," the policewoman said, looking down at Linda Sue. "We believe it's better to make a mistake than to be sorry later."

"And what do you tell the law-abiding Puerto Rican family who gets dragged into a police station because they made the mistake of driving on our block?"

Though I thought Linda Sue was brave to hold her ground, I was sorry she'd sat down next to me, afraid that some of the older people might think I was the one making these comments. Anyone could tell this wasn't the place to say all this. Kim, from Korea was in the room, as was Eleanor, who worked with troubled black teenagers. These were complicated issues, not quite the same as taking a novelty approach to lawn-care chores. If Eleanor wasn't bringing this up, why was Linda Sue?

The policewoman continued, "If the family checked out, we'd thank them for their time and tell them they're free to go now."

Oh, no, I thought. *Please. Just say you'd apologize.*

"You wouldn't worry about them suing you for traumatizing their kids?"

Marianne's face reddened. "If you have problems with this group, Linda Sue, why don't we talk about it afterward?"

"No, I like the group. It's fine." She looked around as if surprised that anyone might have taken her comments the wrong way.

"Good," Marianne continued, her voice tight with the effort to control it. "Then our time is up. We'll meet again in two weeks to nominate officers. Maybe we can take up Linda Sue's questions then."

Linda Sue stood up and lit a cigarette. "Fat chance," she said, exhaling. I wondered if she'd seen Marianne's needlepoint sampler that said, NO SMOKING, LUNGS AT WORK. "Maybe we should go to the porch," I whispered.

Outside, Linda Sue shook out another cigarette. "Want one?"

The last time I smoked was early in college, hardly a time I remember with great nostalgia, but something compelled me to reach over and take a cigarette. Inhaling gave me a head rush. I felt dizzy and nauseated and drunk all at once. I leaned against the porch railing to steady myself. "Why do you say things like that? Get everyone riled up?"

Lind Sue smiled and caught my eye. I saw it then: She knew exactly the effect her words had and it was all an act—the cereal, the clothes, the way she pretended to care about nothing. "When you're not married, you can do anything you want," she said. "It's fun. You should try it sometime. Pick someone and tell them what you really think."

I looked up and saw Geoffrey watching us through the sliding-glass doors. I thought about doing what she'd just suggested, walking over to him and saying out loud, *I think about you more than I should. I imagine us doing strange things sometimes—buying vegetables together or riding an elevator. I know I shouldn't but I do.* I watched him make a face through the glass door, his hands around his neck, as if to say, *I'm dying in here. Let me out.* I laughed and waved him over. *Good old Geoffrey won't ostracize Linda Sue for speaking her mind,* I thought. *He'll probably like her more.*

"Hello, ladies," he said, walking toward us, nodding. "I'm afraid the paranoia quotient is running a little high in there. I thought maybe I'd get some air before I go home and start pricing handguns."

I laughed, too loud. An embarrassing bark. Linda Sue looked at me and shook her head. *Was it obvious?* I wondered. *Could everyone see?*

"Time for me to go," she said, stubbing out her cigarette on the bottom of her shoe and dropping it between the open slats of the deck. A minute later she was gone, leaving Geoffrey standing there, his hands in his pockets, and me wondering—for the first time—which one of us he'd come outside to talk to.

Later, Geoffrey and I walked home together and he told me that back in Florida people were much more obsessed with self-protection. "Down there, if you don't have a gun in the house, people think you're asking for trouble." He often talked about the old days living in Florida as if it had all been part of a different era—wilder, crazier—where he'd gained his fame and all the problems that came with it. "It was great," he said the one time I pressed the subject. "But it couldn't last." I assumed he meant his own overindulgence—too much drinking and sleeping with the wrong women. Corinne saved him from all that. She was a creature of habit who rose at five, worked until eleven, and taught a full day of classes afterward. But sometimes, I let myself wonder,

Would a marriage, embarked on to save him from his own worst impulses, last in the face of his reformation?

Once, I told him my marriage to Paul sometimes felt more like a friendship with lots of sex for baby-making purposes. He laughed and then stopped himself. "Yes," he said. "Corinne and I are like that except she doesn't want the babies." It was the first time we'd mentioned the children neither one of us had. Though he didn't say it directly, I thought I heard the disappointment in his voice, recognized the expression on his face.

"Do you still own a gun?" I asked at the bottom of his driveway. He had his hands in his pockets, and I wondered if he was as nervous as I was, standing in the dark.

"Yes," he said. "But don't tell Corinne. She thinks I sold it before we left."

It was one of many secrets we shared, sure that neither one of us would judge what the other was saying. And I didn't. I went home that night and lay awake in bed beside my sleeping husband, replaying each look, every moment, without once thinking it was wrong that he secretly kept a gun his wife didn't know about.

CHAPTER 10

Linda Sue wasn't killed with a gun. She died from blunt-force injury to the back of the head. Not one blow, but three. We heard this as one of many rumors that were flying around the morning we woke up to the sight of police cars pulling up and parking haphazardly on our street. At first we assumed she'd died of natural causes. When blood was mentioned, and "evidence collection" by one of the police officers standing outside, we assumed that she'd died in some terrible fall down the stairs. *An accident, an accident,* we all told one another. But an hour later it was confirmed: There was evidence of head injury and foul play. Blood spatter on the wall ruled out any chance of accidental death.

By the afternoon we'd gathered at Helen's house and learned, from her brother-in-law who worked as a detective downtown, that Linda Sue had been hit with something large and metal that was found in the house and—we all gasped at this—was cleaned and left behind. Helen filled in more details. "Sometimes these guys try to make a murder scene look like a robbery that's gone wrong. They steal stuff they don't even care about." We sat in her living room, cups of coffee in our hands. "But this guy—nothing. He didn't even take a twenty-dollar bill lying on the coffee table."

It was forty-eight hours before we learned what the murder weapon was, and each of us was struck dumb by the irony: She was killed by one of the dead bolts we'd all ordered from Marianne's police officer at that first Neighborhood Watch meeting. All except Linda Sue, for whom Marianne negotiated a free one, saying, when she delivered it to Linda Sue, that she meant no harm and wanted only for everyone to feel equally safe.

As we heard more and tried to make sense of it all, the cleaning of the weapon became the greatest source of mystery and ultimately, Franklin admitted, the reason my defense never gained traction. Even if the jury had believed that a person could remain in a somnambulant state long enough to cross a street, enter an unlocked house, surprise its occupant and kill her, how did that same person clean up so thoroughly and stay asleep? On the weapon itself, lab testing showed residues of dish soap and bleach, even scratch marks where a steel-wool pad had been used to scrub the hinges. But whoever took such care cleaning it had failed to dislodge the hair and skin residue from the joint. Testing easily confirmed both the damage it had done and the attempt to cover it. Though Franklin could point to cases of assault committed by a sleepwalking assailant, none had gotten busy afterward with a bucket and sponge.

The prosecutors, given only the burden of proving that I was conscious while committing the crime I'd already confessed to, never addressed other peculiarities in the evidence and Franklin never pressed the matter. For instance, my fingerprints were found throughout the house, but not on the front doorknob. Back then we weren't trying to prove the argument Jeremy had made, that I was never there that night, that my fingerprints were from a visit I'd made to Linda Sue during the day. Jeremy showed me a map with X's marking the places my prints were found: on the book beside her bed, on an unwashed glass around the sink where I must have poured myself water. "Do you remember doing that?" Jeremy asked at one of our earliest meetings.

"Jeremy"—I leaned forward in my chair—"it was twelve years ago. No, I don't remember if I poured myself water."

"But it's possible. You touched a glass. You touched the sink."

"I must have," I said.

"Right, exactly." He nodded so emphatically his glasses slipped down his nose.

If the murder weapon struck others as ironic, no one's ever made a joke about it. If I'd gotten a chance to talk to Geoffrey alone after my arrest, it would have been the first thing I'd have done to cut the tension. *Looks like Marianne's locks were a big help. Good thing she got the extra one for Linda Sue.* That was one irony to the murder weapon; the other was the fact that all of us had one. "Were there identifying characteristics? Serial numbers?" I asked, the same day we learned what weapon was used.

"No, Betsy." Marianne rolled her eyes. "Most people don't worry about their *locks* being stolen."

How many people had already installed their heavy-duty lock system by the night of Linda Sue's murder? One? None? Anyone could have brought their lock over, intending to do harm with it. All of us were potential perpetrators.

When I pointed this out after we'd learned what the murder weapon was—before I found the nightgown and realized I was the one we were all looking for—Marianne shook her head. "Oh, Betsy, honestly. You read too much. This wasn't someone we *know*. This was a crazy person who got to us before we could get decent locks installed."

Ultimately I made it easy for the police, handing over my night-gown and, eight hours later, my confession, too. "It was me," I told them. "It must have been me. Who else could have done it?" I'm not sure what I was thinking. I vaguely sensed that my future had been erased and nothing much mattered anymore, so what difference did it make? The morning after I made the confession, I woke up in jail know-ing I'd made a terrible mistake. I called my lawyer and said I needed to change my story. I assumed it would take a few days to clear the mis-take up.

"You're *recanting* your confession," Franklin said, at our first face-to-face meeting. He had snow-white hair and the only handlebar mus-tache I'd ever seen on a living person. "You're saying you *didn't* do it?"

"That's right. I didn't do it."

"Why did you confess, then?"

"I was in a dark mood. I can't really explain."

He folded his hands over his knee. "You'll have to do better than that. Recanting a confession is a bitch, I'll tell you right now. You need solid evidence of physical or psychological coercion. Do you have any bruises or cuts right now?" I shook my head. "Any physical intimida-tion used on you last night?"

"No." They'd played mind games all night, offering to bring me dinner from a sandwich shop, asking my preference and then returning with a broken granola bar, saying it was the best they could do. I hadn't eaten since breakfast nine hours earlier. I was starving, but too proud to eat it on the spot. Instead, I opened it under the table and ate it in furtive bites. After another hour, I gave them my confession because I honestly wasn't sure what had happened and I thought it was possible. I also thought doing so might get me a sandwich.

Franklin was right. Recanting a confession is nearly impossible if you weren't inebriated, a minor, or cognitively disabled when you made it. And there were other problems working against me: The blood didn't follow a clear-cut or obvious pattern. There was a pool of it around Linda Sue's body, and the wall opposite was heavily spattered, but there was no visible blood sprayed in between. Also, no trace spatters on the ceiling or on the wall, which—we were told—would have been expected if an ordinary beating had taken place. One theory was that she was already lying on the ground when she was hit, suggesting that there was an accidental fall and her aggressor might have been someone who was "not physically superior or capable of overpowering her."

There was also this detail that every reporter loved to endlessly repeat: The perpetrator, either before or after the crime (both unimaginable), stopped and fixed a turkey and cheese sandwich. With no sign of it in the contents of Linda Sue's stomach, it had to have been her killer who left his mayo knife on the counter, along with a torn half sandwich—no bite marks, no saliva, no DNA—as if he had made it not to eat but to drive the investigators crazy.

And one more thing: a spiral notebook found beside Linda Sue's bed, folded open to a list that read *Dr.'s appt., Library books, Betsy T.* The prosecution argued that my name on this list must have meant that Linda Sue was awake, writing, when I arrived. The evidence suggests there was no struggle in the bedroom where her few possessions remained undisturbed, her bed comforter neatly folded back, as if she had gotten up to go to the bathroom. There was also no sign of a struggle on the second floor. No telltale handprints clutching at the banister, no fingerprints or blood on the walls at the top of the stairs. Franklin pointed out the illogic. When someone lying in bed sees an unexpected person walk into her bedroom, is her first impulse to write the name down? Absurd, he argued, though no one could think of another reason.

Over the years, I've thought a great deal about this list—all the more mysterious if you consider that Linda Sue had no library card. I've wondered if they ever analyzed the handwriting, if it might not have been Linda Sue's to-do list but *Geoffrey's,* left in her bedroom, along with the nine ghastly semen stains found on her sheets, proof that she cared as little about laundry as she did about her yard. But if it *was* Geoffrey's list, why was my name on it?

In a trial like mine such questions get asked and never answered. Witnesses aren't allowed to speculate; important evidence gets dropped. What matters isn't who wrote that list and why. What matters is the feeling you evoke sitting in a jury's presence day after day. To those people I must have seemed too distant, too unconnected to everything being said. One juror claimed the only time I cried was hearing Geoffrey testify that, yes, he was in love with Linda Sue and had wanted to start a life with her, which isn't exactly fair. After hearing this, I turned around to look for Paul, who wasn't where he usually sat. It took a while to find him, and when I did, he looked so small sitting in the back, so demoralized and ruined, tears sprang to my eyes.

A few weeks after that first Neighborhood Watch meeting, we gathered at Helen's house for a wine and cheese party to launch the "faux-finishing" business she'd been talking about starting for years. "It's a painting technique," she explained after we arrived. "This is Victorian Gothic. And this is Shabby Chic." She pointed at a footstool painted with rose vines, then at a side table crackled to look old. By the time ten people arrived, her living room felt like a very crowded flea market.

"I love it, Helen, I do," I whispered. "But I think I'm going to step outside."

Helen and Warren's was one of the few homes that already had an addition—a covered eating porch out back with an expanded master bedroom/bath upstairs. Around the edges of the porch, she had propped mirror frames and medicine chests, sponge-painted to look old and dusted with mold. I squinted at her price tags and had to sit down. "Oh, my," Paul said joining me. "I don't think I get it."

For no reason I could explain, I felt like crying. Suddenly it was more effort than I could bear, praising Helen's "art," buying the smallest, cheapest piece we could find. Sometimes this happened. I stood in a room full of people and had to stop myself from screaming the bleak truths I felt. *This stuff doesn't look good! We aren't really friends!*

"Are you okay?" Paul asked softly. He knew me well enough not to come any closer or touch me.

"Yes," I said, breathing once, then twice. "I'm fine."

I looked up and saw Geoffrey through the door bent over a flowerpot painted to look like dirt. The smile on his face had dried to his teeth. My heart skipped ahead. He would see us and slip out here. In a minute this party would make more sense. We'd find a piece of furniture to point out and make a gentle joke about. "I like the flowerpot because you don't have to wash it," he'd say, and we'd laugh, and the evening would already be half over.

At his suggestion, he and I had recently started reading *Anna Karenina,* and it seemed as if the dynamic were shifting between us, as if he were ceding some of the authority on literary matters to me. "You understand the modernists better than I do," he'd said last week. When I said nothing, he added, "It's true. You do."

I kept thinking about a conversation we'd had that afternoon. After he clarified a point about Flaubert, I asked him how his own novel was coming. "You'd better hurry up. I need something good to read after we're done with this." Right away, I regretted saying it. I knew he got letters from fans begging him to publish, not realizing how much pressure he felt, how complicated it was for him. I also knew he was having trouble. He was a perfectionist, he'd once said, and he couldn't part with anything that wasn't as good as he'd imagined it could be. It made me wonder if he held himself to impossibly high standards. "Doesn't every book have weaknesses?" I pointed out. "Isn't that the fun for the reader? Finding holes and inconsistencies?"

I thought I'd made a decent point—the book clubs I knew spent most of their time dissecting the flaws of very good books—but he shook his head. "That's not my problem exactly," he said. I could tell he was upset. "I thought moving here would help my concentration, get me more focused. I don't know. I keep letting myself get distracted."

We were standing in the library and I pushed my shelving cart to the farthest corner of the row. "By what?" I asked.

For the last week and a half I'd been afraid of the changes I'd seen in him—the extra nervous energy, the way he brought up topics and dropped them quickly. It felt as if he were on the brink of making some confession I didn't want to hear. Perhaps he was drinking again or moving back to Florida.

"It's not right," he said, shaking his head.

"What isn't right?"

I'd never seen him at a loss for words before. "Corinne and I haven't—" He stopped himself there. Whatever he'd wanted to say, he didn't.

When Geoffrey finally came out onto the porch at Helen's party, Paul smiled and laughed at the joke he made ("I'm looking for the American flag dining room table. Is that out here?"). A minute later, Paul left, which wasn't like him. Usually the three of us looked for excuses to sit alone together at these parties. For a second, I wondered, *Is he trying to give us space? Is he angry with me?*

Even then I worried about how little I intuited about the people around me, basic dynamics, things that were obvious to everyone else. *What's going on?* I wanted to ask Geoffrey. *Explain it to me.* My one flicker of prescience: I felt, that night, as if our world were shifting, changing irrevocably, and I just wanted to know where it was headed.

"Linda Sue is coming, right?" Geoffrey said. It was the first time I'd ever heard him mention her name.

"I don't know," I said. "I guess. Usually she does." For all the distance Linda Sue ostensibly kept, she never missed a gathering as far as I could tell.

"Just curious," he said, looking over his shoulder. "No reason. I mean, she likes stuff like this, I assume. Arts and crafts."

"Are you okay, Geoffrey?"

"Sure, yeah. Just fired up. Did a little writing today."

For what felt like forever neither one of us spoke.

"Inspired by you, I guess," he said, wearing the same dry-mouth smile he'd been wearing earlier, examining the flowerpot.

Say what you mean! I wanted to scream. *Just tell me what's happening.* Then I saw it on his face first: how every muscle relaxed into a real, heart-stopping smile; how he exhaled so deeply, I could hear his relief. I turned and saw what he was looking at: Linda Sue had arrived.

Over dinner, I got stuck with Marianne, who was running unopposed to be Neighborhood Watch block captain. "The most important thing is tell the drug addicts we're *united*," she said. We were standing with our plates, balancing our wineglasses, the assumption being that we shouldn't sit down on chairs Helen was trying to sell.

Across the room I saw Roland staring at me, and for a second I imagined going back to his basement and asking him to explain everything he was working on. I imagined what it would be like to be less afraid of the secrets on this street. I watched Geoffrey and Linda Sue move over to a wooden love seat wide enough for two and sit down as if they hadn't noticed the rest of us not sitting. I had never seen them talk alone before and I tried to imagine what they were saying. Linda Sue spoke so softly, Geoffrey's head bowed toward hers as if he were afraid of missing a word.

I saw Paul notice, too, and raise his eyebrows at me. We were both in conversations we weren't paying attention to. He had Helen Baker-Harrison showing him her sponges and explaining her process. Then we watched Linda Sue and Geoffrey stand up from their bench, move over to the coat tree holding their jackets, and leave without saying good-bye to anyone. A few minutes later, Paul and I found each other. "Did you see that?" he said.

I was surprised, actually. Usually, Paul registered even less than I did in these social situations. I'd never understood the exact nature of the friendship between Paul and Geoffrey. On the surface it seemed like one thing—Geoffrey, the star, and Paul, his earnest and approving shadow—but up close I understood there were shades of gray, periods of discord, old resentments that Paul never specified. "Geoffrey can be self-serving sometimes, but who isn't, I guess," he'd say. Or, "Geoffrey's always had a father hang-up." I'd seen no evidence of this myself. Sometimes I wondered if Paul didn't dwell on the past as a way of staking his own claim on Geoffrey, as if he alone knew the real problems plaguing his childhood friend. At those moments I wanted to touch his hand gently and say, "Actually, Paul, I see him more than you do."

But that would have been needlessly unkind. Geoffrey and Paul had their own friendship; they had loved and fought and forgiven each other. Geoffrey never made light of Paul's inartistic career as an engineer or the boring work stories he sometimes told at parties. I think Paul considered himself the keeper of Geoffrey's secrets, just as Geoffrey had kept some of his, and the truth is I never asked either one too much about the other. I told myself I wasn't interested in secondhand stories, though maybe there was a little more to it than that. Maybe I didn't want to finally hear the secrets I'd managed for so many years to avoid.

When Paul and I left fifteen minutes later, Geoffrey and Linda Sue had made it only as far as three houses up the street. They stood on the sidewalk, heads dropped back to admire the show of stars over our heads. "Oh, my God," Paul whispered, grabbing my wrist. He pulled me back onto the grass and into the shadows. When they walked past Geoffrey's house, then our own, Paul pinched my sleeve and pulled me along.

They crossed the lawn and walked inside Linda Sue's house without any discussion, as if they'd made a plan ahead of time. *I'll meet you there, we'll go to your house after.*

"Maybe they're just talking," Paul said.

I thought of our friendship, the hours Geoffrey and I had spent doing just that. "Maybe," I said. "We could look in the window."

I suppose we both thought a glimpse would calm our fears. If they were sitting in her living room, that meant they weren't racing upstairs, falling into bed. We crept closer to the glowing picture window in her living room. "I think she's making tea," I said, grateful that she was in the kitchen and he was in the living room. *It's nothing,* I almost said, then stopped. Linda Sue had moved to the doorway and Geoffrey was behind her, one arm circling her waist. Her hair fell back over his shoulder. He buried his face in the nape of her neck. They weren't kissing, but what they *were* doing was more intimate than a kiss. Leaning against each other, finding their fulcrum. Her back to his stomach, his face in her hair. It was silent and endless, a moment that seemed to expand and shrink, to include the world and shut it out, as if we'd never understand the language they weren't speaking.

I realized something then, though I couldn't have put it into words. I wasn't standing there watching because I was in love with Geoffrey. I was looking at them, yes, but I was taking it all in. My first glimpse of the inside of Linda Sue's house: how empty it was, how up close there was even less than we imagined. *It's possible,* I thought, my heart beating crazily. *It's possible for someone to live like this—with nothing but the freedom to make her own choices.*

CHAPTER 11

"Oh, my God, IT'S BETSY!" Helen screams to her husband, Warren, when I tell her who's calling. "We've just been watching you on TV. Warren, it's BETSY TREADING." It wasn't hard to find Helen's phone number, listed in the Internet white pages in Montclair, New Jersey. Though Marianne warned me that people would feel uncomfortable answering questions, Helen sounds happy enough to hear from me, and when I ask her about the cat, she remembers the one we collectively fed but not what happened to it.

"Did you ever see it after Linda Sue died?"

"I don't think so. But we were all so distracted then, I can't be sure. I remember telling Geoffrey that."

"Geoffrey asked about the cat?"

"Yes. A few days after Linda Sue died, he knocked on our door and asked if we had seen it."

"Did he say why?"

"He said it was sick and might be dangerous. We thought that it might have gotten rabies."

"But if Linda Sue had just died, why was he worried about *the cat?*"

"We didn't *know,* Bets. We remembered that party at our house. It was terrible, watching all of that happen. The way Geoffrey was trying to seduce both of you."

Seduce?

Because I don't say anything, apparently, she feels free to keep going. "My God, he was shameless. Of course you loved him. He was a writer and you were a librarian. You lived for books and here he was writing them. Though even that wasn't really true, was it?"

Geoffrey never finished the novel that he toiled away at for two years, living among us, giving us updates that struck us as thrilling peeks into the creative process. I assume this is what she means, though maybe everyone knows the truth now, the part I can still hardly bring myself to admit.

"Who could blame you for falling for his cheap tricks? He dragged you into his midlife crisis so he could feel better about all his bad behavior. He thought if you adored him the rest of us wouldn't notice what he was doing. Then Marianne got involved and thought sending you over to Linda Sue's house would open your eyes and solve everything. That's Marianne for you." She sighs heavily. "But we never thought you did it, Bets. We never believed that. How *could* you have?"

Where had Helen been with these theories during my trial?

"We just didn't understand why you confessed. Or why you took that nightgown down to the station to begin with. It could have been *your* blood. It probably *was.* You might have been sleepwalking that night, but that didn't mean you killed Linda Sue. I don't know why your stupid lawyer didn't raise that possibility. Or look at the facts. Ninety-eight percent of sleepwalkers never leave their house."

She seems to have thought long and hard about my case, which makes me feel both grateful and nervous. "What did other people think?"

"Everyone assumed Geoffrey had done it and you found a nightgown with a period stain and dreamed up this story because you wanted to help him and you wouldn't really get blamed because they had so little evidence. And then we got confused. You were arrested and there was all that talk about sleepwalking and no one knew what to think. That was about the time Geoffrey started going around talking to people, telling his side of the story."

"What did he say?"

"That he felt responsible. That he had no idea you had so many issues. All the stuff with your family and your past. He told Warren and me that he felt like it was partly his fault because he'd seen glimmers of your instability."

I feel a queasy burning in my stomach. Why would Geoffrey have done this? Helen speaks into the phone in a breathy whisper. "He said we should all do whatever we could to help you get off on an insanity defense, that you needed to get help, not go to prison, and we had to make that happen."

None of my neighbors stepped forward to testify in my defense. Surely I'm not the only person who remembers this much. "Why didn't you?"

"We were scared, Betsy. That's all."

"Scared of *what*?"

"What if you had gotten off and it happened again?"

It's interesting that in talking to people ostensibly on my behalf, Geoffrey managed to convince everyone of my guilt.

. . .

Downstairs I find Marianne chopping vegetables for dinner. I don't want to think about my conversation with Helen, or the possibilities it has opened up, so I ask where Trish is living these days. Too late, I remember what a loaded subject this is. She lifts the hand holding the knife and pushes hair off her forehead with the inside of her wrist. "Last I heard, Trish was up north. She had some problems after you left. Nothing to do with you. It had been coming on for a while. Roland and I didn't see what was happening until it was too late."

"See what?"

"How angry Trish was with us. How she was doing certain things to express that anger." I think of the cigarette I saw Trish smoking at the bus stop. "It was much worse than most people realized. She had a breakdown and had to be hospitalized, off and on, for a year or so. Afterward, she lived in a halfway house for young adults with mental illness. Five years ago she moved into her own apartment, which everyone was happy about. Or I was, anyway. She was living on her own. I was ecstatic."

I can see from her face that this isn't the hard part of the story. "After she moved out, I went to see her. I thought the visit went fine but at the end she asked me not to come back. She said I made her crazy. That being around me put her in danger of relapsing."

I realize I have had a fantasy this whole time—that Trish's break with her parents might have had something to do with me. That our stories were connected somehow. Maybe she tried to defend me and was ostracized for doing so. Maybe her mother has taken me in out of remorse and with the hope that it might bring her daughter back. Now I wonder where I got that idea when the truth is both simpler and sadder than that.

"She asked me not to have any contact with her at all and I said all right. I've honored my promise."

In prison, when I imagined life with my children, I tried to make them as real as possible, with the problems and challenges that real children face. I gave one asthma and Charlotte, my youngest, a learning disability. Not that I wished hard times on any of them, but because I understood that real parenting brought hard dilemmas. Some children hover adoringly forever, others want nothing from you but their freedom. I know that. I've been watching mothers with their children all my life. I've never thought it would be easy, but I also never pictured heartbreak like this: estrangement, mental illness, love that grows an edge and expresses itself only in the pain it inflicts.

"You haven't talked to her in five years?"

Marianne drops a handful of mushrooms into a pan of hot oil. "That's right."

It was five years ago that Marianne first came to visit me in prison, giving no reason beyond "I've been thinking about you, dear. We all have." But now it makes sense. The regularity of her visits, the sudden involvement. It *did* have something to do with Trish. She was doing what her child had asked her to do, filling a void, finding a way to leave Trish alone.

"Do you know if she works?"

"We've assumed we'd hear from her if money was an issue and we haven't. So my guess is, yes, she's found work doing something." Isn't she curious what it might be? What her smart, passionate daughter has become? "It's hard for me to imagine. So I prefer not to."

I'm only a mother in my dreams. I don't know what this is like or how it feels.

When dinner is finally ready there's so much food I suggest inviting Roland. "Oh, my," Marianne says, as if this had never occurred to her. "Yes, I suppose we could."

When she makes no move to go down, I do it myself, knock softly and whisper, "Roland?" in the dark cement foyer outside his apartment.

He throws open the door, a pen in his mouth, his glasses pushed up on his head. "Yes, Betsy. Hi." He's clearly distracted by whatever he's working on.

"Marianne and I were wondering if you'd like to join us for dinner. We've made a whole pot of spaghetti. Too much for the two of us."

He's already moved back to his desk to finish writing down whatever thought I interrupted. When he's done, he looks up as if he's only just heard what I said. "You want me to have dinner with you?"

"Yes. Marianne and I."

"Ah." He nods and smiles in a way I can't read. "I'm guessing this isn't her idea."

"Well, no, but we'd both like you to join us."

He shakes his head, pats his pockets, and looks down at what he's wearing: flip-flop sandals, drawstring pants that could double as pajamas, an old T-shirt that says UC BERKELEY: FIVE OR SIX OF THE BEST YEARS OF YOUR LIFE. "Should I change my clothes?"

Ten minutes later he appears at the kitchen door wearing khaki pants and black dress shoes with bright white athletic socks. His T-shirt is the same, as if halfway through dressing he decided not to try too hard. "Marianne. Betsy." He nods at each of us. "I thank you for this surprising invitation."

Marianne stares at him. "Oh, please, Roland."

All through dinner I can't help thinking how odd it is that Marianne, who still prizes putting on a good show, no longer bothers pretending she likes her husband much. When I ask about his work, she rolls her eyes, sighs ostentatiously, and reaches for the basket of bread. I've never forgotten that time when he almost told me what he was working on and then stopped himself. Over the years I've tried to figure it out. I've read articles in the outdated magazines in our library—*Science Digest, National Geographic*—thinking of Roland, my mind full of questions. What does he think of wind turbine potential? Did he ever get solar panels heating more than a few gallons of water? Now I wonder about the sketches I saw on his drafting table this morning and how the apparatus drawn looked like nothing associated with solar. Has he been toiling away on his "breakthrough" for the last fifteen years? I know some of the latest on alternative energy developments: hybrid cars, biomass, hydrogen-powered fuel cells. I'll admit that I don't understand most of it, but I know some of the vocabulary at least. "Are you doing anything with this biomass these days? That seems interesting."

"It is," Roland says. "I've always loved the concept of it. Practically, though, for large-scale use, it has lots of problems. It uses a lot of fuel, doesn't burn very clean."

"What about ethanol?"

"Ethanol, yes. Another good idea with kinks to be worked out. But you've been keeping up, I see."

I blush a little and glance at Marianne, who seems to be interested in neither the conversation nor the possibility that we may be flirting a little bit. "I have, as a matter of fact. Prison doesn't mean you can't read a few magazines. It just means you read ones that are four years old."

"I see." He smiles. "So you haven't heard yet about cow-manure cars."

"What?"

"He's joking," Marianne says. Her first contribution to the conversation. "Roland's tried a couple of these alternative-fuel cars. What no one ever likes to mention is the smell. We had one for a while and it was like driving around with a dead body in the trunk. You had to wear a face mask to sit inside it."

"*You* had to."

"Trish threw up, Roland. It wasn't my imagination."

"No, I'll grant you. We had some odor issues."

I wonder about this marriage that feels suddenly so reminiscent of my own parents, locked together in a house neither one of them could bring themselves to leave. "I think a couple of the prison vans were hybrids. That's what was printed on the door anyway. I tried to ask some people about it, but I never got any answers." I'm offering this as a way to get past the tension between them, but it's too strange a story to help much. Instead of clearing the air, it's just reminded everyone of where I've been, sitting shackled on benches behind drivers who never answered my questions. No story of my recent life will apply here.

"I'm not working on fuel converters anymore, or any of that engine-related stuff. I'm back to an old project, actually. Something I think I mentioned to you once."

Marianne shoots him a look. "Roland."

"What? She asked, Marianne. She's interested in knowing what's going on in this house."

Whatever it is, Marianne clearly doesn't want me to hear it. "Betsy has her own issues she's working on now. She doesn't need to get all caught up hearing you explain what you're working on for the next hour."

This seems uncharacteristically cruel, dismissive of both Roland and me. "I am interested," I say. "I've always been curious about your work."

"Basically it has to do with electrolysis. I'm trying to work out some more efficient energy conversion mechanisms, that's all. Where instead of capturing fifty percent, we get seventy or eighty percent." He keeps explaining for a while—that one of the great untold energy mishaps is the vast amounts that are wasted at the source. "It's true for all of them, coal, hydrogen, nuclear. Half the energy they create gets wasted in the conversion process."

The longer he talks, the more eager Marianne seems to move off this subject. Finally she all but interrupts him. "I told Roland I was *fine* paying for these projects as long as he kept living here. And I am. I'm fine. I'd rather have him here doing his crazy work in the basement than have to move myself into one of those security condominiums where the whole neighborhood votes on whether you can put up shutters. No, thank you."

For a long time after this, no one speaks.

Suddenly, Marianne has admitted so much that it only seems to dawn on her afterward what she's said. They truly have no marriage. He is little more than a border kept on to hold her paranoid imaginings at bay for the moment. Sitting cross from them, it strikes me as so sad I feel tears rise up to my eyes.

In prison, my release-readjustment counselor told me to expect mood swings in the beginning: "You think you're supposed to feel happy right away, but I'm not sure it works like that for most people." The truth is that I don't remember happiness very well—the buoyancy of it, the head rush. The components of my old days—walking to work on nice spring days, noticing flowers, remarking on a news story to Paul at night—all seem as hollow as the plasterboard walls in the house of my childhood home, as empty as this marriage I am now living too close to. How well did Paul and I know each other? What did I feel for him except gratitude that he asked so few questions and so readily accepted the surface answers I gave? Sitting here with Marianne and Roland, I feel like weeping not for them but for myself. Was my marriage any better than this? Yes, we had sex (lots of it in our procreation efforts), but when we came up empty-handed, could we think what to say to each other? Would I know what a better marriage should feel like?

During my first years in prison I had an odd habit of drawing closer to the women who seemed the most intractably insane: the masturbators, the self-talkers, the ones who couldn't be given a pencil without trying to cut themselves with it. Though I didn't want to be associated with them, I felt comforted standing in the vicinity of their crazy displays. *This is real,* I would think. *Here's genuine sadness right here.* Later, I was drawn to the motormouths who told endless stories of the men they'd loved and the crimes they'd commit all over again. I wanted to know if I was even in their league of self-abnegation. Had I loved Geoffrey so much that I unconsciously committed this crime to save him? Was I even *capable* of that?

Obviously the jury thought I was, but I doubted my capacity for the depth of feeling such an act would require. Even as I wrote letters protesting my innocence, I envied those who'd owned up to their terrible crimes and carried Bibles around the way they once wielded firearms. They knew the blackened edges of their heart, the bilious taste of their own rage fomenting. Watching those women sob and tear at their own clothes taught me something. I admired them. Crazy as they seemed, I did.

What conscious, bold stance had I ever taken except, possibly, asking Paul for a divorce? I am grateful to have shown that much foresight. Though standing dutifully by his imprisoned wife had become Paul's identity—he talked about me at work, he financed my appeals, he even set up a Web site (freebetsy.com) to outline the circumstantial evidence used against me—the loyalty he showed after my arrest seems only like a sad comment on the absence of such feeling before it. Listening to Roland, who talks on even in the face of his wife's disapproval, I'm struck by his dedication to a cause after all these years working in isolation. He's committed his life to it in a way that I wish I could emulate. Then I hear the tail end of his point: "Basically the whole thing is a souped-up version of an electrolytic cell."

I look up, excited. "I made one of those once. I got second place in a science fair." My contraption separated water into hydrogen and oxygen using a lantern battery, two pencil leads, and some wire. I was one of only two girls who'd entered (the other built a solar oven using a foil-covered pizza box), and my winning second place shocked everyone, including the science teacher, who lowered his glasses in my direction when my name was announced, as if he'd never seen me before.

"Then, you do know." Roland looks over at Marianne. "There you have it. She knows what I'm talking about."

And then I realize he's not telling the truth.

The notes I saw on his desk about the excess heat observed, a thousand times higher than previous experiments, and the tentative conclusion: The temperatures generated weren't chemical in origin. He wasn't designing a prototype for conversion efficiency. Those notes were about heat produced over time. They weren't about energy conversion at all, they were about energy *creation*. Which isn't especially strange, except that he's just spent the last twenty minutes lying about it all.

CHAPTER 12

Here's a question no one has ever been able to answer: If I am not guilty, where did the blood on my nightgown come from? It was a rough oval across the chest area on the front of the gown. Looking at it, one might think I'd been shot. As Jeremy has pointed out, there are no spatter marks or individual blood drops, only one smear that extends like an afterthought toward the back, as if the stain itself were reaching an arm around to embrace me. The afternoon I brought the gown to the police, they were too embarrassed to ask the most obvious question, which now seems quaint and unimaginable to me. It wasn't until that evening, alone with a female detective, that I was asked directly if the blood might be my own. She used the word *menses*, which I'd never heard anyone say aloud before. "You mean, did I start my period that night?"

"Yes."

It shouldn't have been a difficult question. Either I did or I didn't. I hadn't been strip-searched by anyone yet; only I knew if I was wearing a tampon. "No," I said, hesitating slightly. "I don't think it's possible." I told myself I didn't want to get into the grisly particulars of my erratic cycle—that, in the course of my many miscarriages, it was possible for me to have spontaneous bleeds that stopped as suddenly as they started. Once, a doctor dismissed one night of staining as "breakthrough bleeding" only to discover on a sonogram a week later that I'd lost the baby. Though I hadn't bled after the one night, the body can fool itself. I've learned that much.

In the terrible dark hours after I found the nightgown, I wrestled with myself, trying to decide what the blood stain meant. I assumed I hadn't killed Linda Sue. I knew that I'd walked outside and stayed asleep before, but how could I have slept through a rage that turned murderous? I spent that morning at the library and discovered that in the last five years there had been quite a few instances of murderers alleging a sleepwalking defense. In each case the person had killed a spouse or a parent—someone close enough that they didn't need to dress or wear shoes to their crime—and in all the cases domestic abuse was involved. So it was possible. Not likely, but possible.

When I looked up from my research, my heart tripping at what I'd read and what it might mean, I gasped to see Geoffrey standing in the corner, looking shaken. Linda Sue had been dead for three days. The police were no longer pursuing him as a suspect—the phone records checked out, and Corinne was right. They'd been on the line from 10:15 to 11:36. When he caught my eye, his face softened. *We need to talk,* he mouthed.

Outside, I understood that he was not here to offer comfort. "They found half a sandwich in Linda Sue's kitchen, lying on the counter. It doesn't match the contents in her stomach and there're no fingerprints on the knife, meaning it was made by someone wearing gloves or else someone who cleaned their fingerprints afterward. They think it has to be the perpetrator."

I watched his face as he spoke. There could be no mistaking what he meant. I'd told him everything from my past—the sleepwalking, the eating episodes. Who would commit such a crime and eat afterward except someone moving outside of all reason? Who else could have done it except someone with my history? Geoffrey never told me directly to turn myself in, but he nodded gratefully when I told him I would.

He was the last friend I talked to before my arrest. I called Paul later, after the questioning had gone on for so long that I knew I wouldn't be home for dinner. In the police report, I am described as having a low affect and an unusually unemotional response to the events I was describing. Later a psychologist said that I refused to assume full emotional responsibility for my crime by qualifying it in all my answers: "Supposedly I was there"; "I guess I must have been angry"; "I don't remember how I felt."

Now I can explain all of those answers. I didn't know what had happened. When I signed the confession I felt that I was probably guilty, but even back then I also had this thought: *During my questioning, no one mentioned the sandwich.* Even in the swirl of confusion that descended over me that day, I wondered: *If that hadn't been part of questioning a suspect, how did Geoffrey know?*

Had he made it up, afraid the cloud of guilt he'd lived under for past crimes would darken and implicate him for this one? It was a relief when my lawyer went through the first files of discovery and confirmed that, yes, a sandwich had been found on the counter, because it meant Geoffrey hadn't lied. He'd probably learned these details and worried right away about how they might lead back to me. I still remember his face, blotched with emotion, the tears he didn't quite shed, the relief when I told him about the nightgown and said, "I have to take it to the police. I have to see what they say." We were frightened and polite enough to speak obliquely. He squeezed my hand and said, "I'm worried. I don't know what's going to happen." I tried my best to reassure him. "I'll be fine," I said. "I'm stronger than you think." I told many people that until I realized how it implicated me—*I'm stronger than you think*—and then I stopped reassuring people and began accepting the medication that weakened my resolve and muddied my thinking. Looking strong no longer seemed like a smart or noble option.

The more clearly I see how the events played out just before and after Linda Sue's murder, I find myself asking what I should have twelve years ago: *How did Geoffrey know those details from the crime scene?* I had assumed the police told him during his questioning, but now that I understand better how police work, I know that information wouldn't have been given away. Unless he told them right away that he knew of a suspect, a female parasomniac, and controlled the conversation so well that, against usual protocol, they told him things. As unseemly as that thought is, it's preferable to the alternative: He knew because he was there, laying the sandwich out himself.

I haven't let myself consider the possibility that Geoffrey could have done both: loved Linda Sue and killed her. Out of jealousy or desperation, or the fear of losing her. He could have gone over that night, necklace in hand, to cement their future, and maybe she confronted him somehow, about his writing, about the plagiarism lawsuit. I have tried for so long not to think about the necklace that Geoffrey showed me once before giving it to her. Though I still don't want to think about it, I know what it means: It's possible. He would have had eight hours to make a plan and destroy any clothes of his own with blood on them. He could have worn gloves and laid out the food evidence intentionally. He knew the ways I was most vulnerable. To make me look guilty, he needed to plant evidence that only I'd recognize. He had a copy of our house key; he could have gotten in that night and found one of my nightgowns.

I know something else that others don't know. Once when we were talking about our spouses and laughing at their quirks, I told him how Paul slept in his socks. He said that when Corinne was in Princeton, she called him every night and asked him to talk to her until she fell asleep.

"That's sweet," I said, because I wasn't jealous. I wasn't.

"That's expensive," he said.

What it really means is that he could have created his own alibi. He'd done it before—run away from crimes with the help of women who covered his tracks.

That evening I call Jeremy and tell him what I've never allowed myself to say: "Geoffrey's alibi had a hole in it. Yes, he was on the phone with his wife, but she fell asleep every night on the phone." Even now, it's hard for me to form these words. "It was a regular thing. He could have gone over to Linda Sue's without hanging up."

All during my trial, this possibility hovered in the back of my mind. I could have brought it up and never did. Back then I felt too powerless. I didn't think it would work and I didn't want the bad feeling it might provoke. I still remember Geoffrey on the witness stand, wearing a seersucker jacket and with a new haircut so short his scalp showed through. We were reeling in the midst of a late-July heat wave but he managed to look dapper in the oppressive temperatures. Everyone in the room listened closer to his words than they did to the forensic experts who'd analyzed my nightgown.

What kind of "friendship" did we have? His lawyer made air quotes with his fingers in case anyone missed his implication: This wasn't a friendship, it was an aberration of some kind, a one-sided obsession.

"I hadn't experienced anything like it for years," Geoffrey told the DA. "Since college, really. We exchanged books and talked about them. Such a simple thing, really, but it meant a lot to me."

His lawyer looked surprised. "What do you mean exactly?"

"Friendships between men and women are common enough when you're young, but when you get older, it's so much more unusual, isn't it?"

Listening to him, my heart filled. *Yes,* I thought, *he, too, had felt the rarity of it.*

The prosecutor quickly got him back on track. Had he slept with Linda Sue? Had he loved her? Had his intention been to leave his wife in order to marry Linda Sue? Yes, yes, and yes. I didn't dwell on these answers and focused instead on what he had said earlier, what I'd never heard Geoffrey articulate. Our friendship was different, something unexpected and valuable. If he flirted with others, it was different with me, unmuddied by the messiness sex brings along. I should have guessed the prosecution would twist the idea until it seemed dubious, then sad, and finally pathological. Why would a married woman seek out "friendship" with a man? What void was this childless woman trying to fill? When I took the stand—a last-ditch effort, dressed in a pastel sweater, the picture of innocence, of a thousand librarians going back through time—Franklin tried to undercut the prosecution by asking me their questions. *What void were you trying to fill?* I answered as honestly as I could: "After my fifth miscarriage, we were told that my body couldn't sustain another pregnancy. It was devastating for both of us. Then I thought of the idea that maybe friendships—deep, meaningful friendships—could feel like family."

"Didn't your marriage feel like family?"

"Paul and I shared the same loss." I was careful with my word choices. I wanted to be honest and clear. "We reminded each other of what was missing."

Our defense plan involved paying experts to explain disassociation, how it is possible for the mind, under duress, to fragment and act of its own volition. There are textbook cases of split personalities and re-pressed memories. At the center of most, an abused child is warehous-ing terrible episodes in a sealed-off room of his or her mind. Was that possible in my case? Could coming home nightly to the sad specter of a father, his eyes glued to a TV, sitting in a chair he hadn't moved from since the morning, be categorized as trauma? Though I tried not to dwell too often on those memories, I hadn't repressed them, nor had I repressed the even sadder sights of childhood. My mother, waging her own battle with chronic arthritis, struggling to stand up from the couch, blinking back pain to fetch my father's pills. Terrible, yes. Re-pressed? Unfortunately, no.

I went along with the defense because what else was possible? I had no memories of that night. And I'd had blackouts before.

To establish this defense with any validity, my old college secrets had to be aired, along with the roommates who bore witness to them. They must have been stunned by the call, equal parts thrilled and hor-rified to discover they had a role to play in their old friend's murder trial. Did they remember the strange disappearance of food? *Yes,* Polly said, *how could I forget?* Once, a pound of raw bacon disappeared. (I have no memory of that, but I was hardly going to say, *It was raw hot dogs, I'm almost sure.*) In the end, we got two roommates to humiliate me with their college memories of a sleepwalker in their midst, com-mitting acts of aberrant nighttime eating.

Paul was a crucial link in this line of self-defense and, as helpful as he wanted to be, a weak one. We'd been married eight years and shared a bed all that time. No, he admitted in cross-examination on the stand, he had no memory of me sleepwalking, nor did he recall any food disappearances. When he said this he looked up at me sadly, as if in apology. Later, the prosecution made his testimony their final point: "Fifteen years ago, at night, she binged on strange foods most of us wouldn't eat. If that's evidence of a mental disorder, three-quarters of the college girls I know would qualify."

That was how the trial went, the reason I didn't step forward to offer my own evidence of a hole in Geoffrey's alibi. I felt sure I was going to be found guilty anyway.

What would have been the point?

Now I wait for Jeremy to applaud my good work. *We'll get a DNA sample, check it against the hair. How long will it take? Two days?*

"It's not Geoffrey," Jeremy says, stopping me before I can say any more. "We've already had his blood drawn. I just got the results back today. The skin doesn't match. Neither does the hair."

I don't say anything.

"I'm sorry, Bets. But it was someone else."

CHAPTER 13

"I told you about this," Marianne says, pulling out boxes marked "Samples" from the closet. "It's not a party exactly. I like to think of it as a public seminar on personal security."

Ah, yes. Marianne's new side career, what has evidently become of her failed Neighborhood Watch efforts. Now, instead of inviting police officers into her home, she hosts parties where women can order rape whistles, pepper sprays, and what she describes as her most exciting new product, pastel-colored Taser guns that come with their own animal-print carrying pouches.

"Oh, my," I say, as she unfolds a life-sized, human-shaped target with a bull's-eye on its chest, which she tapes to her living room wall.

"I know you probably think I'm crime obsessed, but I'm not really. It's about moving past that, about being *prepared* so you don't have to *worry*."

She seems so agitated that I want to say something supportive, let her know that I don't judge her. "This seems nice, Marianne. Like a new Neighborhood Watch."

"Oh, no. It's not like that. It was never really about crime prevention." She looks up at me as if she'd inadvertently revealed more than she meant to.

"It wasn't?"

"No. I mean, sure, that was *part* of it."

I wonder why I've never asked her this before: Why *did* she start Neighborhood Watch? We all wondered about it at the time when we'd never had a crime in our neighborhood.

"But obviously it didn't work very well. After our third meeting, Linda Sue was killed." I can see her hesitation, trying to decide what she should say. "It was Helen's idea originally." She gestures as if to say, *You remember Helen, her crazy ideas.* "We were worried about you. All the miscarriages you'd had. And then you'd get pregnant again so quickly. It broke our hearts, Bets. That's all."

I stare at her. "You started Neighborhood Watch because of my miscarriages?"

"No, no. Or not exactly. You just—you had these episodes, where you didn't seem like yourself. You'd stand in the garden sometimes and you wouldn't answer when someone spoke to you. I'm sure it was the hormones. My God, what your body must have been going through."

I feel my breath go shallow.

"So much of the time you seemed *fine*. And then, on a bad day, you were so *immobilized*." She goes on, speaking quickly. She tells me they were worried about Paul, how "stretched" he seemed at times, taking care of me and working. "We wanted to help. Helen thought of Neighborhood Watch as a way to let Paul know we were here to help."

"You talked about it with him?"

"Sort of, yes. We told him we were here if you needed anything." She looks at me carefully. "I don't think he knew all of it, Bets. I don't know if he ever saw you sleepwalking."

"But you did?"

She nods and closes her eyes. "Twice. Once at about midnight. You stood on your lawn, in your bare feet. Earlier that day you'd been having one of your spells so I watched for a while. You looked so vulnerable I wanted to help, but then you went back inside. The next day I almost said something, but you seemed fine. Back to yourself."

I don't understand this. Why didn't she speak up sooner and tell Franklin? He spent weeks trying to find someone to testify to recent sleepwalking episodes. "And the second time?"

"The other time. Yes." She looks down and fidgets with a ring. "I think you remember what happened the second time." Her eyes narrow in my direction.

"Yes," I say, nodding, after a painful silence. "I suppose I do."

I'd been praying for a miracle of absolution, that there might have been another episode of harmless night wandering that she'd borne witness to. But no. Before she even begins, I know the night she's referring to. The time I woke to discover myself in Roland's basement sitting on a tattered sofa in the corner, him leaning toward me, offering me a warm mug of peach tea.

"Nothing happened," I say simply. "He woke me very gently, made me some tea, and I went home. I'm not sure why I knocked on his door. I probably saw the light on and went toward it without thinking. He was kind about it. I don't think it bothered him."

"Still."

"Yes."

"You can understand why I worried. A woman in a nightgown knocking on doors in the middle of the night."

"Yes."

"We thought you needed help, Betsy, but none of us knew what to do. When you were fine, you were so efficient and in control. And Paul didn't want to say too much. He told us you'd had more miscarriages than anyone realized. He also said you had premenstrual dysphoria—that it was related to hormones and was a severe form of PMS. He said it usually passed within a few days."

During the worst times it felt like being pulled into a vortex, spinning without bearings, washing ashore on a beach I didn't recognize. Though it happened often enough that I took medication, it still usually took me by surprise. One day I'd be fine and the next I'd stop moving altogether. I lost time, I know. Sometimes whole days. I'd disappear and reemerge having to ask Paul what day it was, and what had happened in my absence. It's hard for me to think about those days of torpor, when lassitude filled my limbs with sand and my mouth with cotton wool. It wasn't that I *couldn't* speak during those times; I was paralyzed by a fear of what I might say if I *did*. I lived in fear of my old selves emerging—as if I might suddenly become the high school malcontent again, or the college freshman party girl. Were those old episodes due to hormonal surges or the exhaustion of watching everything I said? I never knew really.

I learned to anticipate a few of the warning signs—a headache that started in the back of my neck, blurriness on the periphery of my vision. Sometimes Paul would pick me up at work and we'd tell people I had the flu. Having grown up with my father, I should have known such secrets aren't kept for long. People know even as they collude in a show of not knowing. I understood this as a teenager, every time the guidance counselor asked, as if she didn't already know, whether I had any "issues I was worried about at home." She knew my childhood secrets, just as my neighbors knew far more than they ever let on.

Back then I believed only Viola and Paul knew about my spells. Even

Jeremy, to whom I've told as much truth as I know how, doesn't know that I used to have blackouts during the day and unexplained episodes of lost time. The first time I saw Paul after my arrest, we talked about how much we should tell a lawyer. It wasn't a long conversation. We didn't have much to debate—the sleepwalking was enough of an explanation, we agreed.

Now I understand that my memories aren't wholly reliable. If the world saw me as fragile and troubled, then every story I recall of myself functioning normally is a lie. During the weeks and months I thought I was fine, I was a far cry from it apparently, being held aloft by an elaborate charade being played out by everyone I knew.

Marianne is also right about this—the worst of the episodes began after my first miscarriage. After the later ones, it varied. Sometimes it happened right away. Sometimes I'd be fine for three or four months and then I'd start having dreams about babies left in a car or locked in a closet. I'd be at work and think, *Where is he? I have to find him!* I hope I never said this out loud, but how much was I able to control? My heart would race with crazy fears—*My baby might be dead!*—and then I'd remember. *That's right. He is.*

Can I be blamed for this surfeit of unexpressed feeling? When there is no funeral, no ceremony, no condolence cards to mourn the loss of an unborn child? When we have no language beyond salvos of superstition and the terrible suggestion to try again? I stopped telling anyone when it happened. The first time Marianne talked to me about forming a Neighborhood Watch group for the block, I'd had a D & C only a few days before. The pad in my underpants was soaked with blood and the sound of the procedure, the vacuuming slurp, still echoed in my head and made my stomach clench. "Think about the things you don't want to lose," Marianne had said, meaning of course our stereo, our TV. I thought of the only thing I cared about: the stain on our mattress. The closest thing I had to a picture of a baby.

I want to tell Marianne that she doesn't need to worry about these episodes happening anymore. In prison I learned not to shut down the way I once did. There, such incidents meant you were strip-searched and put on suicide watch in an isolation cell with a mattress on the floor and a toilet without a seat. In my first year, two women committed suicide while on suicide watch using bedsheets tied around air vents. If you felt like killing yourself, I discovered, that cell where you might go four days without speaking to a doctor was the last place you should be. When I felt the grip of a dark episode coming on, I rode it out as unobtrusively as possible. I found routines and stuck to them. My library job was an unsupervised blessing. I could sit in the dark if I needed to for hours at a time. If anyone asked, I talked about my troubles as if they were in the past—*I was feeling a little blue, but I'm fine now*. After a while I didn't lose myself in dark patches.

I discovered that in a place where the appearance of normalcy mattered so little, I stopped feeling oppressed by it, and after a few years the darkest parts of those moods faded away. I still got depressed, of course, but I managed to get by. My psychiatrist said I was integrating my personality, taking ownership of all aspects of it, which felt like an apt enough description. In the last five years I haven't experienced the immobilizing waves that used to take hold and close me off from the world. Now I understand the factors that caused it—the stress of keeping up appearances, of trying so hard to seem fine to the world. Maybe I even knew what I was doing, making it clear in some subconscious way: *I'm not fine*.

I also remember that the episodes usually passed as mysteriously as they arrived. One morning I'd wake up able to feel my skin again, taste the coffee Paul had made, read more than a headline of the newspaper. Invariably, I'd look around, giddy with relief, and wonder how much I'd missed. The morning after I found myself on Roland's basement sofa in the middle of the night I awoke even more exuberant than usual.

I didn't remember right away where I'd been or what had happened, only that I felt free, as if a silence had been broken. I kissed Paul right on the lips, which must have taken him by surprise because for two days I hadn't dressed or left the house. I remember clearly how breathless and full of optimism I was.

"Hello!" Paul gasped, when I finished kissing him. "Feeling better?"

We used euphemisms as much as possible. "Yes!" I said. "Much better. Sorry about all that." Force of habit by then—I always apologized after an episode. Not a real apology (it was too large, and too inexplicable, to tell him how truly sorry I was). This was more of an acknowledgment; as if I'd been late or had burned the dinner I was serving. I hadn't yet remembered the night before, only that I'd been in the throes of a bad episode and now it was over, the heavy weight in my heart replaced with elation.

Later that morning, almost like a movie playing in my head, I saw it all: where I'd gone, how Roland invited me inside his apartment and made me tea. He became the first neighbor ever to ask me, directly, what was happening with my pregnancies. Some neighbors knew parts of it—they knew we were trying; that I'd miscarried once or twice—but with Roland alone, I told the whole story: "I've had five pregnancies in four years and lost every one. The doctors say my womb isn't hospitable, but no one says why. They don't *know*."

I told him that one baby held on for almost five months.

That time, I started bleeding at night and the baby came out a few hours later in a bath of blood. He was the only one I got to see and touch, his little webbed fingers and toes, the nub of genitals, the great dome of head. I could have made a footprint—I'd heard of a mother doing that with her twenty-week miscarriage—but I didn't. I held his tiny hand and it wasn't nearly as sad as you might think. He was real, and there, the size of my palm. We kept him in a Tupperware bowl and carried him the next day to the doctor.

I also told Roland something I'd never told Paul, that I'd been pregnant once in college and had an abortion. "I've always felt like that time was different. Like that baby would have lived." In the end, I explained what had precipitated all this. I'd been to the doctor. He told me my body couldn't take any more, that I'd have to give up.

For a long time, Roland didn't say anything, and then his hand moved over to rest on top of mine. His palm was warm and dry. "I'm just so sorry," he said. "About all of it."

I leaned back, meaning to close my eyes and catch my breath. It was dizzying to be there, to realize everything I'd just spoken aloud. Instead of calming my nerves, I fell into the crook of Roland's shoulder, felt my cheek against his chest. I allowed the storm of feelings kept at bay for so long to rise up and began sobbing into his shirt. "Shhh," he kept saying, touching my face and my neck. "Shhh."

After some immeasurable length of time, I stopped crying and looked at him. I understood that I'd humiliated myself beyond any normal measure. I didn't know how I'd ever face him again. Then I let myself look into his face and saw his genuine sadness and something else in the way his eyes moved around my face, as if he were trying not to get away but to remember this moment. "I want to kiss you," he said. "But I don't know if I should."

"You can," I said, grateful for the prospect of something to balance our evening's embarrassments. *Yes,* I thought, *kiss me.* And he did. A minute later, we were stretched along the length of the sofa, our bodies pressed together. It was lovely and frantic and a little overwhelming. When we came up for air, his glasses were skewed.

"I'm sorry," he said, sitting up and speaking quickly, as if finishing a conversation. "I want to move out. Make this situation clearer." He pointed above him, meaning *his home, his marriage.* He took off his glasses and held them in one hand, pinching the bridge of his nose with the other. "I feel—ah! I don't know." I thought for a moment he might be crying. "Tethered." He turned and looked at me for a long time—just my face, taking it all in, as if he already knew that what had just happened couldn't be repeated. "I wish I felt free to make my own choices, but I don't."

That was it. That was all he said.

"I should go, then," I said, pulling my nightgown back into place. Maybe we were both relieved at the prospect of escaping our swan dive into madness.

Back home, I lay in bed and thought over the simple truths we'd each revealed. I was barren; he was unhappy. If I had exposed myself, he had, too. Though we never repeated that night, I never forgot it. Sometimes in prison when I got tired of imagining a life with the children I never had, I'd go back to that night and remember as much of it as I possibly could. His drawings spread out on the table in front of us, his soft hands, the blue faded T-shirt he wore, the way he tried at the last minute to rectify things by grabbing my hand and saying, "You can come back, you know. Anytime you want."

Now Marianne studies me with an expression that suggests she knows more about all this than she's ever let on. That maybe she's kept up a friendship with me for reasons that have more to do with keeping enemies close than with compassion. I don't know. Maybe inviting me to live here was a test of some kind, of Roland's loyalty, or of mine.

Later that night, I call Paul, who says I shouldn't read too much into anything Marianne says or does. "She's always been a little strange. Maybe you're forgetting."

Just hearing his voice makes me a little emotional. I want to ask if what Marianne implied was true—if being married to me felt like a burden. "She said the whole block used to worry about you, the way you had to take care of me sometimes."

"She said that?"

"She said everyone knew."

He seems to think this over. "We took care of each other, Bets. That's what married people do."

"I wonder why Marianne invited me here at all. I keep thinking maybe she knows something and feels guilty that she didn't come forward during my trial."

"Knows what?"

"I have no idea. Something about that night. About who else might have done it. She keeps saying I shouldn't talk to any of the old people from the block. If you think about it, wasn't it strange that none of them were at my welcome-home party?"

"They all moved away."

"But we were friends, weren't we? I talked to Helen, who lives an hour away. She says she would have come but she never heard about it. Why wouldn't Marianne have wanted Helen to come?"

"I don't know. Marianne and Roland always had their own things going on. To be honest, I never liked the idea of you staying there. Going from prison to their house. I just never thought it was a good idea."

He may not have liked it, but he never offered his own place. He still doesn't. "I don't know how long I'll last here," I say.

Then he surprises me with an idea I hadn't thought of. "Maybe you should get out. Meet some of the new neighbors."

I know what he means, but isn't saying. He wishes he could help me more, in the ways I need most, but he can't because doing so would send us both back in time to the fragile house of cards that was our marriage, filled with so much sweetness and so much disappointment. "Maybe I'll do that," I say.

CHAPTER 14

"Hello!" Finn says, when I knock on his door. It's strange to stand here, on Geoffrey's old porch. Finn is wearing jeans, holding a cup of coffee. "Did you want to hear more stories about Bill's bad old days at prep school?"

"No." I smile. "I have a favor to ask. I'm wondering if I might borrow your computer for a little while to do a little research. Marianne has a personal safety seminar she's getting ready for. I'm just trying to get out of her way."

"Oh, of course," Finn says. "Come in, come in. I almost forgot—she invited us to that, where everyone gets to try out Taser guns."

"Something like that."

He says I'm welcome to stay as long as I'd like, that I can even spend the night if I'd like. They have a guest room finished for Bill's mother, who was going to move in and never did. "She has a hard time staying here and pretending Bill isn't gay, I guess."

I ask Finn if he knows how I might find some of the old neighbors online if I have no idea where they live now. "Do they have search engines where you can look by names and ages? Something like that to narrow it down?"

"Oh, please," Finn says. "Wait'll you see what we have now." He tells me to write down a list of names, which I do. A few minutes later, he has found the first name: Baylor, B. and K., in New Haven, Connecticut.

Barbara Baylor was the closest thing we had to an eyewitness at the trial. She took her dog for a walk from 10:00 to 10:20 the night Linda Sue was murdered and reported seeing no one on the street. She walked past Linda Sue's house and heard no voices, nothing resembling a fight, which the prosecution took to mean that it couldn't have been a domestic dispute if Linda Sue was killed at 10:50.

"Oh, Bets. I just never expected to hear from you is all," Barbara says when I tell her who it is. She sounds a little breathless, as if I've caught her in the middle of something. "Kevin is out of work these days. I didn't recognize your number on the caller ID. I was hoping it was one of those headhunters he's waiting to hear from."

When we knew them, Kevin worked on Wall Street and they were the first family to put a two-story addition on their house, which at the time we thought was a little ostentatious. "It's been terrible," she says. "He hasn't worked in three years and we had to move down here to a smaller house. I know I shouldn't complain compared to your life. Never mind all that. How are *you* doing?"

"I'm all right."

"It must be strange, I guess. Being back on the block."

I tell her it is, and ask if she'd mind answering some questions about what she saw the night Linda Sue died. It's awkward. She repeats exactly what she said at my trial—that she saw and heard nothing—but she speaks slowly, as if she were weighing her words. When I ask if there was anything that she didn't tell the police, she doesn't answer right away. Then she says, "It wasn't related to the murder. It wouldn't have helped your case or anything."

"What do you mean?"

"There were some things we weren't supposed to tell anyone. About the accident earlier and what was going on with Trish. Sometimes I think it all started with that accident—"

"What accident?"

"No one knew if it was related or not. They just kept saying they needed to keep it confidential—wait, Kevin's just got home. I need to go. I'm sorry. I'll call you later."

After she hangs up I call Paul back to see if he remembers anything about an accident.

"Like a car accident? No."

What puzzles me most is the fact that no one was supposed to talk about it. I ask him if he remembers what Trish was doing around the time that Linda Sue was killed.

He is quiet for a minute. "She had some hard times, I remember that. I don't know too much more."

"What kind of hard times?"

"Didn't she leave home for a little while and they didn't know where she'd gone?"

How did Paul know this when I never did? It's unsettling, to say the least—as if people were intentionally keeping things from me.

"She came back later, for a little while anyway. Then she left again."

"Did you know that she was hospitalized?"

He hesitates. "Yes. I heard something like that."

"Why hasn't anyone looked into this more—or figured out if

there's a connection between her disappearance and Linda Sue's death?"

"I did, actually. I told Franklin all this and he couldn't find any evidence that Trish and Linda Sue knew each other. The more I looked into it, the more it seemed like he was right. She was a pretty troubled girl, but all of her problems were focused on kids at school. I couldn't find anything that connected her to Linda Sue."

Except that she lived next door, I think. And this: Geoffrey's inscription in her copy of *Middlemarch.* Evidence that at some point he befriended her the same way he befriended me, with books and talk.

Paul keeps going. "Turns out she ran away from home two weeks before Linda Sue died. That's where Marianne and Roland were the day Linda Sue's body was found—picking her up and sorting things out. She wasn't even around for the murder."

So if Trish had been gone for two weeks, the last night I saw Trish, or any of us did, must have been at the last Neighborhood Watch meeting. I ask Paul if he remembers seeing her there, if she looked different or distraught.

"You forget," he says. "I never went to those meetings. That was when I decided that Marianne reminded me too much of my mother."

I laugh because I do remember even though I never understood the comparison. By the time I met her, Paul's mother had become a free spirit who lived in an artist community in Arizona. When Paul was a child, the youngest of five children, she was entirely different, weary and distracted from coping all the time. "Five was too many kids," she once told me. "Four more than I should have had." Honesty was something she'd discovered in middle age, along with Eastern religions and poetry writing. She was blunt about everything, even, on the eve of our wedding, her feeling that we shouldn't get married. "It's just a sense I have," she whispered privately to me. "It's probably nothing."

The first time she visited, she stood on the front lawn and said it was hard to imagine why Paul had wanted to live here, on a block so much like the one he grew up on. "Maybe he's forgotten how unhappy he used to be."

We learned to brace ourselves for her tactless observations.

"Is no one here interested in doing their own thing?" she'd ask, looking around the neighborhood. "Could someone paint their house chartreuse if they wanted to or is that against the rules?"

"It's not against any written rules, Mother," Paul would say. "It's just *understood*."

Her visits drained us and I could see in Paul's face how hurt he was by her. "It's not your fault she wasn't happy back then," I once said to him. "Think about it, Paul—your mother disapproves of you living the same life she *brought you up in*."

"It's not that. Sometimes living here makes me feel like a child again. I can't explain it."

It was an odd thing to say, when buying this house meant we looked and acted older than anyone else our age, but I knew what he meant. Sometimes I'd look at Paul and see the child he must have been, the youngest and the shiest, the one his mother waited on to leave, which she let herself do when he was fifteen. He never talked about that time in his life. I heard about it only from her when she insisted, "He was *fine*. I knew he would be. That's why I left."

Paul never chimed in on those conversations, never said, in so many words, *Yes, I was,* because he wasn't. That was my discovery after I married him. Paul still needed everything his mother took with her when she left him in a big rambling house, alone with his father—reassurance, protection, a feeling of self-worth. My fondest memories of our marriage were the moments when I most felt her absence—making him a sandwich and cutting it along the diagonal, or standing in the bathroom fitting a Band-Aid around the finger he'd just cut. All those times where I thought: *Here is the mothering he never got.*

"You *could* have gone to those meetings, Paul," I say now. "You *chose* not to."

"That's right. No, you're right."

"You didn't because you said the whole idea of Neighborhood Watch was creepy and strange." What's strange, actually, is how easy it feels to go over all this with him.

"*Wasn't* it, though?"

"Yes," I say, letting myself laugh. "It *was* a little strange."

CHAPTER 15

We had three Neighborhood Watch meetings altogether. At the second, Marianne introduced a retired police officer named Norman with the wizened, folded face of an apple-core doll and a special fondness for doing home security on the cheap. Every idea he showed us had a price tag under ten dollars. Who needed an alarm system when you could glue a telephone pad to your wall and paint a red dot on it for seven dollars? Why buy a dog when a bowl of dog food and a BEWARE OF DOG sign will achieve the same effect? We were charmed by his parsimony; beside him, Marianne beamed.

If Linda Sue was there that night, she didn't speak up or ask any questions the way she had at the first meeting. She saved that for the last meeting, after everyone was seated and Marianne announced brightly, "Tonight we have a very special guest."

We all looked around the small living room. We knew everyone there. "Give me a sec," Marianne said, and returned a moment later, followed by a middle-aged man wearing a denim jacket, brown corduroys, and a baseball cap pulled low. "This is Gary," she said, walking him up to the front of the room. "And he's a former burglar."

We looked around. Beside me, Linda Sue whispered, "What is she *thinking*?"

"Gary is enrolled in a rehab program that provides supervised housing in exchange for participation in community outreach groups. Gary has graciously agreed to share his life story with us and answer any questions we might have."

Linda Sue put her hand up.

"Later, Linda Sue. After he's spoken." Silently I prayed Linda Sue wouldn't use this as an opportunity to pick another fight. In the month since we followed Linda Sue and Geoffrey home after Helen's party, I'd been watching from my window for any sign of a repeat visitation. The night after we saw them standing together in her living room I slept maybe an hour or two at best. I woke early enough to make coffee and sit all morning watching Linda Sue's yard, waiting to see Geoffrey walk across it. He never did. When I finally had to leave so I wouldn't be late for work, I found him outside on his driveway, lying on the rolling board he used to work under his car. I was fully prepared to walk past him when he called out, "Bets!" and slid over to the grass strip that separated our driveways. "Quite a party last night, wasn't it?" he said, smiling. I could hear the teenage joke he wasn't saying: *NOT.*

"Helen's work might take a little getting used to," I said diplomatically.

He asked when I wanted to get together to talk more about *Anna Karenina*. I tried to remember which one of us had suggested this book and why. Why had he put me in this position of knowing so much about him and yet nothing that mattered? He acted so cordial and so *normal,* asking me what page I'd gotten to, when I was off work, if I'd be ready this afternoon to talk about our book, that I began to wonder—honestly—if I'd imagined the scene at Linda Sue's house the night before.

"I'm a little busy this week," I said, shaking my keys as if to prove I had a real job here, with responsibilities.

"Okay," he said, pushing himself back. "Maybe this weekend?"

"I don't know, Geoffrey," I said. "Maybe you should spend time with Corinne. You said you hadn't seen much of each other recently."

"Hmm." He nodded. "She's away this weekend, actually. At a conference." We usually knew ahead of time about the weekends Corinne wasn't around. We always had him over for dinner at least one of the nights, sometimes both.

"I didn't know that." I let the silence open up, with no mention of dinner.

"Well, then." He pushed himself as far away as he could. "Let me know when you want to talk about the book."

I didn't say any of the things that crossed my mind. *I never want to talk about this book with you. You shouldn't be sleeping with Linda Sue. She's vulnerable and strange and not worthy of you.* Or what I was finally beginning to feel: *You manipulate all of us, Geoffrey. You listen to our sad stories and then you tell your own and you get all of us to excuse you for your bad behavior.*

When he didn't show up at the library that day or the next, or anytime at all the following week, I knew something was different. It became a mystery and I watched Linda Sue's house more. Anytime I wasn't at work or obligated to attend to Paul in some way, I stood at the kitchen window with the clearest view of her yard. I never saw

Geoffrey go in or come out. What did it mean? A few days later, I called to tell him that some things had come up at work and I wouldn't have time to read our book. "It's a little too much right now," I said, hoping he'd get the gist of my meaning—the book was about an adulterous affair that didn't end well. *I know what's going on,* I wanted to yell over the phone. *You weren't exactly subtle.* But the problem was that I *didn't* know. I didn't understand—what did he and Linda Sue have in common?

"Okay," he said, as if the enormity of what I was saying—*I don't want to read with you anymore*—meant little to him. For the next week at work, I watched the library door and waited for him to come. Some days I felt the buzz of expectation, an electric tingle in my neck, and I'd think, *Yes, he's coming today.* I couldn't explain it except to say that I felt like a child, left behind by the first real friend I'd ever made. I lurched between moods, one minute sad, the next irritated by the endless demands of patrons, always looking for something slightly different than what we had on the shelf. Large print, paperback, a different translation. Once I actually snapped, "What difference does it make?" to an elderly woman looking for an edition of Emily Dickinson that she remembered as having a *yellow* cover. After that I went into the bathroom and sat inside a toilet stall for the better part of an hour. *Calm down,* I told myself. *Just calm down.*

I thought about calling Geoffrey and saying, *I never wanted to sleep with you, you know,* which sounded adolescent even though it was true. I didn't. Why would I want stolen kisses and hand-holding when we had topics to discuss and ground to cover?

I was beginning to understand that the end of a friendship could break your heart as cleanly as the end of a romance. Maybe I did behave like a teenager. Paul implied it more than once and we started bickering more. "I don't understand you," he said one night over a dinner I'd thrown together, a box of macaroni and cheese with sausage cut up into it. We both lifted the tasteless food into our mouths. I narrowed my eyes at him as if to say, *Oh, don't you?*

Though presumably Gary's life of crime was behind him, he began his speech in an unsettling present tense. "Okay, so. Let's say I'm out, looking for a house. I want one that looks vulnerable, right? Windows half-open, no screens or bars. I also look for blinds closed all the way. That means when I get in I can do anything, look for the jewelry, find the silver. What have you."

Marianne's smile looked like it was caught on her teeth. "You *used* to do this."

"Right," he said, nodding.

Gary was a dreadful speaker. He blinked nervously and picked at his teeth. Later, he talked about looking for jewelry in a bathroom and touched his zipper. To conclude, he hiked up his pants and said, "I forget what else. "When Marianne asked for questions, we sat in silence. He might have been reformed, but he was a sad sight and no one wanted to drag this out. Except for Linda Sue. "Do you mind telling us what jail is like?"

He seemed game enough to answer the question, but Marianne stopped him. "That's not what we're here for, Linda Sue. This is about *preventing* crime."

"It seems like it's been more about glamorizing it. Isn't that what he's been doing all night?" She turned around and looked at all of us. No one said anything. "I feel like leaving here and becoming a burglar. We've just learned about twenty great tips for doing it. I think it's worth his telling us a few reasons why we shouldn't."

Marianne fumed until Gary said he'd like to take the question.

"Look, the thing about jail is—" He looked at each one of us, sitting with our notebooks open in our laps, pocketbooks tucked under our feet. "Don't go there, okay? Seriously. Jail is like your worst nightmare times ten. It's scum of the earth in your face all day and all night, sleeping on top of you, pissing on the floor. The reason I'm here tonight is I'd rather do *anything*—I'd rather do *this*—than go back to jail."

We shifted awkwardly in our seats at the unkind implication he'd made about our gathering. Only Linda Sue laughed at the answer, so hard I feared she might lapse into a choking fit. "Thank you," she finally said, catching her breath.

Because it was our final meeting, Marianne had planned a party with a rum punch, crystal cups, and a handwritten folded sign that warned: ALCOHOLIC! She laid out her spread and disappeared into the kitchen. After a few minutes, I went to check on her and found her standing alone with tears in her eyes. There was no point in pretending I hadn't walked in. "Are you okay, Marianne?"

"I'd just like to know why she moved here."

For weeks I'd been asking myself the same question. "I wish I knew," I said.

"Helen keeps saying she's harmless, but I don't think she is."

I hadn't dared articulate such a thought, but the minute Marianne said it, I knew what she meant. "It's like she watches us," I whispered. "And judges everything we do."

She looked up and caught my eye. *"Exactly."*

This wasn't fair. Even as I said it, I knew I was wrong. I'd stood with Linda Sue at three parties now, had walked home with her twice, and I knew the simple truth: She didn't think about us nearly as much as we thought about her. The real problem with Linda Sue's cavalier jokes and laughing with a felon about our gathering was the kernel of truth that lay behind it. We were a joke. We favored practical hairstyles and dressed in bright pinks and greens that made us look like an army of cautious women trying to look cheerful. We kept conversations light and on predictable topics. If one expected anything more interesting—like the conversations I'd had with Geoffrey all spring—one would only be disappointed coming to this group.

Marianne wiped her nose with a paper towel. "Part of me thinks she needs our help, and part of me wishes she'd just *leave*."

I thought about my own contradictory impulses—offering to help with her curtains one minute, peeping in on her private life the next. In the other room, I could hear Linda Sue's voice above the others. "Look, I never even lock my door. If anyone wants to rob me, they can."

Standing in the dark kitchen, I surprised myself: "She'll leave soon, Marianne," I said. "She'll be gone. I know she will."

CHAPTER 16

After I hang up with Paul, Finn appears with a pitcher of something he calls "sun tea," which he tells me is made by putting a pitcher of water in the sun all day with tea bags floating in it. "It's one of those things gay men who work at home do with their extra time."

I laugh as he pours me a glass. He's been so helpful and reassuring, I hardly know how to properly thank him.

"Oh, please." He sticks a sprig of mint into my glass. "You'll need this," he says, pointing to the mint. "Otherwise it just tastes like brown water. That's the problem with sun tea. It doesn't really work."

I ask if he knows any way to look up old police reports about an accident that would have happened more than twelve years ago.

"Hmm. That might be tricky, but we can try." He takes me into his office, where two computers sit on desks facing opposite walls. As he works on finding police files online, I ask about the other names on the list and point to the two that I wrote down at the bottom: Trish Rashke and Alocin Bell, the name I saw on the envelope at Marianne's house. "Nothing so far, but I'm going to work on Trish Rashke next. I remember her and I've got some ideas about how to find her."

"You *knew* Trish?"

"She lived here with her parents when we first moved in. We hired her to walk our dog for a while. She was always very sweet with him. She bought him toys and came over to visit with him. Then the dog died suddenly and we hardly saw her after that."

"How did he die?"

"A kidney infection. It happened so fast the vet thought maybe he ate some pesticide. We never knew exactly what happened."

That evening Marianne starts her Personal Safety Seminar by asking everyone to say their name and what they currently use for personal protection. A woman in the front goes first. "Sharon. Mace spray." Her sister, beside her, is next. "June. Brass knuckles." No one makes the joke I would have expected. *Condoms sometimes, diaphragm occasionally.*

There are more people here than I ever remember at our old Neighborhood Watch gatherings. She keeps going around the room until finally one woman admits that she doesn't carry anything. "I don't like thinking about this stuff."

"What would be nice is not having to think about it at *all*," Marianne says. I have to admit she's pretty good. She doesn't seem obsessive or disturbingly fixated on threats that don't exist. She seems like a problem solver. "Look," she says, holding up the pink Taser gun she's laid out for demonstration. From far away, it looks small and harmless, like a fun grooming gadget. "No one wants to think about being attacked. No one is looking to be one of Charlie's Angels."

When the sample guns come out, Marianne demonstrates one, warning everyone about the sound it will make when it hits a target. "It's like a bug zapper and it makes my skin crawl. You wonder if this thing is going to burn someone up. But I'm told no, that it feels like a very powerful jolt—painful, yes, but also temporary."

After one woman volunteers to try first and hits Reynolds Wrap, as Marianne has named the foil-covered target, everyone lines up for a turn. Marianne calls out pointers: "Aim for his chest if he's farther than forty feet, his jugular if he's closer. Does everyone know what the jugular is?" No one answers because no one's listening anymore. They're waiting for their turn, wielding their gun. A commotion of laughter and applause erupts every time the target sizzles with a hit. I move to the refreshments table in the back. I realize that Marianne is so flush with the success of this event and the checkbooks already being pulled out that she probably won't notice if I slip away.

Downstairs the door is open, almost as if Roland knew I might flee the party upstairs. "Hi, there," he says. A bottle of wine sits open on the U-shaped plank of linoleum that serves as a makeshift counter. "Care to join me?" He holds up a glass.

I take it from him, careful not to let our hands touch, and take a sip. At the party on my first night home I didn't drink anything, probably because Marianne never offered it. She must be worried about triggers for me and inadvertently unleashing my old black moods. Though why she thinks the gathering upstairs would be fine but not a glass of wine seems strange. "This is nice. Thank you, Roland."

"You're welcome. I imagine none of this is easy for you." He rolls his eyes upward, meaning, I assume, *this party*.

I tell him what Marianne said this morning. "She was awake when

I came here in the middle of the night. She saw me crossing the street."

"She *did*?"

"I told her nothing happened. That you were nice and made me some tea and that was all. I wondered if she ever said anything to you."

"No." He looks down. There is more to say and I wait—to see if he'll have the courage to start. Apparently not.

"I'm sorry I never came back," I say. "I wanted to, and then—I don't know. I felt too self-conscious." Though I've pretended not to remember that time, I do.

"I'm sorry, too. I wanted to step forward during your trial, but I was afraid it would do more harm than good." I look at his face, his eyebrows raised in lines of worry. For so long, I wondered about this. Before my trial, desperate to prove any recent episodes of sleepwalking, I gave Roland's name to Franklin with the promise that he would testify to one episode. Two days later, Franklin returned empty-handed and said, "Nothing. The guy says he never talked to you in the middle of the night."

"I went to his *apartment*," I told Franklin. "I woke up on his sofa, wearing my nightgown. He made me a pot of peach tea."

"That may be, but he denies it."

All these years, I've wondered what Roland's denial meant. Was he embarrassed, or guilt-stricken, or just a terribly frightened man? I haven't stayed angry for twelve years but I also haven't forgotten.

"I wanted to talk about that time your lawyer came," he says. "I saw you sleepwalking, yes, but I also saw you wake up pretty easily when you heard my voice. I couldn't even say you seemed disoriented or disassociated. You didn't." He has a point. Testifying to my episodes would have also meant testifying, *Yes, she sleepwalks, and yes, she also wakes up easily.* "I was scared I'd have to tell them what you'd told me about your miscarriages. I thought the prosecution would turn it into a motivation argument, saying you were jealous of Linda Sue." He's right. They would have. "If it would have helped you, I'd have told Franklin what happened that night. I hated lying—I did a terrible job of it."

I take another sip of wine. "I assumed you didn't want Marianne to find out."

"No." He starts to laugh, then stops himself. "No, that wasn't the issue. The truth is—I thought about that night a lot. I kept hoping you'd come back. I left my light on for a long time so you could see your way if you needed to." He looks out the narrow window that faces my old house, long enough for me to imagine him sitting here, watching my front door. "And then you didn't."

"I wanted to." For a moment, I consider telling him the truth: *I did*.

"Yes," he says and lifts his glass.

It's hard to imagine how important appearances seemed at the time, how I didn't want anyone to think I was approaching another woman's husband. Better to have them think it was Geoffrey rather than the one I really wanted. Something happened that night we peeked in and saw Linda Sue and Geoffrey standing in her living room, a tectonic shift in the focus of my longings. I no longer wanted *him*, I wanted *that*.

Roland takes another drink and keeps going. "If I could, I'd do it all differently now. Back then, we were hearing so many different things. Geoffrey kept reassuring us that everything would be fine. He said he'd given the defense information that would guarantee you wouldn't get convicted." I remember what Helen said, how Geoffrey returned after my arrest and talked to everyone.

"Do you remember what he said?"

"He wouldn't get very specific. He just kept telling everyone that it would work out fine and you wouldn't get convicted. He was a little strange with me. I wondered if he knew what happened that night."

He's asking as if, even now, the answer matters.

"I never told him. I never told anyone."

Strictly speaking, this isn't true. In prison, I once told Wanda who asked if I'd ever had a kiss that made me so dizzy I forgot to breathe. "Yes, I have," I said, recalling my one night on the couch with this man who stands now an arm's length away from me. Upstairs, we can hear the party breaking up. Sitting close enough to see the lines around his eyes and the way his hair has grayed around his ears makes me think of Leo. How I memorized these details about him and lay in bed at night going over all of them, laying claim to him in my mind.

I look at the clock and realize it's almost eleven P.M. Enough revelations for one day, I think. Enough truth and honesty and all the talk that goes with it. We all have mistakes and regrets, pieces of our past that don't fit in. There is an electricity between us that's impossible to ignore and impossible to act on. I have too many specters crowding my thoughts, too much I still need to figure out.

Over the last three days I've hardly slept at all. After my conversation with Marianne, I fear I may never sleep again. It's a danger zone for me, the place my unconscious runs freely. In prison I had a locked cell and neighbors accustomed to activity all night. There, I weaned myself off sleeping pills and started dreaming again. Night became my private time, a chance to visit with the children I gave myself. Whatever I did in the night—laughed, talked, used names none of my block mates had heard of—it was brushed over the next day. Now such freedom is impossible. Even sleeping over at Finn and Bill's won't help in this regard. I can't run the risk of sleeping so deeply I might get up in the middle of the night, so I sleep in guarded, light snatches, waking every hour or so to make sure that I'm in bed, where I'm meant to be.

Finally Roland says, "You're welcome to spend the night here if you want."

It's such a surprise that I say nothing.

"We don't have to do anything. But if it helps you sleep better."

How does he know that my body aches with fatigue? My legs can't stop moving, as if they want to run a marathon and win the right to rest. "I haven't been able to sleep at all," I whisper.

He nods. "I've been worried about that. With all Marianne's hovering. I've kept thinking, how can she relax?"

I feel an old humming start in my brain, a noise that drowns out all other sounds and thoughts. I remind myself: *Breathe in and breathe out. It's a feeling. Not an attack. I'm here with this man who is flawed in his own ways and forgiving of mine.*

But it scares me. It reminds me of lying on my prison mattress, writing letters six and seven pages long to a man I'd spoken with only once about when we'd meet again at the next picnic. *I know a place we can go,* Leo wrote. *Though I won't pressure you in any way. I'd be happy just holding you.* For years, I'd made fun of my fellow inmates who had sex in broom closets and on top of washing machines, but by that point I understood exactly how they felt. *I'm happy to go to a Porta Potti if we have to,* I wrote back. *I just want to be alone with you.*

"You can use my bed," Roland says now, and gestures toward a door in the corner. "Marianne doesn't have to know. I'll stay out here and make sure nothing happens."

We both know what he's saying. That he'll make sure I don't get up and do anything untoward. Of all the generosity I've been the recipient of, this seems to me the simplest, kindest act of all. I can't say no. My body won't let me. I need to sleep and I can't do it unwatched, alone in Trish's room. "Thank you," I say.

And then, because it's late and I'm scared of ruining this moment with more talk, I lean over, kiss him on the lips, and stand up. "I'm going to go to bed now."

He looks flustered for the first time. The kiss is nice, but not lingering and not a reprise of the one twelve years ago that I've never forgotten. It's more of a nod, a thank-you that defies my ability to say: *I'd like to sleep with you, but I can't.*

That night I lie in Roland's bed and think about things I can't forget. Leo was the one who pulled away first. At least that's how it felt, though in prison, with unreliable conduits running letters back and forth, it's impossible to be sure what really happened. He'd introduced a note of caution into his declarations of love: *I'm not sure why I feel this way or how long it will realistically last. I understand that we don't really know each other and we are bound to be a disappointment sooner or later. That's how it goes.*

Was this his way of saying he'd heard about my crime? That if his bore the weight of shortsightedness, it was also inarguably unintentional. Mine was the fatal bludgeoning of a woman's head. Quite a difference on any level.

I want to work these things out, but I also want to be able to talk honestly with you about our differences.

I read that line as an accusation: You're a real murderer, I'm not.

Fine, I wrote back. *Maybe we should take a break from these letters for a while.*

He protested (halfheartedly, I thought), and then, when I made a test out of refusing to write to him for a week, he responded in kind and wrote nothing at all. I grew so desperate, I solicited Wanda's help. "What are you, twelve?" she asked when I told her what was going on. "Just write him again."

"I'm afraid to. I've written him so much." I hesitated. "I'm afraid he's seen the real me and that's what he's backing away from."

"All men back away, honey. That's what they *do*."

"And then what?"

"You keep all your options open and play a few games. You say, maybe I'll see you at the next picnic, and then you talk to everyone but him for the first hour."

"I'm forty-five years old."

"Right."

"I don't have any options. I'll be sixty-two when I get out of here."

"Look, honey, no one's a pretty picture in here. You work with what you got. You show him who you are, then you say, you want me, you gotta do some work. I want some pipe cleaner necklaces and some nice long letters. I want to feel the love again."

I took Wanda's advice. I decided I wouldn't regret my earlier honesty, but I also wouldn't sell myself short. I wrote him a note saying I'd be at the picnic if he wanted to talk but I wouldn't expect anything. In the span of three weeks we managed to devolve from marriage talk to junior high. *Maybe I'll see you there, or maybe not,* I wrote.

For the first two hours of the picnic I sat huddled with the same women I'd ridden over with. When I finally broke free, I lost my courage walking over to him. I started talking to two older men who asked why I was called the Librarian Murderess. Did I beat people up with books or what?

"I used to be a librarian," I said, smiling, so that if Leo was watching, he might think I was having a good time.

"Seriously," the moon-faced man asked. "I thought that was, like, a joke."

"Oh, no. No joke."

"So what? You stamped dates?"

"Right. Among other things." Out of the corner of my eye, I saw Leo and it sent me backward, performing a dance of nonchalance. I could feel his eyes on me—it was possible to *feel* them—but I couldn't imagine what he was thinking. This was our only chance to talk after four months of letter writing and neither one of us was taking the first step to do so. Even if we technically weren't supposed to touch, we could do what everyone else did—hide behind a tree and touch until someone told us to stop. Or we could sit, as we had last time, tell our stories, and laugh.

But he wouldn't walk over. And the longer he refused, the greater the gulf grew.

In the end, we never spoke.

Wanda said it was the saddest thing she'd ever seen. "You two shoulda hung signs around your neck, I'm not gonna talk first. My kids used to do stuff like that. Course they were in second grade at the time."

"Please, Wanda," I said, lying down on my bunk. "I don't want to talk about it."

CHAPTER 17

"We missed you at the end of our Wild West shoot-out," Finn says the next morning, pouring me a cup of coffee when I come back to keep researching. "You missed the tinfoil target man going up in flames. That was exciting. Everyone had to throw their terrible wine on him."

"I'm sorry I left."

"No, no, you got out of there just in time. We actually wondered afterward if maybe Marianne is losing it a little."

"Really?"

"I don't know. We've always liked her, but last night raised the bar to a whole new level of strange."

Poor Marianne. I think about the days when Roland had expensive cars parked in front of their house and work that wealthy men wanted to invest in. Maybe there was a simple explanation for that odd gathering. Maybe Roland's work had never amounted to much and they needed the money. "Were other people feeling the same way?"

"Who knows? She sold a few guns to the people who seemed the least likely to ever use them. I don't know. I'm too judgmental, I'm sure." He pours milk into a creamer and pushes it toward me. "So the real question Bill has forbidden me to ask, but I will anyway, is where did you go and where did you sleep?"

"I went down to Roland's."

Finn raises his mug along with his eyebrows.

"Nothing happened. Roland's an old friend and I've been having so much trouble sleeping. It's made me—" I stop myself before I say *a little crazy* or *afraid I'll start sleepwalking.* "We got to talking and I was so tired, I fell asleep on his couch."

"That's it?"

"That's it. I woke up this morning still wearing all my clothes."

"Oh, Bill will be disappointed. We've always thought that Roland was so cute. I used to watch him through the window sometimes, working on his little experiments." He points through their front window, where you can see into Roland's basement. I have to wonder: *If this had been my view, how much time would I have wasted watching that window?* "Wait, what experiments?" I say.

"I don't know what they were. Something with beakers of water and measuring temperatures."

Was he back at work on solar heating? I never saw any beakers in his work space.

"I don't think that's going on anymore, though he's still working on something. I see him up at night. Speaking of which, I did a little of my own work last night."

I follow him into his office, where he pulls up old police blotter columns that list car accidents significant enough to have been noted in the police report. "There were two highway accident reports the night of Linda Sue's death, both about twenty miles away. I checked through the column for the whole week before Linda Sue's death. Nothing on Juniper Lane, until I found this about two weeks before the murder: 'Hazardous Waste Spill Reported at 32 Juniper Lane.' According to the item, which is only three lines long, the spill occurred between two properties—32 and 34 Juniper Lane—and was contained. An inspection team came in 'to assess the area, and made recommendations, which were followed up on by the homeowners.'"

"Do you know what constitutes a hazardous waste spill in a residential area?"

Bill comes in from the kitchen, holding a bowl of cereal he eats standing up. "Antifreeze, maybe, or refrigerator coolant. At my school, some kid once stabbed a barrel of Freezone outside the hockey rink and the stuff was so toxic a team from the EPA came out to remove two feet of dirt from an area the size of a soccer field. It freaked us all out because we were standing right there when the guy did it. Everyone said we were contaminated now and we'd never have babies. Of course that might have also been because we were all gay."

Linda Sue's old house was 32 Juniper Lane, right next door to 34, which was Marianne and Roland's house. I don't remember anything about a toxic spill, but I do remember that it was around this time that Marianne began warning us about a new study on the pressure-treated wood we'd all used to build our decks. Apparently they'd just discovered dangerous levels of lead leeching into the soil. She circulated flyers telling everyone not to plant vegetable gardens within fifty feet of our decks. I took her flyer and worried that maybe this was an explanation for my miscarriages, but we hadn't built a deck. Everyone else seemed to ignore her warning completely. They couldn't get a lawn of grass to grow. Why would they undertake a vegetable garden out back? "Be safe!" I remember her calling from her yard. "I just want everyone to be safe!"

Now I wonder what was in the beakers of water Finn saw. Finn says he asked once, and Roland told him they were ocean water, hardly a toxic substance.

Finn also thinks he might have found something on Trish. "I was doing all these different searches, variations on her name. Patricia. Pat. Tish. On one of them, I accidentally left off the *R* in her last name—I typed in *Patricia Ashke*—and look at this: Here's a woman listed, the right age, living in Connecticut about an hour north of here."

"You're kidding."

"Any chance our Trish could be a writer these days?"

I clap my hands. "Yes! That's what she always wanted to be!"

"It's a Library of Congress listing. She uses a pseudonym as her writing name. If this is her, she writes a fantasy series for middle readers, ages eight to eleven. There have been three books so far, all written under the name Cat Ashker." He has notes scribbled on a piece of paper.

I look over at where he's written it down. *"Cat?"* I say, my heart quickening.

"That's what she goes by."

There it is in block letters: CAT ASHKER.

It takes only a minute to see that it's an anagram: three letters from *Patricia* and the letters in her last name rearranged. In front of my eyes, the letters jumble again and rearrange themselves, as if they've become a message meant for me: *Cat, ask her.*

"Where in Connecticut does she live?"

"Bridgetown, which is up north about an hour away. I Googled a white pages search and her address isn't listed, but look at this. Here's a press release for a reading she's doing tomorrow afternoon at a book-store in Middletown." I lean over his shoulder and read the notice. My mind races ahead. I can't drive myself, and I can't ask Marianne.

Finn scratches his head and smiles. "I don't know about you, but I'd like to go."

CHAPTER 18

The library has all three books by Cat Ashker. I check them out using Finn's card and wait until I get outside to Geoffrey's and my old bench to start reading the first one. It's about five children, ages five to fourteen, who live in a development marked off by cornfields on one side and woods on the other that are full of tiny fairies who have grown tired—bone-tired, they say, though they have no bones—of eating the dried corn. One day they see the children alone in the woods on an evening picnic, eating from a bowl of ambrosia salad. They move closer to admire the bits of fruit covered in sticky white. They want that salad more than they've ever wanted anything before, but surrounding it are the five children, three boys and two girls.

I stop reading for a moment and wonder, *Can this be a coincidence?* Then I keep going and feel my breath catch:

The tallest was Shannon, fourteen and pretty, but not in
that way that boys at school noticed. They saw it, though, the
fairies did: The way her eyes sparkled. Her teeth were so
straight and white ever since her braces had come off. Her
middle brother, Peter, a year younger, was handsome but
irresponsible, just the kind of boy, frankly, that fairies don't
like. They preferred Ben, the oldest, bespectacled and kind,
bad at all ball sports. Henry and Charlotte—the little ones,
the babies, were favorites because everyone loved babies, even
though these babies were five and six.

For a moment I can't breathe. Even Wanda never knew about the children I've imagined, that they have lives of their own, names and personalities. In all this time, I've told only one person. And she's dead.

"Betsy? Is that you?"

I look up, so startled to hear my name, I gasp. "Paul!" I close the book and slide it to one side. "What are you doing here?"

"Oh, I stop by occasionally these days." He's smiling cheerfully, holding a plastic file case in one hand. "I like to check up on them. You'd be surprised. They've let a few things slide. No one can get the whole *New York Times* on one roller like you could."

I move over so he can sit down. "There's a trick to that actually."

"You'd better tell them what it is. Poor Viola gets yelled at for throwing away the sports section." I laugh and he touches the back of my hand. "So I've been thinking about our conversation." He says he's got a new theory. It has to do with the sandwich found on Linda Sue's counter. "We've always assumed the perpetrator made that sandwich, right?"

"Right."

"But why couldn't it have been someone *else*? Why hasn't anyone thought about the possibility that *two* people came into her house that night? One who went looking for valuables upstairs, and one who stayed downstairs because he was hungry?"

I should be grateful that he's still working on my case, trying to help, but I can't help thinking about an observation Franklin once made: *Paul doesn't have the greatest instincts. He doesn't mind barking up a lot of the wrong trees.* If it was a team of burglars, why would they have chosen Linda Sue's empty house? Why would they have taken nothing afterward, including a twenty-dollar bill sitting on the table?

Paul's right about one thing—the sandwich has always been hard to explain. Franklin tried to use it as part of my sleepwalking scenario. In his version, I crossed the street and walked into Linda Sue's kitchen believing I was still in my own house. He displayed the identical blueprints of our houses as evidence—stove, refrigerator, countertop, all identical. Thinking I was in my own kitchen, he argued, I made a sandwich in my sleep state and was interrupted by a sound that frightened me. Not Paul's voice, but a stranger's. In this scenario, her death was entirely unintentional. I grabbed the closest weapon at hand, the new lock, walked upstairs, and there, in the dark, was violently disoriented by a stranger's appearance in what I believed was my own house. "What we have is a case of self-defense," Franklin argued. "Fear of crime had become a neighborhood obsession, and tragically, Linda Sue, who spoke out against the dangers of community-sanctioned paranoia, was herself the victim of it."

It was the strongest argument we had, even though it had holes. It didn't explain the cleanup afterward, or the choice I must have made not to seek help.

Paul offers another theory. "At first I thought maybe it was inexperienced teenagers who didn't know enough to look inside a window before breaking into a house, but you're right, that might be a stretch. So then I started thinking about Gary, the burglar who came to that last Neighborhood Watch meeting."

Gary was a suspect early on. Linda Sue was murdered three nights after our meeting at Marianne's house, the one where she announced to everyone that she never locked her doors. A promising lead, dismissed when staff at his residential house provided an alibi for him that night.

"What the police never followed up on was the *other* men living at that halfway house. Gary could have gone home after that meeting and told the story of Linda Sue. How she lived alone and didn't lock her doors. How she stood up at the meeting and announced that fact. Everyone living there had at least one felony conviction. Most of them were already repeat offenders."

I know these statistics all too well. Having been incarcerated, I'm at a precipitously high risk for becoming one myself. "How far away was Gary's house?"

"Nine miles. None of the residents had cars, but they could have hitched a ride down the highway or walked. Whoever it was planned for one crime but not the other. They wore gloves and knew how to get inside, but they didn't bring a weapon. Meaning they had experience, but weren't hard-core, which lines up with the Cleary House residents at the time." Paul opens his case and pulls out a file. "Here's the list I got of the residents. I've flagged two who shared a room with Gary. It was supposed to be a single, but they were overbooked and it's possible that made Gary angry. He knew the best way to free up his living space was if those guys went back to prison."

Sometimes I wonder, does Paul work this hard to prove my innocence, or is it more complicated? Is he trying to prove Geoffrey couldn't have done it either?

By the time Geoffrey moved here, I'd already begun to suspect a reason for the distance I felt in our marriage. I never put words to it and couldn't say exactly when it started. Was it the first week after we moved onto the block, when Marianne gave us a tour of her house and I watched Paul pinch the fold of one curtain, feel its weight, rub the texture with his thumb? Or did the possibility strike me later, when I saw the way he sometimes watched Geoffrey from across the room? When did looking gay turn into a question of *being* it? I don't think that came until later, when I got to prison and could look back with some clarity on the marriage I'd left behind.

The first time we had sex, I remember Paul saying afterward, "We did it!" so triumphantly, I wondered if I'd just taken his virginity. No, he told me, it had just been awhile and he was nervous about all the parts working. I can say that it's possible to have an active sex life and still wonder about your husband's attention to small matters of personal vanity, about how sensitive he sometimes seemed to what other men said.

Now we sit side by side not talking for a long time. He seems to sense my reluctance to keep pursuing threads of my case with him. "But if Gary wanted them to be caught, why weren't they? Why wouldn't he have just turned them in afterward?"

"Maybe he felt bad. Maybe the murder freaked him out."

"Have you found the old roommates?"

He nods his head. "One of them is back in prison at Bellington State. I've written him a letter but I haven't heard back."

Of course he hasn't. He never will.

I tell him I've been doing my own research, talking to more neighbors. I tell him what I've heard about Geoffrey calling people before my trial.

"He was trying to help," Paul says. "He told them he didn't think you were guilty."

I'm sure he did, but I wonder what else he communicated. Geoffrey knew he was vulnerable and many people were still suspicious of him.

Did he talk to neighbors, ostensibly on my behalf, and say softly under his breath, *Her childhood was hard. Her father had mental illness.* Was he planting the story in their minds, watering the seeds of doubt? *It wasn't really her fault. She is the victim of hormones and memory loss.* Paul could have supplied him with my diagnosis, could have acted as an accessory without even seeing how Geoffrey had manipulated him.

"He told them I was mentally ill, Paul. That I should be going to an institution, not a prison."

"We were trying everything, Bets. We got a little desperate by the end. We thought it might work if we reminded people about your episodes."

"Insanity defenses almost never work."

"I told him that. I'd spent all the money we had, I'd paid for half a dozen different outside experts to weigh in on the evidence. We were told this was the smartest way to go. In the end, Geoffrey talked me into it. He said we had to commit to one line of defense and throw all our resources into it. That's why he went to all the neighbors. We thought they'd step forward voluntarily, and then nobody did. It was such a—" He struggles to find the right word. "Well, a disappointment."

In a trial, I've learned, what isn't said can be as significant as what is. Silence can be deafening, and in my case it was. The jury assumed I was a neighborhood version of a malcontent school shooter—quiet and unnoticed until the night my hidden rage propelled me across the street. With no testimony stating otherwise, what else could they think? We'd been neighbors for six years, participants in one another's lives, but when mine hung in the balance, no one spoke up in my defense. Franklin told me he wasn't surprised. Suburban criminals, especially women, often get abandoned. He told me not to blame anyone individually—the group fear response won out.

But was this why Marianne remembers my bad episodes so well?

Because Geoffrey gave her details? Is this why everyone I talk to sounds so nervous to hear from me? It's certainly possible. It's hard to blame Paul, whose face wears the terrible weight of these misguided efforts. "It wasn't your fault, Paul. When I look back, I see how Geoffrey manipulated all of us."

"I know he did," Paul says softly. "Still, I can't help it—sometimes I miss him, don't you?"

I think about the way Geoffrey listened to my stories, how powerful that was. I know this much: We were both in love with him. Paul for a lifetime, me for a year. Strangely, it wasn't a source of tension between us. It gave us something private that we shared, though we never discussed it. Even as I remember this, I think: *Maybe Paul, in his own way, has been a truer friend than I realized*. We shared certain truths we couldn't speak of aloud. We respected the privacy we each seemed to need.

"All this time I've wondered if Geoffrey killed her. If maybe I turned myself in and confessed in some unconscious, complicated act of friendship."

"No, Bets, I wouldn't have let you do that—"

"It turns out he didn't do it, though. He took a DNA test; it wasn't him."

Paul must know this already because he nods. "I knew he couldn't have. He loved Linda Sue. In a way I'd never seen in him before."

"So where does that leave us? Who *was* it, then?"

Instead of answering, he hands me another file, a report from a blood spatter expert, saying it was possible that Linda Sue coughed the blood up the wall, that the spray hadn't necessarily been caused by repeated blows to her head. It takes me a minute to realize what it says, and the difference this could have made if it had been included in the trial. It would have at least introduced the idea that her death was not a bludgeoning but a possible accident. "If the blood spatter could have come from her coughing, did anyone say she might have just fallen down the stairs?"

"Unlikely, given the fingernail scrapings and the hair in her blood."

"But it's possible, right? Maybe someone was there, maybe they struggled before she fell, but this person isn't responsible."

"I tried. After I read that blood spatter report, I sent it to three experts. Two out of three ruled out accidental death. They pointed to the bruising on the neck as evidence of intent. Whoever it was tried to strangle her and couldn't manage it. Eventually the fight came to the top of the stairs, where she was struck in the head and forced down."

"What did the third expert say?"

"The third said it was remote, but accidental death was a possibility."

For a long time, neither one of us speaks. "It could have been an accident, Paul. That's what I've always thought. But who was there with her?"

It wasn't Corinne, she was in Princeton. It wasn't Gary the burglar, who had an alibi. Who was Linda Sue happy enough to see that she invited him or her in, put on a kettle for tea, then went upstairs and ended up getting killed? One of the other women on the block? I go through all the names—Helen, Barbara, Kim, Marianne. "She didn't like any of them. If they showed up at her door she would have done what she always did with me, stepped out on the porch and smoked a cigarette so the conversation could end when the smoke did. So who did she invite in?"

I haven't mentioned this new idea I've only just hatched: that Trish could have been there, somewhere inside the house. Paul's already dismissed Trish as a possibility and I don't want to lose my focus.

To my surprise, Paul hardly seems interested in going over the list of suspects. Instead, he seems determined to dwell on the mistakes and what went wrong twelve years ago with my defense. "I wish I'd done a lot of things differently. Starting with Franklin. Boy, if I could go back in time, I never would have chosen Franklin."

"I was there, too, remember? Making the same mistakes."

"I should have seen things clearer. You were sitting in jail, how could you judge? I was weighing everything, getting advice, and still I managed to screw it up."

He turns and looks at me, his brown eyes soft. He's a sweet man, and well meaning. It doesn't surprise me that he's kept blaming himself for what happened. I wish we had a different history. I wish I could ask him if he's fallen in love or if his current life is less lonely than the one we had together, but I can't. There are some questions I simply can't ask out loud.

CHAPTER 19

Instead of going back to Marianne's house, I stop by Finn's and ask if I can borrow his computer again. Typing in Trish's pen name leads me to a Web site designed for young readers to talk to other fans of her books. Currently posted are two weeks of messages, about twenty in all.

> Are you a huge Peter fan? I am! Which book is your favorite?
> I say number three is best!

I went to prison just as the Harry Potter craze was beginning and I missed what I imagine has been an exciting phenomenon. Trish's books seem to have attracted an equally loyal, albeit smaller, fan base. One girl writes to complain that there hasn't been a new book in a year and a half, which means she's had to reread her three books over and over.

Please, Cat, if you're reading this, finish the new one soon!
An eager sixth grader in Portsmouth, NH

I can't get over the casual way everyone talks about the characters:

Henry and Charlotte are my favorites. I know they're usually
the cause of all the trouble, but that's why I like them. Has
anyone else noticed they make everything happen?

Henry and Charlotte. They're alive in their own way.

I've figured out one part of the mystery already. I don't know what Trish would have been doing inside Linda Sue's house, only that she must have been there that day, hiding somewhere, like the cat.

Maybe she was the reason Linda Sue was so nervous.

I remember standing at Linda Sue's door that afternoon, how she looked—what was my first thought?—*relieved* to see me. As if I'd interrupted something when I knocked. "What are you doing here?" she said. Did she look behind her? Am I imagining that?

It was three days after our last Neighborhood Watch meeting and Marianne had come over to my house that morning with a catalog of personal security devices from a company called Safe-T-First. "I'm worried about Linda Sue," Marianne had said, her voice low. "I believe she's in danger. She needs to start protecting herself." She wanted me to show Linda Sue one product in particular: an inflatable doll that looked like a man, with lifelike hair and real clothes. The idea was to prop him in a chair by a window with a newspaper in his hands. "The best crime deterrent is a house that looks full," she said.

I tried not to sound cruel. "I don't know, Marianne. This doesn't look like something Linda Sue would go for."

"You have to convince her."

The more I resisted, the more insistent Marianne became. "She needs to install her lock right away. She might laugh all she likes, but she won't after she's attacked."

She made me promise I'd go over that afternoon. "This is too important to play around with," she said.

I wanted to ask her then: *What is it, Marianne? What's made you so afraid?* I didn't know how to tell her that Linda Sue didn't need a fake man to sit in her living room, that she already had a real one.

"She likes you, Bets. You have things in common."

I didn't say anything because I knew what Marianne meant but wasn't saying. Linda Sue had lost babies, too. The first time she told me, I held my breath and prayed she wouldn't say more. I was superstitious and believed in the power of suggestion, that it might be contagious. If I heard her sad stories, my body would discover new ways to break its own heart. A few weeks earlier, when the doctor told us I wouldn't survive another try at pregnancy, Paul and I drove home forty minutes without speaking a word. Once home, I got out of the car, crossed the street, and knocked on Linda Sue's door. I wanted a cigarette, I told myself. I wanted to dull my senses and my nausea, the feeling that I had driving home, both ironic and true: Grief moving through a body feels like pregnancy.

I wanted Linda Sue to tell me how she went on. For so long, Paul and I circled around this subject and never discussed it. We always said, *We'll try again,* or, *We're good at getting pregnant.* Never once had we said, *What if it never happens?* I had to ask someone: *How do you go on after you know this?*

Then I stepped into the emptiness of Linda Sue's house with its stale cigarette smell and began to weep. For a minute I couldn't speak at all, couldn't form a single word. She found me a paper towel in the kitchen. "Here, take it," she said, her voice impatient, as if I were not the first person to stop by and cry in her foyer that day. "I don't know. Sometimes it seems like everyone here is so sad."

I have a reason, I wanted to say. *And we share it*. But I couldn't catch my breath. I couldn't speak. Finally, after she'd brought me water in a plastic cup, I managed to say, "Sometimes I think I'll die living here." I meant to add, *without children, without a reason for all this*.

"Yeah," she said. "I can see why."

Later, when I explained—*I can't have children, I just found out*—she looked flustered, as if my revelation had no connection to her life.

"I don't know," I told Marianne as she pressed me to take the catalog. "I don't think Linda Sue likes me very much."

"Please," Marianne said, her voice grave. "She's in danger. This is important." She leaned forward, as if she were afraid of being overheard. A day later, when her paranoia looked like prescience, I wondered what Marianne would say when I saw her. I assumed she'd blame me because the visit had gone so badly and I forgot to tell Linda Sue to install her lock.

But I did go over. I stood on Linda Sue's porch, holding the catalog upside down so she wouldn't read it too quickly and know what this was all about. "Can I come in? Marianne wants me to show you something," I said.

I knew Linda Sue didn't like having people inside, but she turned around and stepped away from the door. "Sure. Come on in."

"We wanted to find out if everything is all right."

She shrugged. "I guess."

Suddenly, standing in her living room, empty except for three canvas folding chairs circled around an ashtray, I felt scared for Linda Sue in a way I never had been before. She no life, no belongings, nothing except for Geoffrey. "I've noticed Geoffrey's been over," I said carefully. She nodded and looked away. "I didn't know you two had become such good friends." If she broke down and told me she loved him, I decided, I would tell her it was okay, I knew how she felt. Maybe I'd even joke and say, *Join the club*. If she cried, I wouldn't be embarrassed. I would cross the room and put my arms around her. I would tell her love is hardest when it feels the most real. But instead she shrugged and said, "Not really. I think his writing is a rip-off."

"You do?"

"I don't know." She lit a cigarette. "It's just pretty unoriginal."

"What do you mean?" I said, though of course I knew what she meant. I'd spent the last three days at the library defending him with clumsy, far-fetched arguments about how his admitted act of plagiarism wasn't really his fault. "It was only a problem on two stories, the shortest and the weakest ones in the book. It doesn't mean he can't write, it means he was stupid." Even as I said this, I knew it was hopeless. Why *had* he been so stupid? Why steal stories that weren't as good as your own? "We know Geoffrey pretty well, Linda Sue. He has a good heart but he also has weaknesses. Impulses I don't think he can really control."

"Did he already tell you?"

"Tell me what?"

"Oh, skip it. Never mind."

For a minute, I couldn't breathe. "Tell me *what*?"

She didn't say it out loud, but I saw it on her face. *We're having a baby.* Then she cleared her throat. "We're having a baby, okay?"

I didn't say anything. I was terrified I might throw up right there.

"What was it you wanted to show me?" she finally asked.

I held up the catalog that had gone damp in my hands. "Marianne thinks you should get a blow-up man doll."

She laughed as if I'd made a joke. "Seriously?" I nodded and she shook her head. "Marianne's got problems. I'm sorry, but maybe *she* needs a blow-up man."

"She has Roland."

"Oh, right. I forgot."

In that moment, I saw it all. Our pity for Linda Sue had been misplaced. Marianne was right, everything she said *was* loaded with judgment. She didn't come to our meetings to participate but to make fun of us all. We were a joke to her, a reminder of the life she'd happily left behind along with the husband she never mentioned. She hated us and lived here to remind herself why this was so. Now she was going to take Geoffrey for herself, the one thing that made my life bearable. I turned around and started back toward the door.

"Wait, Betsy. I'm sorry. I shouldn't be like this. You're not like those other women. Geoffrey always says that." I stopped but didn't turn around. "He's not sure he would have stayed here if it hadn't been for you. He thinks of you as one of his best friends."

Was this true? Geoffrey knew certain things about me but suddenly it seemed as if he knew nothing that mattered, nothing about the babies I'd lost, or the infants that lived on in my mind. "I should go," I said.

"Yeah, okay. I probably won't see you again because now—what? You hate us, right? I don't know what to say about that. I'm sorry, I guess."

I did hate her then. As much as I'd ever hated anyone. "Don't be," I said. "I wish you good luck. You'll need it. I'm afraid Geoffrey is going to disappoint you." It was the meanest thing I could think of to say.

She walked back to the folding card table where she kept her cigarettes, pulled out a fresh one, and cupped her hands around the end to light it. I thought about snapping the cigarette from her lips. I thought about taking a drag, blowing smoke in her face, and saying, *That's how a baby in utero feels when his mother smokes.* I thought about saying something so bitter and inappropriate it would be talked about for years. *Women like you don't deserve to get pregnant.* But as I gathered my courage, the expression on her face caught me off guard. There was no look of triumph.

Now that I've known plenty of bad mothers—ones who'd been criminally negligent, who'd left babies alone in apartments to go out to buy drugs—I know that it eats at one's soul to fail at this. I've sat in therapy groups where everyone talks about the school meetings they missed and the beatings they delivered. Children's lives may be destroyed when mothers abandon them, but no one ever talks about this: The women are ruined, too. Doomed to obsess over their failure every sober moment of their lives. Even back then, I knew this.

Suddenly, instead of resenting Linda Sue, I felt sorry for her.

Maybe she had succeeded in fertilizing a viable egg, but what else could she offer this child? She had no job or source of income that anyone knew of. The father of this baby was a long shot at best. Even I had to admit that in the two years he'd lived here, Geoffrey had gone from seeming like a celebrity in our midst to a question mark. (Had anyone ever *seen* him writing? Was he really working on anything beyond expanding his female friendship circle? I never thought these things, of course, but I knew people who did and recently I'd begun to see their point.)

"I know you've had miscarriages," Linda Sue finally said. The daylight was draining out of the sky. "I have, too. Three altogether."

I didn't say anything.

I could barely see her face but I remember every word she said. "No one understands, do they? They never let you grieve for those babies. You go in for your D & C on the obstetrics floor next door to women delivering healthy newborns. No one thinks about what that does to you."

That had happened to me once. I wasn't sure if she knew that and was pretending to understand or if it had happened to her, too.

"I named all my babies," she kept going. "You have to, I think. You go crazy otherwise. You have to acknowledge it. God, otherwise you walk around all day with everyone telling you it's a blessing since the baby was probably disabled anyway."

This was true and it was excruciating. To see it on someone's face, to know they were about to say it: *Usually those babies are pretty disabled. Maybe it's a blessing.* Was it crazy to want to say once for all the world to hear: *It's not a blessing. Say whatever else you'd like, but it's not a blessing.* My throat hurt so much I wasn't sure if I was talking or if she was simply saying everything I'd felt. "No one understands how awful it is."

Was she crying? I couldn't tell. I couldn't see her face.

Finally I said, "I named mine, too. And I think about them sometimes. I imagine this life where they're all with me."

"Yeah," she said softly. For a long time neither one of us said anything. Finally she asked, "What are their names?"

And I told her. Ben, Shannon, Peter, Henry, and Charlotte. I kept going, told her more about each of them, what they were like.

"That's good," she said. "That's really good."

After I got to the end, she asked me if I'd like to see something upstairs. I followed her, past a pile of flattened boxes and a trash bag full of Styrofoam peanuts. "This way." She opened the door at the end of the hallway. When I looked inside, my heart moved into my throat. There it all was, exactly as I'd imagined it. Ceiling stars, yellow walls, and gingham curtains with little ribbon ties. A white crib stood in the corner with a mobile above it of black-and-white clowns. The baby nursery I'd dreamed of setting up, the one I'd planned for and once got close enough to that I let myself buy three cans of yellow paint. My palms went slick.

She wasn't even showing that I could tell. Didn't she know what could happen? That setting all this up was like arranging a wedding before you had a groom, and if no one arrived, you'd have this as a testament to your heart's folly forever? I'd only ever decorated rooms in my mind, and still, they were there. "Linda Sue—" I said.

Before I could get my thought out, she snapped off the light. "Don't say anything." She kept going with the tour as if I'd come up to see the master bedroom and bathroom suite identical to my own. "Here's . . . whatever. My bedroom. The bathroom. The vanity." Her bedroom was as sparsely furnished as downstairs. A box spring and mattress, a sheet and thin spread. "Wait here a sec," she said, and disappeared down the hall.

I walked over to her side table, picked up the book lying open, *Your Pregnancy and You: A Month-by-Month Guide.* I don't know how to describe my feelings except as a complicated mix of pity and envy. I understood that she had something I did not: access to her real feelings, and the freedom to make choices based on them. She had no husband or money, but she was better off than all of us, anyone could see it. I moved over to the bathroom, out of curiosity, I suppose—all bathrooms hold secrets, don't they?—and that was when I saw the pink box with the white stick lying on top of it. A pregnancy test with a plus sign on it.

According to the trial record, I touched other items in her bathroom and beside her bed. My fingerprints were found on a glass, her tissue box, and a pencil, for some reason. The prosecution pointed out that a house tour doesn't usually involve examining personal items on a bedside table. "Nor does a murder," Franklin said, but his delivery was off. One juror rolled her eyes.

At my trial, the prosecution argued that I began, right then, to disassociate. They said I went home and sat alone in my darkened living room for close to six hours to plot my revenge on my neighbor, who had both the man I loved and a child on the way. They said I waited for Paul to return late from work, eat dinner, and fall asleep before I let myself go back across the street. They said I didn't bring a weapon with me, because my intent, when I went there, was not to kill Linda Sue but to push her down the stairs and cause a miscarriage.

"Five miscarriages," the DA repeated for the jury, not once but twice. "Elizabeth Treading had had five miscarriages and wanted Linda Sue Nelson to know how it felt to make assumptions, to plan too far ahead, to have her heart broken by a baby who didn't come." For my defense, Franklin saved our only piece of surprise evidence for his cross-exam of Geoffrey. We intended the moment to turn the tide of the trial, expose their scenario as a house of cards built on a fabrication. He asked if Geoffrey had seen the results of Linda Sue's autopsy report.

"Yes," Geoffrey said.

"Do you know what the results were?"

"Blunt-force trauma to the head. Intracranial bleeding," Geoffrey said. We'd heard the injuries described in detail; no one was surprised.

"Anything else?"

Geoffrey shook his head.

Franklin asked, "Did you know there was no evidence of a pregnancy?"

At the very least, this fact altered the story the prosecution had painted against me: that I was an infertile woman in love with Geoffrey, blind with anger at Linda Sue's good fortune not only in winning Geoffrey but in defying her own body's long odds and getting pregnant as well. Here was Franklin's point: It wasn't that simple. Linda Sue wasn't pregnant and Geoffrey must have known this. Everyone was keeping secrets. No one could be trusted. Then we all watched Geoffrey's reaction on the stand. First he looked around the courtroom, his eyes darting from one face to another, as if he were hoping to find Linda Sue in the gallery. As if he needed an explanation himself, because we could all see, from the way his face went pale and tears formed along the bottom of his eyes, that this was news to him, too.

Watching a man weep soundlessly before a courtroom of spectators convinced everyone there of one thing. Geoffrey knew nothing about Linda Sue's deception. In no time, the prosecution recalled enough witnesses to establish the *illusion* of pregnancy. The decorated room, the books beside her bed, a positive pregnancy test in the bathroom. How did a woman infertile from endometriosis accomplish that? No one could say.

In the end, the information clouded the story but not the case against me. Yes, it was unclear why she'd perpetrated such a fraud, but wanting a baby wasn't a crime. Murder was, the DA reminded the courtroom.

CHAPTER 20

In the car driving to Trish's reading, I think about how best to approach this situation. Surely Trish must have been in Linda Sue's house the same time I was on the day of the murder. She overheard our conversation, the only time I spoke the names of my children aloud. If Trish didn't kill Linda Sue, she must know who did. And whoever wrote me the note knew her pen name and was trying to point me in her direction.

As we drive, I avoid all this by getting Finn to tell me about his childhood spent in Oklahoma. How he joined the Cub Scouts and 4-H Club trying to fit in but it never really worked. Going away to college—even to Norman, Oklahoma—was such a relief, he pierced both ears the first week and started wearing eye makeup the second. "I was trying for a David Bowie thing, but I was about eighty pounds too heavy.

In the end, I looked more like Jimmy Osmond wearing mascara." When he finally moved to New York, he realized he was more like his small-town, aging parents than he'd thought. "I kept falling in love with all these boring, clean-cut men who reminded me of my father."

I almost interrupt to defend Bill—*He's not that boring*—when he clarifies his point. "Bill came much later. He was wearing a kilt when I met him. Very cute. He turned out to be a balance between the two."

So why did they want to live in suburbia, in this neighborhood, on this block?

"That's a good question. I thought it seemed like a simpler life than the city. I wanted that. We had enough that was complicated."

"Are you happy?"

He turns and gives me a look. We never asked questions like this back in my day. I don't think it occurred to me before Linda Sue came along saying and asking anything. Now I want to know. "I think so, yes. Most of the time."

I feel nervous before we even get inside the bookstore. I haven't planned what I'll do if Trish doesn't want to talk to me. Then she stands up, looking surprisingly like her old self, except now she's not wearing black rings of eye makeup or holding a cigarette cupped in her hand. Her hair hangs softly down to her shoulders, and I realize she looks not so much like an older version of the girl I remember but a happier one.

After she's introduced, she steps up to the podium. "Hi, everyone, thanks for coming—" She stops talking when she sees me. "Oh, my gosh! Mrs. Treading! I can't believe you're here!" I know she's had twelve years to practice not letting on what she knows about Linda Sue's death, and I expected her to put on a show of politeness, but I didn't expect this: unmitigated delight.

She turns to the audience. "This is my old librarian, everyone. It's so funny to see her because I always think of her when I do a reading. She was the only librarian I ever knew who read chapter books to preschoolers. I still remember one about a witch who rode on a vacuum cleaner with a cat who could fit in one of her pockets."

I can hardly get over her saying all this, though I remember the book—*The Wednesday Witch* by Ruth Chew. A favorite from my childhood that had fallen out of print.

"Mrs. Treading was the first adult I knew who took children seriously as readers."

I was?

"She read books that she loved and passed along that passion. I've always wanted to thank her publicly for opening the world of books to me. I came from a house that favored science over fiction and I don't know if I would have been a writer if it hadn't been for her."

The crowd—now around thirty—applauds politely, and after an awkward moment where it's unclear if I'm meant to say something or not, she continues with her reading. It's from her newest book, in which cousins from England are introduced, a girl named Grace and a boy named Thaddeus. She reads their dialogue with an English accent, then laughs self-consciously, tucking hair behind her ear.

Afterward, Finn and I get in line to get books signed. I'm grateful to him for buying two copies of each book. "My treat," he whispers, handing them to me, and I wonder if he knows how much this means to me. I want to take them home and read them, sleep with them at night, wake up with them lying next to me in bed. I want my own copies but of course I have no money.

"Thank you for what you said, Trish," I say when we get to the table where she's signing books. "I was very touched by that."

"It was all true."

After we've talked for a few minutes, managing to avoid all the loaded topics like my incarceration and the characters she's named after my imaginary children, I invite her to join us for a cup of coffee, which she seems happy to do. At a table in the café section of the store, she starts to look more nervous than she did in front of an audience. After we order drinks, Finn asks why she chose to write for this age group.

"I'm not sure. Someone once said you write for the age you remember being the happiest. Ten was probably my peak. Things went a little downhill for me after that. I'm not sure, maybe you heard." She peeks up at me. "I did some stupid things."

"Like what?"

"I don't know. I got in trouble. I went home with guys I shouldn't have. They'd ask if I wanted to hear the new Pink Floyd album and the next thing I knew I'd be in some fat boy's bedroom taking my shirt off."

It's hard to know what to say. Finally Finn leans over and pats her hand. "I did that, too. Only I was the fat boy and we listened to the Electric Light Orchestra."

She laughs hard enough that some whipped cream on her hot chocolate blows off onto the table. "I've never heard of them," she says. "It's just a funny name."

We drift back to the safer topic of her writing. She tells us she's planned seven books for her series, each one with a different suburban foe—a real estate developer leveling the forest, a school superintendent cutting art programs—each enemy vanquished by a combination of the children's nimble wit and fairy magic. "The last book will be the darkest of all. About toxic pollution spreading first through the gardens, then killing pets, and finally people, too."

I think about the mysterious spill next to her house. Is this whole series based on our life back then and the dangers we didn't even recognize?

"I've only read part of the first book so far but I loved it," I say. "You're a wonderful writer, Trish."

"Thanks. I think about you a lot when I'm working. In some ways, you're responsible for them being written at all."

I can't get over the credit she's giving me. *"How?"*

"My parents would have insisted I be more practical. You were the first person I told the truth to, that I wanted to be a writer. Do you remember what you said?"

I don't.

"You said, 'I think you should be.'"

I hardly know what to say. It's more than I ever imagined, that I played a role in her life, affected her without even realizing it. As sweet as she's being, I still have to ask: "Trish—about the names of the children in your book." Suddenly, my voice is shaking. "How did you pick those?"

"I did it for you." She takes my hand and squeezes it. "I wanted them to have a life—something you could read about."

"Were you there? In Linda Sue's house when I told her?"

"Yes."

I can't believe she's admitting this so easily, as if it means nothing. "Were you there when she died?"

"No."

In the timeline we constructed of that day, I left Linda Sue's house at 4:00 P.M.; she died almost seven hours later, at 10:50 P.M.

"I left around six o'clock that day," Trish says. "My parents came over and said if I didn't come home with them they'd call the police."

"What were you *doing* there?"

"I'd been there for a while."

I remember what Jeremy said: that police found evidence of another person living there—toothbrush, shoes. It's possible the police called her combat boots men's shoes. Then I remember the list we all puzzled over trying to understand: *Dr.'s appt., Library books, Betsy T.* Is it possible this is the explanation? That Linda Sue didn't write it, *Trish* did?

But it seems so improbable that Trish ran away from home and then went only a hundred yards next door.

"I'd been there almost two weeks without my parents figuring it out. It was amazing, in a way. I watched them through the upstairs window making calls and freaking out."

Had she done it as a cry for attention from her parents? "Why did you run away?"

"I had to leave. They were going to make me do something I didn't want to do." Trish seems to consider saying more and then stops there.

"How did they figure out where you were?"

"I was never sure. I always wondered if maybe you saw me and told them."

"No. I had no idea." Even as I say this, though, it's strange. I'm remembering some fragment. Weeping in the dark because Trish chose Linda Sue's house to go to and not my own. When would that have happened? When did I know enough of the story to feel saddened by it? "Even if I had seen you, I wouldn't have told your parents."

"Now I wish I *had* let them call the police. If I did, Linda Sue would still be alive." Her eyes are rimmed not with girlish tears but with adult ones.

It's a relief to realize Trish didn't kill Linda Sue. She couldn't have. She is still the book-loving, well-intentioned girl I remember, but a larger question remains: Does she know who did? Is she estranged from her family because one of them went back to exact revenge for the two weeks Linda Sue had hidden her next door without saying a word? I think about the clues that have never added up—the tea kettle and two mugs set out on the counter, such a welcoming gesture for a woman who never invited anyone inside. The killer didn't force his or her way into her house looking for a confrontation. It was someone Linda Sue was happy to see, someone she offered a choice of teas to. That wouldn't have been Marianne.

And then my breath catches. I think about the time I showed up in Roland's apartment, and the steaming mug of peach tea he'd made for me. The easy way he had of talking to women in the middle of the night. "I need to ask a favor of you, Trish."

"What?"

"You need to come back with us and talk to your parents again."

"No." She shakes her head. "I'm sorry, Mrs. Treading, but I can't do that."

"I know it's been a long time since you've seen them, but if I've ever been an inspiration to you, or a help, I'm asking you to do this for me."

"I'm sorry, but I can't. I'm terrible around my parents. It's like I become this different person. These books I write are—" She stops herself.

"Are what?"

"They're about kids who haven't been *parented,* really. They have to go out and find fairies to help them because that was how my childhood felt. My parents were never *there*."

"That's not true, Trish." I think of Marianne bringing her to the library, carrying in her bags of books.

"You don't know what it was like."

She's right. I can't imagine what it was like to grow up in her house.

"Look," Finn says, leaning in. "Here's one thing I've learned about parents. It takes more energy to stay angry at them than it does to forgive them. That's my experience anyway."

Trish stares into her milky cup and says, "My parents aren't bad people, but they've done some bad things."

I lean closer to her. This is what I need to know. "What did they do?"

"They never *saw* me. They never had a clue what was going on. They worried about John all the time. How depressed he was, and anxious. I was always supposed to be *fine,* but I wasn't."

Finn smiles. "My parents thought my biggest problem was sensitive skin. That's why I cried in public and blushed. Because rashes make you attracted to men."

She laughs and looks over at him. "And you still see them now?"

He holds up an index finger. "Once a year, whether it kills me or not. Sometimes it almost does kill me. But here's the thing I've learned about parents: They never change. You can get down on your hands and knees and beg them to and they'll say, 'Yes, yes, we want to change.' And they still won't."

Finn may have a point, but he's missing a larger one. I say to Trish, "You say being with your parents isn't good for you, but sometimes we don't have choices in these things. We have a responsibility to tell the truth."

"I've been trying to do that."

I look in her eyes and try to decide what she means by this. "You have, haven't you? In your books. You're trying to tell us something, aren't you?"

She nods. "Yes."

"There's something about your parents we need to know, isn't there?"

She nods again.

"Please, Trish. Come with us. I promise you won't have to be alone with them if you don't want to."

"What do you mean?" she asks carefully.

"I'll stay with you." I lean toward her so that she understands the urgency. "This will never end without your help. The police won't do anything. They don't have enough evidence." I don't know if she understands what I'm saying. "I need this, Trish."

She closes her eyes and finally nods. "All right."

In the car, she sits in the backseat, quiet for most of the hour-long drive. I watch her face grow more anxious the closer we get and wonder if I'm doing the right thing, forcing a confrontation like this. For twelve years, my case has gotten nowhere because this family has managed to hide whatever the truth was about their participation that night. Not only was Trish there earlier in the day, but Roland and Marianne were as well. Having spent two weeks in the private hell of their daughter's disappearance, they had finally found the engineer behind it, their next-door neighbor, a woman Marianne had always resented.

"Thank you again for doing this, Trish," I say when we finally pull into her driveway. "I know it isn't easy."

"I don't want you to go in with me," she says.

"You don't?"

"No."

"Are you sure?"

"I need to do this by myself."

For a second, I wonder if this might be a mistake. Will she go inside and warn them that they need to escape? "How about if we call you in an hour?" Finn says as she gets out of the car.

She nods and walks toward the house. "What's the worst that can happen?" Finn says, watching her go.

CHAPTER 21

’m beginning to remember more from the week before Linda Sue died. How the whole block was unsettled, in flight, though nothing showed yet. Things had changed for me, too. By day, I’d grown quieter. At our monthly library staff meeting, I made no mention of the reference books I found misshelved, or the “bookmarks” I’d been collecting under the desk for my lobby display. What did it matter with a friend too busy to take any notice? I knew I was being childish in the way I moved past Geoffrey without a word if he was standing in his yard. Childish in a way that I’d never been as a child. Eventually Geoffrey did notice. How could he not as I grew bolder with my silence and once looked him in the eye and turned up my own walkway without a word? *There,* I thought, closing the door behind me. *That’s what you get.* It was glorious and satisfying and a perfect communication of words I couldn't speak. *You can't have it all, Geoffrey. My friendship and her, too.*

For two weeks I moved under that cloud. But such anger is draining after a while. I tried a new tactic and made a show out of laughing with neighbors on the street, in case Geoffrey was watching. *See,* I tried to show him, *I have other friends, too.*

Roland was part of that. Their house sat directly opposite Geoffrey's. The night I left Roland's basement, I felt someone watching me and hoped it was Geoffrey. The revelation that it was Marianne has unsettled me more than I want to admit. As if I were putting on a show for the wrong audience entirely. Though it didn't feel like a show. That night with Roland broke the back of my anger. I saw how easily a body could respond, how it opened up and reacted without any forethought. *I want to kiss you,* he'd said. *But I don't know if I should.*

It was a relief to realize how senselessly bodies acted, but it didn't stay that way. In that mind-set, one obsession replaced another. For one day and then two, I thought nearly nonstop about Roland. At work, stamping a sheaf of overdue notices, I'd remember the moment of leaning across for a kiss, the messy urgency, the way our bodies pushed against each other, and a minute later I'd realize my hands had gone damp. It was wonderful and terrible to be kissed by Roland. To carry that memory around in my head, already crowded with so much I was trying not to think about.

A break from all this electrified stasis came when I least expected it. One morning, as Heather, another assistant librarian, was checking in returns, shaking each one for loose contents, as I'd asked her to do for my collection, an envelope dropped out addressed to me.

"Look," she said. "Here's something for your bookmark collection." She raised her eyebrows as if she already knew what it said.

I carried it to the back office and opened it privately:

Can I talk to you, please? I'll be out back in the garden at
lunchtime.

Love,

G

So simple and direct. A peace offering. A plea. I was filled with a
sense of largesse. We were each having our flings, and still we needed
the touchstone of our friendship to sift through and understand what
we were doing. All morning I waited for lunch hour to come.

When it did, I walked outside to find Geoffrey looking withered
and exhausted on the bench, brown bag on his knee, a backpack beside
him, in which he carried the notebook that he wrote his novel long-
hand in. He looked as if hadn't slept in days, maybe weeks. My heart
softened at the sight. He was suffering, too. Maybe more than I was.

We got through our apologies without specifying exactly what they
were for. "I'm sorry we've gotten so distant," he said vaguely. "I didn't
know if you were angry with me or just preoccupied for some reason."

"No," I said gently. *Why spread it out now like dirty linens between*
us? I thought. "I'm not angry anymore."

He looked at me and waited for something more.

"I've been worried," I said. "You don't look too well."

"Right." He looked down.

I couldn't get over how the balance between us had shifted. As if I'd
become the only person who could steer him out of a dark hallway.
"What is it, Geoffrey? Tell me what's going on."

I'll tell him, too, I decided. *I think I might be falling in love.* This is
what friends do—they try out grand ideas and see how they sound.

"I'm being sued," he said. "For plagiary, if you can believe it."

I couldn't, actually. Then he told me the details. It was an old student, and involved two of the shortest stories in his book, written last,
after he'd sold the manuscript. They were the weakest stories in the

book, more like voice exercises than stories with any weight. He said the suit was valid, yes, but the plagiary unintentional on his part. He'd read the student's stories five years earlier and must have remembered them subconsciously. When he sat down to write two new ones, he was amazed at how quickly these came. Now the student had sent proof to his publishers, copies of his old stories with Geoffrey's comments written on them.

My face burned with shame for him. I thought of what my colleagues inside the library would say, how the world of minions waited for such stars to fall from the sky. "What does this *mean*?" I whispered.

"Not that much actually," he said, shrugging and pulling his backpack into his lap. "I still feel pretty good about the novel. I just finished another chapter this morning."

He was being sued for plagiary and wrote another chapter this morning?

"But what about these stories?"

"I'll have to pay the guy something. But it'll die down after that, I expect." Was he serious? Could a writer be so cavalier about something so fundamental? "If the book hadn't been a best seller, the guy wouldn't have cared. He's in law school now. He hardly reads fiction. He only picked up mine when he saw the sticker on it."

I remember the steady and deliberate tone of his voice, as if the fault lay not with him but with the marketing of his book. That silver embossed sticker shouting his award nomination, compelling people to reach out, pick up the book, and find fault with its contents. No, Geoffrey had lost no sleep over this matter, nor, I was beginning to suspect, over the near loss of his friendship with me. Something else was eating at him. Something that had nothing to do with me.

He fingered the toggle on his backpack zipper, opened it a little, then shut it again. *What's going on?* I thought. *Just tell me, Geoffrey.*

I don't remember exactly what he said—"I'm nervous about some-thing," or, "I don't know what I'm doing"—but I do remember the way he reached deep into his backpack and pulled out a long silver box with a tiny gold bow pressed onto the top.

Please let this be a pen, I thought. It wasn't.

"Will you look at this," he asked. "And tell me what you think?"

It was a beautiful necklace, with a delicate gold chain and a sapphire charm shaped like a faceted blue sunburst. He hovered as I looked at it. "She doesn't wear much jewelry is the thing. Hardly any, really."

Of course he wasn't speaking of his wife. Or me, for that matter. We both wore ordinary amounts of jewelry. Earrings, bracelets, our wed-ding and engagement rings. Linda Sue wore none of those things. "It's pretty," I said.

"You really think so?" His desperation was palpable, embarrassing to witness. I thought of him at the party, going mute at her arrival.

After two weeks spent in agony, I realized I wasn't jealous of Linda Sue or the necklace she was about to receive. I was jealous of him, of feeling this way—consumed by passion, overtaken by love.

CHAPTER 22

When I call an hour later, Roland picks up. His voice sounds changed. "Is this Finn?" he asks.

I'm not used to these new developments—cell phones, caller ID. "No, it's me, Roland. I'm checking in on Trish."

I've just spent two hours reading the rest of Trish's first book, and it's extraordinary, really, how she describes this neighborhood, this block, with cornfields and woods that aren't menacing but magical, alight with spirits who watch over the humans. It's heartbreaking to imagine the complicated reality behind the story she's written.

"Why did you bring her here?" His anger is arresting, even over the phone.

"I thought you wanted to see her."

"Why would you force the issue? Why would you intrude on such a private family matter?"

In spite of everything I now suspect Roland of, I'm not prepared for this. "Because it's not private. It involves me."

"Not really."

How can he imagine that I'm not involved in the murder I've just served twelve years for committing? "Your family knows more about Linda Sue's death than you've ever told anyone. I asked Trish to come back with me so I can find out the truth."

"Do you know why she was at Linda Sue's house? Did she tell you?"

"Not exactly. I suspect she was trying to get your attention."

"Did she tell you she was pregnant?"

I take a deep breath. *Pregnant?* "No, I didn't know that."

Roland tells me to come to his basement apartment; he doesn't want to talk about it over the phone. When I get there, he tells me the whole story. Trish was fifteen and they'd been worried about her for months. She'd started pulling out her hair and skipping school, letting her grades fall, crying out for attention in so many ways, it was hard for them to know what was really going on and what was an act. As he speaks, he fiddles with a grid-lined drawing pad on his desk, open to a page covered in notes. Then she disappeared, leaving behind a hastily written note: *I'll come back when it's over.* They called her friends and no one had any idea where she was. One admitted that lately Trish had been talking about killing herself, which scared them enough to notify the police, the school, everyone they could think of.

Though no neighbors, I want to point out. *You never told any neighbors.*

As the days went on their only hope was the regular, untraceable arrival of notes in their mailbox, unsigned but written in Trish's hand: *Don't worry. I'm fine. I'll explain when I see you again.* Another: *I had to do this, okay? I didn't have a choice.* Though that worried them, of course, they took comfort in the purposeful notes, their clarity, that they suggested that she wasn't far away—that, in fact, she might be somewhere close by, watching them. *Tell Mom to stop staying up all night,* one note read. *I'll be back when I'm back.*

Finally Marianne figured it out, walking through the neighborhood at night, peeking in windows. It was her worst fear and also a relief. Trish was sitting in Linda Sue's kitchen, eating crackers.

Yes, Marianne had sent me over to Linda Sue's in the hope that I might see Trish and talk to her, get her to come home. "Trish had always been fascinated by you. You represented the world of books. Marianne was always envious of that. She thought you might have better luck than she would."

Marianne and Roland watched me walk across the street, safety catalog in hand. They watched me go inside and come out again forty-five minutes later, so visibly shaken by whatever I'd seen that I had trouble walking in a straight line. They waited for an hour, hoping to hear from me, and then walked over to Linda Sue's front door and demanded that Trish come home immediately. To their surprise, she appeared behind Linda Sue looking exhausted and—though it was impossible to say for sure—grateful for their presence. Back home, Trish told them the reason she had left—that she was pregnant and didn't want to have an abortion. She wanted to have the baby and give it away. By that point, there wasn't any argument to have. She was past her first trimester, too late for an abortion, which must have been her intention. He and Marianne sat up all night making phone calls to adoption agencies and lawyers, trying to decide what to do. Trish was still so volatile and unpredictable. Yes, she'd come home with them, but who knew how long she'd stay? That was their main fear that night when they locked the door to her bedroom, afraid that if they didn't, she'd run away again, go farther this time and not let herself be found.

I understand what he's trying to make clear. She couldn't have gone back and killed Linda Sue. She was locked in her room. "You don't know what it's like to have a child who's out of control. In crisis like that. It's terrible. You do whatever you have to and that's what we did."

It's as if he doesn't realize that it's not Trish I'm most suspicious of. As if it hasn't occurred to him that he might be a suspect.

But it's also clear that his guilt is complicated and based far more on evasions and silence—on what they *didn't* do and say—than on anything they did. He tells me that neither he nor Marianne left the house that night, and I believe him. They didn't sleep much either, he says, which made the scene the next morning all the more mysterious at first, and then terrifying: the fire trucks, the police cars, the ambulance that drove away empty. Before they went into Trish's bedroom to tell her what had happened, they talked about what they'd say—*There's been an accident. Linda Sue has been hurt.* They wouldn't lie, but they would do it in pieces, carefully, because they both understood how much Linda Sue had meant to Trish.

I watch his face shift as he gets to the last part of the story, the one that is the hardest for him to tell. They walked in her room that morning with the news of Linda Sue's death and what they found propelled them back out and onto the telephone, with psychiatric hospitals, this time because they finally understood that what was happening to Trish was more than they could handle alone: She was lying in bed asleep, beside the dead body of the neighborhood stray cat.

CHAPTER 23

"So Dad told you, I guess, right?" Trish says. She is lying on one of her twin beds, her head resting on top of a lopsided stuffed pink hippopotamus.

"He told me you had a baby," I say, though he didn't get much farther than that. After he got to this part—that she gave birth while still a patient in the psychiatric wing of Hartford Children's Hospital—Marianne called down and asked him to come upstairs.

After he left, I poked through some of the drawings on his desk, what he'd described as a souped-up electrolytic converter, though even I could tell that it wasn't. They were meant to be blueprints, and included some instructions (*deuterium—room temperature; palladium cathode, 6cm or less*). I stayed, hoping he would come back down, and then I heard them both get in the car and drive away. I went upstairs to see if Trish had left with them. She hadn't.

"Are you all right?" I ask her now.

"I guess. I'm tired mostly. My parents are screwed up. Maybe you noticed."

"They told me you were in a hospital for a while. I'm sorry."

"I'm surprised they told you. It's not something they like to advertise too much. Our daughter, the nutcase. My roommate there used to eat her fingernails. Not just chew them, but eat the whole thing. Her fingers were these bloody stumps. Another girl pulled out all her hair. Quite a lively crowd." She closes her eyes and for a minute doesn't say anything. "Sometimes I think going to the hospital made me crazy."

It felt that way to us when my father came home shrunken, a shell of the man who'd left home two months before. He never recovered, really, until after my mother's death, and then he emerged, inexplicably alive and capable again.

"Of course that's not true. I had problems before. You don't get pregnant by some jerk who barely says hi to you at school without having a few—" She rolls over to look at what she's lying on. When she sees how she's flattened the hippo, she plumps it up again, straightens its bow tie and what appears to be a homemade black satin vest. "Whatever—self-esteem issues."

"Who was the dad?"

"This guy Ian. He played trombone in the band. He wasn't that bad. He cried when I told him and then said I had to get an abortion. That's why I ran away. I didn't want an abortion. I wanted to have the baby."

I almost can't bring myself to ask. "How come?"

She shrugs. "I saw people around me who wanted babies and didn't have them." She doesn't look at me. "I asked Linda Sue if I could stay with her. When I got there, I told her my plan, that I wanted to have the baby and give it to you."

My breath catches in my throat. "You did?"

"That was my big idea. I'd heard about your miscarriages, and I thought maybe this baby could take their place. I'd tried to talk to you about it once and you said you were really busy and didn't have time to think about children too much."

I remember this. I was standing by the magazine racks at the library and Trish appeared out of nowhere, looking pale. "Can I talk to you for a second?" she'd asked. It was a hot day in the summer and she was wearing short shorts, a tube top, and flip-flops on her feet. Recently we'd had trouble with teenagers coming to the library after the swimming pool closed to lie around our basement, drawing graffiti on our baseboards and making trouble. We decided the only solution was enforcing some dress codes. "You can't be in here wearing those," I said, pointing to her flip-flops.

She looked like she was going to cry and I thought, *Oh, for heaven's sake, Trish, just put on some shoes and come back. I can't make exceptions just because I like you.* "I wanted to ask you about something," she said. "Whether you think about having children at all?"

I remember what I thought: *She knows too much. Knows that I sometimes pretend she's mine.* How could I let anyone see this? "Of course I think about it, Trish, but not at the moment. At the moment, I'm too busy to think about it. Now, why don't you run home and change and then you can come back."

Did she come back that day? Did she ever approach me again? I don't think so.

"I'm sorry, Trish. I didn't understand what you were saying."

"Linda Sue was the first person besides Ian who I told. And she was so positive right away. She kept saying I should have it. When I told her I wanted to give it to you, but wasn't sure, she said it was still a wonderful idea and that you weren't the only person."

Of course she said this.

Why didn't I see any of this before? The books Linda Sue bought, the decorated room. The cigarette she lit. Of course she wasn't pregnant. No woman who has been pregnant and lost a baby would smoke a cigarette. If she had been pregnant she wouldn't have decorated like that, announcing it so boldly. Everything I saw during that visit was preparation for a baby she knew she could count on, but also—and here was the important part—a baby she had to *woo*. Why else would she have set up a nursery when she cared so little about decorating? She was doing it for Trish, who needed attention and also needed to see proof: *I want this baby. I will take care of it*.

I think about the other things she did, showing me the room, turning on the light and then snapping it off as if she recognized the risk and changed her mind. Trish must have been up there, hiding in the third bedroom, and Linda Sue was making a point of some kind, letting Trish know, *Look, it's official now, you can't back out*.

Linda Sue knew I was the competition and, in many ways, the more natural choice. I was married, for one thing. If we didn't have plenty of money, at least we had two jobs between us. Maybe Linda Sue was putting on a show because she wanted me to break down again. She wanted Trish to know, *This woman seems fine and then she has episodes and acts crazy. Watch, I'll show you*.

"When did you tell Linda Sue?" I ask now.

"A few days after I found out. I was looking for Geoffrey over at her house and he wasn't there. I started crying and she asked what was wrong."

Which meant Linda Sue had known for weeks, maybe even months, when she started those fights at our meetings. We thought she sounded like a teenager, but now I understand what it really was: the effort to *please* a teenager. Trish was there, at those meetings, forced to come by her mother. How could Marianne have guessed what was really happening, that Linda Sue was working to win Trish's trust, prove she was different than everyone else? Maybe seducing Geoffrey was even part of it. I had a husband in my favor, and she knew no single woman would have an easy path to the adoption. She'd need a man. Why not pick the one Trish liked the most?

"Then it got strange. I wasn't sure what was happening. She and I started fighting. . . . I think she wanted me to leave, but didn't want to come right out and tell me to. She and Geoffrey got in a fight that morning before you came over." She stops herself, though I can tell there's more to the story.

"What was the fight about?"

"I don't know. Me, partly."

"What happened later, when your parents came to get you?"

"I was upstairs, but I heard them talking on the porch before they came in. My mom said, 'She's probably already told her everything,' and my dad said, 'She doesn't know anything to tell.' That's when I knew they hadn't really come for *me*. They didn't even realize I was having a baby. They were just worried that I was telling their secrets."

"They didn't know, Trish. You never looked pregnant."

"She was my *mom*. I wanted to hide it from everyone else, but not from her. I thought, my God, sooner or later, she's got to see. She'll look at me and *see*."

"What were the secrets they didn't want you to tell?"

"It doesn't *matter*. That was the point. That's what I told your husband when he came to see me in the hospital."

"*Paul* came to see you in the *hospital*?"

"He asked if I'd still consider giving the baby to you and him. He didn't think your case would make it to trial. He said they didn't have enough evidence, that you'd get released within a few weeks, and he asked me to at least consider you two as parents."

I try to imagine Paul doing this. What makes me want to cry is that I can—I picture his earnest good intentions, his hopeful heart thinking I'd be out soon and we could have a chance at a new life. "What did you say?"

"That considering everything that happened, I didn't want to put my baby with anyone I knew. And I didn't want it to grow up on our block. Then he said if I ever saw you again I shouldn't tell you about the conversation. He said you had some psychological issues and couldn't handle certain kinds of stress and this would be an example of something you couldn't handle."

It's still light enough outside to see the view from Trish's window across a strip of lawn, two rows of hedges, and into Linda Sue's house. This must have been what Trish looked up and saw every night: Linda Sue moving through her empty house, Geoffrey joining her.

"Were you friends with Linda Sue before you ran away to her house?"

"I wasn't supposed to be. My mom made all these rules about who I could talk to on the block. She didn't think I should have adult friends, but what else was I going to do? The only other friends I had were boys who wanted to sleep with me."

I flash on a memory of my own indiscretions and the terrible price I paid. I remember my own lonely youth spent thinking, *I don't blame them for not saying hello. I wouldn't say hello either if my friends were all around me. If I had any friends.* I want to reassure Trish, tell her she wasn't alone in doing stupid things, just to feel a connection. "It wasn't easy growing up on this block, I'm sure. I thought it would be so great for kids and maybe it was the opposite. Too much pressure to look and act a certain way. Maybe it was a mistake."

"It *was* a mistake."

"Maybe so."

"Those people weren't your friends. Trust me."

I look up, slowly. "What do you mean?"

"They just talked about you sometimes. About the problems you had."

I feel my face go red. "That's not true."

She shrugs. "Well, I mean—sorry—but yeah, it is. I used to hear people talk about what you could handle and what you couldn't. They weren't supposed to let you drink too much, that was one thing. Linda Sue wasn't sure what to say when you came over to her house that day. That's why she came in to talk to me while you were there."

That must have been where she went while I stood in her bedroom. "What did she say?"

"That you were freaking out."

I remember that part, the end of the visit after I found the pregnancy test in the bathroom and felt a panic attack start to close over me. Vertigo, shallow breathing. I was sweaty and hoarse. "I have to go," I'd said.

I suspect Trish is right about this much: There was a collusion behind my back that started before Linda Sue's murder and extended long after I turned myself in. If it's true, it means Paul must have been worried right away, and looking for ways to deflect suspicion from me. It means the canvassing the police did and the initial questions they asked were more pointed in my direction than I ever realized. Did my neighbors assume I'd done it? Did they start Neighborhood Watch to help their mentally unbalanced neighbor and then close ranks so tightly that I got shut out completely?

Whatever they did must have reaffirmed every suspicion the police had about me and cemented the weak case they built against me. Yes, my neighbors must have whispered in confidence and off the record. *We've been worried about her for a long time. She seems to periodically break down and disassociate.* The implication was there all through my trial. Even my coworkers talked about my "bad patches." In theory, we asked for this. Building a corollary of the insanity defense meant that we had to establish that I was not in control of my actions at the time of the murder. But Jeremy was right; there was far too much evidence of calculated cover-up for that defense to have ever worked. So why did we use it? Why did Paul suggest a lawyer who would agree to argue a losing insanity defense when there were other, better options out there?

I have to assume the answer is that Trish is right, that "keeping an eye on me" meant protecting me, ostensibly, but it also meant protecting themselves *from* me. In my neighbors' eyes I must have been more unsettling than Linda Sue even, with her home-glued clothing and her Bohemian ways. I was trying to fit in, to pass, and she was not. I was outside every weekend, weeding and gardening, trying valiantly to seem normal. My presence was a reminder that we were all vulnerable to forces we couldn't control. Talk of miscarriages makes every woman take a step back in fear that a mysterious problem could be contagious. My neighbors might have pretended otherwise, but they blamed me and helped convict me in part because they wanted me out.

"What happened with the cat?" I ask Trish. I have to hear the end of the story, how she ended up that night in bed with it.

She doesn't say anything.

"The cat they found you with. The morning after Linda Sue died." Roland told me they were never able to figure out how the cat died. By the time they found it in Trish's bed, it had been dead for a while. According to him, Trish wouldn't talk about it, wouldn't talk at all in the terrible confusion of that morning as they shuffled her, nearly catatonic, out to the car and to the hospital. "If there was any chance she'd seen something or knew what happened to Linda Sue, we would have stepped forward," he told me. "But she was locked in her room from seven o'clock that night and Linda Sue died just before eleven o'clock. We were on the telephone talking to people. Even the doctors agreed. If she didn't see anything, she shouldn't be forced to talk to the police."

"That cat was really sick," Trish says softly now. "I was trying to take care of him, but he kept drinking water and peeing all over the floor. Then his back legs stopped working and he started walking sideways into walls. Right before you came over, he'd fallen down the stairs and Linda Sue brought him up to me and said it was time to take him to the vet and put him down. I put him in the bathroom cupboard because I didn't want her to find him. I'd made him a nest. He liked being in there. That was one of the things we were fighting about. She thought I was too obsessed with it, that I needed to focus on taking care of myself and my baby, not some stupid cat. She kept saying the cat wasn't our responsibility. But it was. It was my responsibility."

"Why did you think that?"

"Because it *was*."

It's all so strange and hard to piece together. If the cat was sick at Linda Sue's house, what was it doing in Trish's bed the next morning? "Why did you think it was your fault?" I ask.

"Because I killed him. Just like I killed everything else."

CHAPTER 24

This is what happens: Bodies believe the lies they're told at night.
Or mine did, anyway.

After our wedding, Paul and I took two days to drive down to Florida for our honeymoon, stopping along the way to have sex and sleep in cheap motels. Neither one of us liked the beach particularly, so we chose St. Augustine because of its history, Ponce de León and the Fountain of Youth. We went on tour buses for the air-conditioning and visited an alligator farm, where we watched a mother alligator carry her newly hatched baby across the water in her mouth. I loved the way we disappeared there, like other tourists. There was another newly-wed couple at our hotel and I once caught the other bride's eye sitting at the bar. We both rolled our eyes at our sunburned husbands, who were wearing matching flip-flops and had cameras hanging around

their necks. *What was I thinking?* she mouthed, and we laughed. That
was how I imagined our neighborhood would be—that seeing ourselves as mirror images would solidify what sometimes felt liquid and
uncertain.

I had so many questions on that trip. Did other women sit down to
dinner with their husbands unsure of what to talk about? Did a meal
feel like a long time to other couples, too? Our marriage had sweet
times, yes, but more often than not it felt like an effort. A happy one at
first, and later less so. I know this much: It went gray and empty long
before I found the bloody nightgown balled up in my hamper. Even
before that doctor's fateful declaration, we were both starting to wonder if our relationship would survive its inability to procreate itself. I
seemed to love him best when he came to me with an injury, or a need—
when he became the child we would never have. We never talked about
what the doctor had told us because by then we were well practiced in
avoiding difficult conversations. Why talk about something hard when
you could just as easily not talk about it, too? It was a way to go on. A
holding pattern, yes, but it contained a thread of optimism. *We're holding on until we can't anymore! We're not there yet!* But even if it wasn't
over, we'd each begun to give up in our own ways. I stopped cooking
elaborate dinners with recipes I'd clipped from magazines, stopped
setting the table with place mats and flatware we'd gotten for our wedding. Instead I used the microwave and we ate some nights with two
books open on the table. *Why not?* I thought. *No one's watching.*

He stopped feigning interest in my life or what I wore. I stopped
caring. If my body had failed me, why should I attend to it at all? I
didn't know if we'd bother with sex after we got the news from the
doctor that no babies would come of it. What had once felt like a private delight had become hard work that reminded us too much of our
most basic failure.

Maybe he's right not to talk about it, I told myself, knowing there was a corollary advantage. If we never discussed our children who'd died, I could keep them alive inside my head. I could name them and visit them when I needed to. Shop for them at Christmas, and worry when I read certain articles in the newspaper. It's true that I began living in my head long before Linda Sue's death. I heard voices crying out. I stood up at work sometimes believing I was needed when nothing had happened or been said aloud.

I said I had been to Roland's basement apartment twice, which is true. Once carried over by my restless unconscious, once not. The second time I went, I was fully awake, in a heightened state, keyed up and agitated. I'd been awake for days, unable to settle the jumble of thoughts crowding my head for the last week and a half. *I have to go back and talk to him,* a voice would say one minute, and the next another would chime in, *Leave it alone.* Sometimes those voices were cruel. *You'll only embarrass yourself, knocking on his door like a teenager when you're thirty-three now.*

Lying awake night after night, I'd feel the fierce urgency of my father's old panic: *I can't take another night. I'll die doing this.*

I kept imagining our one kiss, that delirious cliff-falling. I convinced myself that another visit would get it out of my system. *I'll disgrace myself once and be done with it. I'll sleep again after he tells me there's no chance of this ever happening again.*

The night of the murder I lay in bed for hours thinking about the fool I'd made of myself at Linda Sue's earlier that day. How I stood in her bathroom, folded over myself to catch my breath. She thought I was sick and asked if she should call a doctor. "No," I said, pushing her hand away.

"Don't call anyone. Don't do anything." It's a terrible feeling, not knowing if your legs will work long enough to carry you out of a place you must leave. They did, eventually. I got out of there and went to bed, where my mind traveled for hours on its own roller coaster.

Finally, I decided: *I will do it tonight.*

I waited until ten-thirty to leave, a half hour after Paul had fallen asleep, as he always did, reading a magazine. There was one light on in Roland's basement but no sign of movement, none of the rolling shadows that I sometimes watched for.

I remember the yellow glow of Roland's window. I remember crossing the street and feeling the world drop away, the silence developing a sound of its own, a mute roar that filled my head. After that, I remember nothing. And then, in flashes, way too much.

Do I still hear voices in my head? Yes, sometimes.

Are they real or imagined? That's the problem, isn't it? In solitary confinement in prison, where silence is pervasive, is it sane or insane to hear voices in your head? To hold whole conversations with people who, you understand, aren't really there? If therapy were provided in the parting package of nothing that I got from the state, I'd ask these questions and listen carefully to the answers. What constitutes insanity and what is a sane response to insane conditions? If I have memory gaps—hours and even days that are foggy and clouded with ominous feeling—does that mean I know more than I'm able to say? If I remember pieces, the smell and feel of blood on my hands, am I responsible for committing terrible acts? I remember this much: When the police cars pulled up to Linda Sue's house, I knew what they would find inside. The body at the bottom of the stairs. The oval-shaped pool of blood splashed up on the wall and already dried by the time I got there.

CHAPTER 25

I don't tell Finn what Trish said about the cat. I fear it would get him thinking about his dog, who got sick and died after being in Trish's care. It has me wondering if Marianne's paranoia began not because she was afraid of losing her daughter but because she was afraid of what she'd glimpsed her daughter becoming: dangerous, aggressive, a pet murderer, even. And if Trish had done this, was it possible she'd done something worse? The evidence presented at my trial was clear. Linda Sue's injuries could have been inflicted by someone smaller and weaker, by which they meant a woman. But could it also have meant a child, a fifteen-year-old girl, pregnant and terrified? Had playing the pawn in the complicated adult dramas around her simply pushed her too far?

Instead of telling Finn this, I ask him if he would do a search on some of the terms I found in Roland's drawings. I keep thinking about one detail from Trish's account of when her parents came over to Linda

Sue's. *They weren't worried about me, they were worried that I was telling their secrets.* "It must have been about his work," I tell Finn. "That's the thing they were always secretive about."

"Why would Linda Sue have cared?"

"Exactly. I don't know."

Before I left her house, Trish revealed one more tidbit about her family that I'd never heard before: that Roland wasn't her real father. Her real father, who died when she was five, was more like John, her mom always said—meaning too cerebral, too intense, apparently. He was the real scientist of the family and it was his work that Roland was trying to complete. "Her dad's name was David Bell," I tell Finn. "Maybe we should start there."

It's hopeless, of course. Far too common a name, and he died too long ago, to have any relevant information come up. We try *David Bell, chemist; David Bell, physicist.* Nothing. We get many listings and no hits until, in a very random stab on Bill's computer, I try *David Bell Free Energy,* and then I don't just get a listing. A Web site pops up: *The Free Energy Society of America, David Bell, Founder.*

"Look at this," I say.

Finn is across the room on his own computer, doing his own search. He rolls his chair over beside me.

"Oh, my." He reads through the goals listed on the Web site, which seem broad and insanely optimistic. All cars hydrogen-powered by 2012; decentralized power grids by 2015; combinations of wind, solar, biomass, and nuclear-fueled communities by 2030. His mission statement ends with this: *We envision a world with no utility companies, imagine a globe with no wars to be fought over fossil fuels.* Imagine indeed.

"Can anyone make a Web site these days?"

"Pretty much."

"So a lot of crazy people do, I imagine."

"Sure." He scrolls through a little farther and reads some more. "The thing is—this is kind of interesting. He's got all this Nikola Tesla stuff in here, and he wasn't so crazy. He was an electrophysicist working around the same time as Edison, and everyone says he was this great unrecognized genius. He invented a whole bunch of things— wireless radio, alternating electrical currents, radiant energy—and then did a terrible job holding on to his patents."

Bill is in the other room making us tea, though he must be listening in on the conversation because he calls out from the kitchen, "Wasn't that the pigeon guy?"

Finn turns to me. "All right, he *was* crazy at the end. After he died, they found his notebooks and hoped they'd be filled with more amazing inventions, and instead he'd spent his last years writing about this one pigeon. I guess it flew into his hotel room pretty regularly and at some point he married it."

"Married the pigeon?"

"Right."

"And David Bell's Web site is dedicated to his ideas?"

"That's the thing. Yes, he went crazy by the end, but his ideas about energy weren't crazy. Now everyone looks back on him as a real visionary. He saw the problems with coal pollution and carbon emissions a hundred years ago. He anticipated all the issues with utility companies having exclusive monopolies on electricity. He said there would be global conflicts over fossil fuels if we didn't diversify energy sources early on. No one else had that kind of foresight."

"Or a wife quite like his," Bill jokes, handing me a mug.

Something occurs to me. "A few days ago, there was mail across the street for someone named Alocin Bell. I thought it had something to do with John because it was from a company based out of Alabama, where he lives. I wonder if there's a connection."

"Someone must be maintaining this Web site. In fact, if the guy died years ago, someone must have set up this Web site in his name. He wouldn't have had anything to do with this. This looks like it's three or four years old at the most."

"Maybe he's not dead?"

"Maybe not. Especially if he's still getting mail across the street. How do you spell the name?"

I write it down so I can see how it looks: ALOCIN BELL. Then I study it some more. Alocin seems like an odd derivative for either John or David. It might be Italian, or Spanish, possibly. But it also might be a code of some kind. When I turn the paper upside down so Finn can read it, I realize it is. It's another anagram.

"Look—" I say. "It's *Nicola* backward."

We search for *Alocin Bell* and get no hits on Google, and nothing on any of the other search engines, either. We get loads of other *Bell*s, and assume that we must be misspelling the first name. "Does this mean this person doesn't exist?"

"No. It means he or she hasn't been named in any public documents available on the Internet. It's more common with young people who haven't bought houses or been around long enough to get their name listed. I'm not sure what it tells us except that this is probably a pseudonym and whoever's using it hasn't made their work public."

CHAPTER 26

S ometimes my children come to me at night, speaking so authori-
tatively on teenage matters that I don't see how it's possible I made
them up. "No one wears those jeans anymore, Mom. Look around,"
Shannon will say. In prison Ben used to talk about my life as if he was
there, alongside me, watching it all. "Let it go, Mom. Taneesha's jealous.
She's not really your friend."

Last night they were with me and saying the same thing. *Remember
what he did. Remember pouring him the tea and how he'd look up at you, weeping. The cough syrup was never his idea, was it? You thought of it yourself.*

My memory points me in different directions at once. Nothing is clear,
no thought more than a fragment. I know I went to Roland's the night
after my panic attack in Linda Sue's bathroom. I've never lost my memory
of this because I knew what I was doing. I had to see him again.

I'd gone over it in my mind again and again. Had our kiss opened a door or had we tried something once and shut it again? The more I thought about it, the less I slept and the less sure I was. Why had he told me about his loneliness, the duty he felt to his children? The whole business left me foggy and distracted, not thinking properly about anything else. Instead of doing my work, I imagined different futures. Moving out of our houses, starting new lives where no one knew the people we once pretended to be.

I went to Roland's door because I couldn't stay away.

When I arrived, the door was open slightly, lights on and music playing. There was even half a glass of wine on the counter, every indication that he was enjoying the same sort of evening I'd interrupted five nights earlier. Except for one thing: He wasn't there. I called softly from the doorway and then again, louder. I pushed the door open and walked inside.

I stayed for a half hour at least, hoping he'd miraculously appear with food from upstairs, or a bottle of wine. I arranged myself in various casual positions so he wouldn't be alarmed when he walked in. Then I heard Marianne's voice in the kitchen speaking in a whispered hush to someone else, and after that, two sets of footsteps on the wooden stairs. I couldn't stay. I had my answer as clearly as I was likely to get it: He did visit his wife at night. Their marriage may have been moribund, but it wasn't dead yet. I left his apartment when I saw the time—almost eleven-thirty—and knew he wouldn't be coming back that night.

Now I understand that they must have been upstairs, dealing with the news of Trish's pregnancy and her determination not to abort the baby.

I keep trying to remember what happened next.

As I walked out of his basement apartment, my breath went short at the thought of returning home to the bed I'd slipped out of hours earlier. I couldn't go back, couldn't lie down again beside a man I hardly knew anymore.

In that state of mind, why did I go over to Linda Sue's house? I don't remember except that a light was on downstairs and it seemed to offer a momentary alternative. Did I think I would find Geoffrey there? Did I consider peeking in the way I had that other time, walking home with Paul? I suppose I thought, *I'll just check and see if he's there.* Of course I hoped he wasn't. I wanted some glimpse of her, awake and as alone as I was.

I went because I couldn't think what else to do. My body was alternately sweaty and dry, my thoughts fragmented, my words slipping away. At work that day, I'd alphabetized forty request slips, and then, without thinking, dropped the batch in the wastepaper basket.

I'd had no choice, really. I had to push my life off the edge in one direction or another. I went to Linda Sue's house because I couldn't make my body go back home.

I wanted to find her alone.

Instead, I found her dead.

CHAPTER 27

The next morning I can tell right away that something is wrong. Marianne and Roland are talking downstairs. The twin bed across the room where Trish slept last night is empty.

Last night when I came in, I stood over Trish for a while and asked myself again: Could she be a murderer? Could Trish have gotten out that night, climbed through the window, and crept back to Linda Sue's house without her parents knowing? I don't have a lot of evidence, just an unstable girl who has admitted to killing a cat, and a letter, written three years ago, imploring me to *think about the cat*. Any lawyer would tell me this doesn't add up to much.

Downstairs, Marianne asks if I know where Trish is.

"I don't know. It's eight-thirty in the morning. Where could she have gone?"

"That's just the point." Marianne shakes her head. "You never should have brought her here. The timing was—just terrible."

What timing? What is she talking about? "She's your daughter, Marianne. You haven't spoken in five years. I assumed you'd want to see her."

"You involved yourself in something you shouldn't have. She's gone now. Let's just leave it at that."

Does this mean Trish has run away? That my suspicions are right? I go back across the street and find Finn looking as if he hasn't slept at all. He tells me he hasn't seen Trish, which worries me more. Has she taken a bus home? It's possible, I suppose. More than possible, I fear, if she'd started to wonder about my suspicions. She may have written me that letter three years ago, may have wanted to confess and free herself from this prison of guilt, but when it comes down to it, no one is going to sit around and wait to be taken to a real prison.

I don't blame her, really. In all the complicated, stormy mess of this, I don't.

She was fifteen, mentally ill, and pregnant. Could voices have taken hold of her that night? Told her to go back and harm Linda Sue?

Last night, after I returned here and let myself in with the key Marianne had given me, I found Trish asleep and no one else home. I stayed up and read the rest of Trish's book. I didn't want it to end; I loved all of it, especially the details I'd never thought of: Shannon wishing for breasts, trying on lipstick; Peter wearing wide-wale corduroys his mother has bought, all wrong, so dumb-looking, it makes him wonder if his mother shops with her eyes closed. How can I not love the gift that Trish has given me?

"I have no idea where Trish is," Finn says. "But I've found something interesting. You've got to look at this." I follow him back to his office as he explains. "I worked with some of the elements you saw on Roland's drawings, deuterium and palladium. Do you remember that business with cold fusion in the late eighties? Where the two scientists in Utah made this big announcement that they'd discovered a way to

create nuclear reaction using nothing more than ocean water in a beaker with a cathode of palladium stuck in it?"

I do actually. I remember that Paul came home one night and talked
about it excitedly.

"No one could believe it at the time. They'd financed their own research and done it all in a lab they set up in a basement. The whole thing
was so simple that everyone was skeptical. They held a press conference
about their results and it was all there, these beakers of ordinary water
producing excess heat, tritium, and isotopes of helium-4, all by-products
of nuclear fusion. They'd done it. They'd made ocean water a fuel source.
The government had spent billions of dollars trying to do it with hot
fusion and these guys did it in their basement. They were a sensation,
on the covers of *Time* and *Newsweek*. Everyone said if it worked it would
be the end of global warming."

I remember some of what happened after that. The announcement
that generated worldwide buzz was disproved six months later when no lab
could replicate the same results the two scientists had gotten in their basement. A year later, they were the butt of jokes and scorned for their hubris.
Finn tells me the rest: "The whole idea died, theoretically, except that if
you hunt around a little bit, you realize that it didn't. A few years later,
there's a scientist in Georgia saying he achieved intermittent bursts of
spontaneous energy with palladium in ocean water. About three years after that, two groups, in Italy and Japan, did it again—a sustained elevation
of temperature with tritium and helium by-products. It was finicky and
unpredictable. The palladium had to be from a certain mine, cut a certain
way, which explained the difficulty reproducing the results. But they came
right out and said not only was this possible, but they'd gotten it to happen in one out of every thirty trials, which meant it had some reliability.
Not enough yet, but some. After that, more people started to set up their
own experiments. Privately funded, very underground experiments."

It finally occurs to me: the beakers of water, measuring temperatures. "You think this is what Roland's working on?" I think back to the old days, when strange, expensive-looking cars drove up our street looking for Roland. Each time it happened, we'd wonder, *Wait, could he be working on something significant?* Finn shows me a printout of some of the early material, and as he speaks I flip through an old *New York Times* article with a rough drawing of a cold fusion prototype that is remarkably similar to the blueprint drawing I found on Roland's desk.

"Here's the strange part, though," Finn continues. "I found a Web site dedicated to cold fusion research. It's now gotten big enough internationally that they have annual conferences for scientists to get together and exchange updates on their research. I'm looking it over and in the back of my mind, I'm thinking maybe I'll find Alocin Bell. That maybe Roland's been using that name for his research. Sounds logical, right?"

"Right."

"Except there's no Alocin Bell, but there is, lo and behold, someone named *Macias* Bell. So I look through their archives of old newsletters, where you can find group photographs of award ceremony recipients, and here's one where Macias Bell is listed in a photograph."

He points to the photograph: a group of old men, standing in a row in front of a fountain. "Okay, so I look through the names and study them. After a while I can recognize a few. Here's Martin Fleischmann, who started it all. Here's Victor Foulard. But look at this. I was trying to count across the rows. Twelve names are listed but only eleven people are pictured. Macias Bell is meant to be standing between these two people, but look—he's not there. If you look very closely you'll see something that looks like it might be a shadow except that it also looks light colored. Do you see that?"

"Yes."

"Couldn't this be somebody's shoulder behind Fleischmann?"

It's a stretch, but it's possible.

"Now look at this one." He flips through to a newsletter dated three years later and points to another group photo, this one with twice as many faces and names. Or almost. Twenty names with nineteen faces. Macias Bell is listed but he is not in the photograph. This time, there's a more blatant attempt at subterfuge. An outline of a head has stepped out of the light and looked down in time to let hair and shadow obscure the face. Someone is there, but it is impossible to see the face.

Finally we get to the newsletter and roster for 1996, the last year Macias Bell attended the conference, according to published rosters. And the same year as Linda Sue's death. That year the news at the conference was all pretty troubling. The EPRI, Electric Power Research Institute, which was providing what little private funding there was for cold fusion research in the United States, announced the termination of all funds. During the same year, the Japanese Ministry of Trade and Industry also announced a pullout from all cold fusion research. "Most of the talks at the conference were about being on the cusp of finally putting together some reproducible working models, going into some experimental production, and suddenly all the money had dried up. Attendance fell off after that year. Bell stopped coming, along with a lot of others."

"Are there pictures from that year?"

"Just one group shot—maybe fifty faces, impossible to identify anyone, I'd say." He shows me the picture and he's right. It looks like a blurry class reunion photo. I try anyway—count over on the row where Macias Bell is listed to see if it's another shadowy blur, and this time, I'm surprised. It's gray and indistinct, but this much is reasonably clear—Macias Bell is a woman.

CHAPTER 28

"I've called the police," Marianne says when I get back to the house.

The police, I think. *She's brought the police into this?* "Why?"

"We had to. We had no choice."

"Trish probably called a friend last night and asked to get picked up. I'm sure she's fine, Marianne."

"That's what you think." She sounds like a child. Certainly not like the scientist she's been pretending not to be for twenty years. The more I studied the picture on Finn's computer, the more certain I was. It was her hair, her jawline. I even recognized the shirt. I want to sit down at the table, grab her hands, and say, *Why Marianne? Why were you pretending all these years to know nothing about what Roland did in the basement?*

"We found blood in the bathroom," she says. "A lot of it. And bloody towels. Like someone tried to clean up."

My heart quickens. *Blood?* I left the bathroom at midnight, after I'd finished reading Trish's book. There was no blood in there.

"The police are on their way over. They've asked that you stay here until they can talk to you."

Hasn't it occurred to Marianne the harm this could do? That the likeliest scenario right now is that Trish has had a breakdown of some kind or tried to kill herself last night?

That some part of her might want to confess but another part is—quite rightly—terrified of getting caught?

Last night I decided that I wasn't going to tell Jeremy or anyone else what Trish said about the cat. Nor would I remind him of the cat letter. If Trish managed to get out of her house that night and returned to Linda Sue's, where they got in an argument—over the baby, over the cat, something—that ended with Linda Sue's death, what good will be served by sending Trish to prison at this point? I know all too well what prison does to its youngest inmates. Her gifts would be ignored, her weaknesses exacerbated, and in no time she'd be medicated into a shuffling state of mute compliance.

"Please don't bring the police into this, Marianne. Think about it." Surely Marianne knows what I mean by this. Surely the explanation for their silence all these years and the tension of this reunion is that she's known or suspected her daughter's guilt. "It could be a terrible mistake."

I think about Trish yesterday, her perfect willingness to admit to all her mistakes, the confessions she made with such little prodding. *I did some shitty things; I was a mess; I slept with too many boys.* How long would it take before the police wrestled a murder confession out of her, too? Five minutes? Seven?

"You don't remember what happened last night, do you?"

I try to read her face, but I can't. "No."

"You were up and roaming the halls. Screaming names—Shannon, Ben, Peter."

I don't know what to say. This happened occasionally when I first got to prison, but it hasn't for years.

"The police want to know what you did to her when you were up in the middle of the night, screaming at everybody."

Me? Screaming? I feel a cold chill rising up from the base of my spine. Has my subconscious ever been something I could control? Have I ever understood what prompted me to rise and wander darkened hallways in my sleep? I can't imagine what I was thinking, or dreaming, or—God help me—doing, but suddenly I understand that anything's possible.

"I didn't do anything to Trish, Marianne." I try to keep my voice calm. I think about the picture we found of Marianne on the Web site, hiding in the shadows, behind a false name. My tone says what my words don't. *We've all got secrets, okay, Marianne. Let's not jump to any conclusions.* I remind her that there's no blood in the bedroom, and none on my clothes or hands or in my bed. "I didn't touch her last night. I love Trish, I always have," I say, which is true, though I've never said it out loud.

It's more than that, though. What drove me to her reading and propelled me to invite her back here? If Trish was a child in search of attention, driven by a need she couldn't name, for a love that would fill the void at her center, I understood her and I recognized pieces of myself. She wanted a baby to change her life and so did I.

I couldn't have hurt her, I think, and then I imagine what I haven't let myself think about yet. Trish had her baby, she got to hold him for a night, feel him breathing against her chest. I never got that much.

My whole life, I have waited for something that hasn't happened.

Though it's been twelve years, long enough that I don't talk about it anymore, I still hate every pregnant woman I see, their hands cradling their backs or resting on their bellies. Once a prison counselor told me that most people learn how to reconcile themselves to loss eventually. This was the counselor who liked seeing me and talking about books we'd both read. She was younger than I was, and had done her clinical work on female psychosis and aggression. She told me about the cases she'd studied, and the results she'd gotten. "Why Women Kill" was the flashy title they gave her dissertation when it got published, which she hated. "The point was most women *don't* kill. They do harm in other ways. For women, violence is a last resort in extreme circumstances."

I assumed she told me all this forgetting what I was in for.

Or maybe she didn't. Her words got me thinking about my innocence again. They stayed with me for months. *Most women don't kill. They do harm in other ways.* Later I asked her to elaborate a little. "It's not appropriate really. I shouldn't be talking to you about my work." I wondered then if our sessions were being watched somehow. If she had higher-ups waiting to chastise her. Later, she gave me a copy of one of her articles, in which she wrote: "Women assume responsibility as a way of taking control over a situation. They will admit guilt more readily, find fault with themselves. They confess to crimes they've only imagined committing, believing that this alone seals their culpability. For other women, killing is the completion of entering a man's world. To participate, to belong fully, one must act in every way like a man and this is the final and ultimate test."

I think of this and it occurs to me: Which woman among us has been trying all this time to enter a man's world?

CHAPTER 29

I go back upstairs and search around Trish's bedroom for any sign of what might have happened last night. I remember slipping into the darkened room and standing over Trish in the bed. After that, nothing. No dreams of my children, no nightmares that might have propelled me out of bed, afraid for their safety, crying out in search of them.

In prison I did a little research on sleepwalking with what I had available: legal cases that involved a sleepwalking defense. With my own as a notable exception, a surprising number were successful, even in instances involving outlandish acts of cognitive awareness. Two years after my conviction, Kenneth Parks in Toronto claimed to have been sleepwalking the entire time he got in his truck, drove fifteen miles, broke into the house of his wife's parents, and stabbed them both. He was acquitted after neighbors testified to his gentle disposition and past sleepwalking episodes. Except for a little compulsive gambling prob-lem, he was as sweet as a lamb, and always—it was noted by many neighbors—fond of his in-laws.

A year after that, a chef in England was accused of bludgeoning his wife to death. He claimed he was asleep the whole time, and woke up to discover he was standing over her body, holding a claw hammer.

The sleep scientists who testified at their trials said these cases were the result of random misfiring of a poorly wired brain, not the expres-sion of deep-seated desires or psychopathic aggression. The sleepwalker who attacks has never consciously entertained the idea of hurting that person. The event is entirely out of his control. Even as I looked further into their studies, though, I started to question them, the way some behaviors seemed to divide curiously along gender lines. One doctor declared, "Somnambulists do not act out latent desires, their actions are random." Yet he also cited the study where sleepwalking men are most inclined to battle unseen intruders and women are most likely to roam farther and longer, in search of lost infants.

How could this be considered random? Surely there was meaning behind these late-night wanderings, our minds in search of solace with-held from us by day.

My case is listed among the others and our testimony rings similar notes. We all have a long history of waking up in rooms and houses al-tered by our night movements through them. We all know the heavy dread of remembering nothing. In every case, there was a genetic com-ponent to the disorder—all (except me) were acquitted in part because family members had a documented history of night wandering. Though my father's hospital would not release his records, I know it was a prob-lem there, that he arrived and finally began sleeping again only to wake up more than once and discover himself in another patient's bed. I know this news did not wholly shock my mother. Instead she was quietly grateful that no charges were pressed and, after two incidences, had a lock placed on his hospital room door.

I resisted bringing this into my trial until I was told I had no choice, that sparing my father could be tantamount to going to jail. How many people have made such choices and gone to jail anyway? When I finally relented, the revelation was broadcast on our local news, as so much of my trial was, and eventually, like a virus, it made its way across the country. My father, a widower by then, wrote Paul a letter succinctly apologizing for "harm done in the past, genetic and otherwise." I understood this to mean I shouldn't expect to ever hear from him again. And I haven't.

Though it's Wednesday morning and I know Jeremy goes to church with his family, I call him and tell him what's happening, that Trish is missing and they suspect there might have been foul play involved.

"Jesus, Betsy."

"I know."

"Are the police there yet?"

Roland is in the kitchen, though he doesn't look at me or acknowledge my presence. Jeremy arrives fifteen minutes later, while the police are in the living room talking to Marianne. I tell him what has unsettled me as much as Trish's disappearance. "I'm starting to remember more about that night. About Linda Sue's death."

Jeremy exhales and looks in the direction of the police. "All right, stop right there. First, we concentrate on Trish." We go upstairs to Trish's room, where I tell him everything I've learned about her over the last few days: her books, the baby, the tension with her parents. I don't mention anything about the cat or remind him of the letter I showed him long ago. Given the choice of her pen name it will raise too many questions, get everyone wondering how much she knows.

"Did it make you angry when she told you about wanting to give the baby to Linda Sue? That she didn't pick you?"

Yes, of course. But it was my own fault, wasn't it? She'd wanted to give it to me and I hadn't given her the chance. *"No,"* I say. *"No. I wasn't* angry with Trish. I wanted to help her." He seems to be missing the main point I'm trying to make without saying it out loud: Trish might have killed Linda Sue and I don't want these police officers to know this.

"Look—I'm going to be honest with you, Bets. If her body turns up, or if she's disappeared for good, you're going to be their first suspect, okay? You've got to be careful every step of the way here, about everything you say."

I understand this and I don't. *I am trying to protect someone I also might have hurt.* Jeremy walks me back downstairs to the living room, where two officers wait, one seated on the sofa, the other pacing behind it. I recognize the technique—one in motion, inviting agitation and unease, the other inviting stillness and confession. The older one, sitting, tells me right away, "We've found some more evidence in the bushes outside the bathroom window—a T-shirt saturated in fresh blood."

"Okay," I say, aware of him watching my response, weighing it carefully.

"We need you to tell us everything you remember from yesterday."

I'm a different person than I was twelve years ago, the first time I was questioned like this. I know that we're not on the same side, that everything they ask is for a reason and everything I say will be interpreted as negatively as possible. The balance is skewed against me. I know that a bloody shirt thrown out the window suggests a hasty and desperate stab at cleaning up, not unlike the job done at Linda Sue's. In a minute, the younger cop is going to start with his questions, pressing these points and pushing me to admit that, yes, there are some simi-larities here. He'll probably be ugly in his insinuations. Yes, I might have been exonerated, might have gone to prison innocent, but I no longer am. The police assume I've been brutalized by the twelve years I spent warehoused in the prison system and am now capable of worse offenses than I ever was back then.

As I retell the story of the afternoon, the older one nods in agree-ment and shakes his head in wonder at everything I say. He's all affir-mation and sympathy, while the younger one, with darker hair and skin, listens skeptically in the corner, arms folded over his chest. "Did you ever suspect anything? See any signs of Trish's pregnancy?"

I think about the conversation we had at the bus stop when she talked about wanting a book from the library with a cigarette folded into her curled palm. She must have been pregnant then. It was maybe a month before Linda Sue's death. "No."

"Did you notice her gaining weight?"

"No."

"But yesterday, when she told you this, you believed her."

He's trying to have me admit that I knew all along about her plan for the baby. That my resentment, gone underground, has seethed all these years. "I know young girls can sometimes hide pregnancies. It's happened before."

"But you must have felt pretty angry, right? After you'd tried for many years and hadn't had a baby? And she had one so easily?"

"No."

"And she wasn't even going to keep it. She was going to give it away to your neighbor, no less. It must have been infuriating."

I need to be clear. "I don't have the same intensity of feelings that I used to about pregnancy. I can hardly spend the rest of my life resent-ing every woman who's carried a baby to term."

"Still. This one might be different." He looks down at his notes. "Didn't you tell Roland, her father, that you always felt a special connection to her? Something you couldn't explain exactly?"

Roland told them this? "I did. She was a precocious reader as a little girl. I was a librarian. That's not so strange."

"Why did you get a neighbor to drive you an hour away to a reading yesterday afternoon? Do you do that with all your old library patrons?"

"She's an author now. I was staying with her parents."

"Did her parents go?"

"No."

"Did they ask you to bring her here?"

"No."

"You took it upon yourself to invite her into a house you've been staying at for only three days?"

"She's their daughter. She's been estranged for a while and I thought I would help them reconnect. Trish wanted to come."

"Did you have any other motivation in bringing her back here?"

I need to say this carefully. "I wondered if the family had information about Linda Sue's death that they might be keeping from me. I thought it might be an explanation for their estrangement from Trish. If I brought her back here, I was hoping I'd find out what it was."

"Did you know Trish was a suspect in the murder of Linda Sue Nelson?"

This is a surprise. "No—she's never been a suspect for the murder."

"Her fingerprints match the fourth set found in the victim's house. She was in the house that day. She admitted this to you, right?"

How do they know so much? "Yes, she told me she was at Linda Sue's house that day. But she left four hours before she was killed. When it happened, Trish was back in her own home, locked in her room."

"Did you go to the reading yesterday hoping she would confess?"

"No."

"Do you think she killed Linda Sue?"

The biggest mistake I could make now would be telling an outright lie. "I've thought about it, but in the end, I don't think she did it."

"Her mother has called her an intense and troubled girl." I see where this is going. "And difficult at times."

I know what they want to hear. They want me to admit, *It's possible, yes, Trish could have killed her.* My heart begins to race. I know how easy it is for the appearance of guilt to become guilt itself. How it feels like quicksand.

I look through the doorway to where Marianne stands with Roland. They're all talking about me, about the strange things I've done and said. This is no longer about protecting Trish. If she is guilty of the old crime, I must be guilty, too, of some new crime we don't even know the specifics of yet. I've made this mistake before—sat with police officers convinced of my guilt until I saw the picture they'd painted for themselves. *Yes,* I think. *You're right. She was a difficult girl. Infuriating. Yes, I could have hurt her. It's possible.*

I can feel eyes on me. Everyone in the room is pretending not to look at me.

I have felt so out of place and disoriented this whole time. I don't belong in this world that has moved on without me. I know the statistics. The odds of reoffending are highest in the first week after a prison release because voices whisper everywhere you go: *Prison is where you belong, where it is safest.*

Calm down, I tell myself. *Breathe in. Breathe out.*

Then I imagine Wanda, a paintbrush of nail polish in one hand, waving hello, happy to see me. The relief it will be.

"I know what I did," I say. "I remember now."

I can't speak yet.

There's a flurry of activity, a need for protocol. Jeremy is called in. I hear someone, somewhere, reading me my rights. They need a tape recorder, they say, and leave me alone in the room with Jeremy, who looks saddened by this turn of events. I'm not his poster girl for innocence anymore.

This story is more complicated, as am I, apparently. He looks at me for a long time without speaking, as if he wants me to tell him without words whether I am guilty of something here. And of course I can't, because nothing is simple, and nothing happened the way it looked.

CHAPTER 30

I t has come back to me slowly, what happened that night.

I see the oval pool of Linda Sue's blood and Geoffrey's necklace lying in it. The necklace is so vivid in my mind that I know it can't be my imagination. I remember the way it seemed to float on top of the blood, until I tried to pull it out and discovered the clasp caught on Linda Sue's nightgown. Getting it off her involved lifting her up, smearing blood all over myself. I'd wanted only to get rid of the jewelry that implicated Geoffrey, and in trying to do that I'd made such a mess. I had no choice. I had to clean up what I'd done.

Here is the truth I need to tell Jeremy: I'm the one who cleaned up the crime scene, which means I altered the evidence and rendered much of it inadmissible. I don't remember everything about the hour I spent alone with a corpse, a bucket of soapy water, and a sponge, but I remember my first thought when I walked into her house and found her lying there. *Geoffrey must have done this.* I assumed there had been a terrible accident, that they'd had a fight about his plagiarism and it turned physical.

In theory, Geoffrey might have loved Linda Sue's raw honesty at our Neighborhood Watch meetings, but he didn't love it as much as he loved the illusions about his life, that he was a great artist and a man of letters. I knew his marriage to Corinne was based on those illusions, along with the dark places she'd reached in and pulled him out of. Now she was withdrawing into her own world, home less and less, available for picking up fewer pieces of the life he continued to shatter.

I thought about the man I'd grown to love in spite of his flaws. The friend who had read my old favorite books, listened to my stories, and prodded me with questions. I'd married a man who asked none and I'd never felt this before. Whatever pain Geoffrey had caused me in the past two weeks, he'd also awoken a great cistern of feeling that some-times left me breathless. *Corinne can't save him this time,* I thought, *but I can,* and I got to work cleaning.

I found the lock beside Linda Sue's body and cleaned it for a while. I returned to the kitchen a few times and found sponges and gloves, though I don't remember seeing the sandwich or the mayonnaise. They might have been there, but I didn't see them. I was working with only the one light in the foyer on. I also missed the catalog I brought over myself that afternoon, the books I'd touched, the glass I must have drunk from. I was aware enough of the need to protect myself that I wore rubber gloves while I cleaned and then missed all those items and I'm not sure why.

Jeremy sits beside me for my official statement, helping me say as little as possible to incriminate myself. They can't arrest me yet without a body or more evidence that a crime has been committed. Two days ago, my picture was on the front page of every newspaper in the area with a headline about the twelve years I'd spent behind bars for a crime I didn't commit. The police need to be careful. They can't make another mistake.

CHAPTER 31

For a day, then two, nothing happens.

Trish doesn't return to her apartment in Bridgetown. A canvassing produces no sightings or information. Because of the blood, police have identified this as potential foul play and brought dogs in to search the woods and the cornfields behind the house. A story appears on the front page of the local paper under the headline YOUNG AUTHOR MISSING, with her photograph, which appears on none of her books. If Trish wanted anonymity in her writing, she's lost it forever by disappearing.

I'm trying to be helpful in any way I can. I've confessed to cleaning up the crime scene at Linda Sue's house twelve years ago, but have continued to say I don't know where Trish is or what happened to her that night. I can feel the tension my presence creates and am grateful when Bill and Finn invite me to stay in their guest bedroom for the time being. I pack what few belongings I have, and before I leave, I find Marianne sitting alone in the kitchen, with a pamphlet titled *FIND THEM: What to Do When a Loved One Goes Missing* open on the table in front of her.

I sit down at the table across from her, thankful for the tentative truce that has grown between us. Two days is a long time to hover by phones and wait while people in uniforms tell us what to do. Every few hours, we've learned a little bit more. For instance, Trish has done this before, gone missing for days when she had appointments and meetings scheduled. When her agent first heard about her disappearance, he actually said, "Oh, no, not this again," then quickly backpedaled, calling her the most talented young writer he represented. "She's astonishing," he said. But yes, he admitted, she can be unreliable. He told about her reading at the Book Expo last year where three hundred people waited, and she never showed up. After that, she didn't call or send an apology, didn't contact anyone for almost two weeks. "I worried that time," he said. "But eventually she turned up."

The finger of suspicion pointed against me is softening. Marianne is no longer sure if this is my fault. I suspect she's no longer sure what to think. When I sit down, she shakes her head, as tears I've seen only once before rise to her eyes. "I don't understand. For five years, I was fine not knowing where she was. Now I can't bear to have this go on another day."

The doorbell has been ringing with neighbors stopping by, checking in, dropping off food. All of this reminds me of the feeling after Linda Sue's death. As if we've all been poised, waiting for this to happen, expecting it somehow.

For the moment, though, we are alone and I take advantage of the silence around us to ask Marianne about her work. Her eyes widen and then she must assume Roland has told me everything. She looks toward the basement door and shakes her head. "We had to keep it a secret. We didn't have a choice. My first husband, David, died doing this work and I needed to keep us all safe."

"How did he die?"

"Pancreatic cancer. But there were other people on his research and development team getting the same cancer and no one wanted to investigate the connection or figure out what was really going on."

"Was it from the chemicals they were working with?"

"He didn't work with the chemicals. I did. None of the men who got the cancer worked in the labs. They were analyzing our results and drawing up designs. How do three men under the age of fifty get cancer from pencils and computers? No one would ever answer that question for me."

I can't get over how easily she's shed a twenty-year charade of pretending to do nothing. It's as if, with Trish gone, there's no point in any of the old secrecy anymore. She tells me I'd be stunned by what an amoral bunch scientists can be, especially if they think their precious research funding might be endangered. "David used to complain about it. I thought he was being ridiculous, and then he died under circumstances that no one would look into. There were people obsessed with stopping cold fusion research. He thought it was someone putting carcinogens in our water supply, which I thought was crazy until all these guys got cancer and died within six months of each other."

"Who wanted to stop work on cold fusion?"

"Hot fusion got all the government contracts and money in those days—billions and billions. They had to hold on to it." It all started when they were at Texas A&M after Fleischmann and Pons made their announcement. Their lab went to work the next day trying to replicate the experiment. After four months with no results, the tide began turning. Georgia State was the first to say it wasn't replicable; MIT came out a few weeks later, calling cold fusion a hoax. Soon after that, the money disappeared. Basically, the government funded it long enough to look like they'd tried but not long enough to threaten the twenty-five years they'd invested in hot fusion. Without government subsidy, the university cut them off, even though most of the scientists they were working for agreed they hadn't had enough time. She and David were postdocs at that point, low enough on the totem pole that they were able to move around under the radar. They stole equipment from the lab to continue the work in the basement of their tiny rented house. Their feeling, the whole time, was that the higher-ups knew and approved of what they were doing. They believed cold fusion had potential, though it might take ten years or more to get reliable results.

A year later, in their makeshift basement lab, it finally happened: One of the beakers began to boil. "We couldn't figure out what we'd done differently. Why this one and not the others? It's addictive, a question like that. If you can answer it, you know you'll change the world. We had to stay with it. We had to."

Committing to this after they got their degrees meant forgoing university jobs and mainstream research. It put them on the fringe, where they met Roland for the first time. "He'd been working in solar for a long time, and wind a little bit. He was less of a scientist, more of a designer, but he came out and saw what was happening with our research, that we'd gotten reactions going in one out of ten setups, higher percentages than anyone else was getting."

He was amazed and asked if he could join them. Soon after that David got sick, and Marianne's world fell apart. "I had two young children I had to protect. I couldn't put them in danger. I didn't know if I'd been exposed or if I was going to get sick. Of course I married Roland. He was good to my kids. I had to make sure they'd be all right."

All along I've wondered if their marriage was a little like my own, born of circumstance, two people clinging to similar life rafts. They took Roland's name and moved here to disappear. If David had been a target, they didn't want to be found. The intention was to leave all the old work behind. "Then about three months after we moved here, I woke up one night with a question about the presence of trace carbons in our cathodes. I told Roland I wanted to set up one experiment. Of course there's no such thing as one experiment, we both knew that. One set of answers opens up new questions and you need a new trial."

They built a lab downstairs, hidden in an annex, and kept going. Money quickly became a factor and, as isolated as they were, they had to play games to keep some coming in. After five years, they found themselves at a crossroads. The work was going well, but the minimal funding sources were drying up. Roland thought they were a year away from creating a viable hot-water heater. Anything like that, any commercial application, would have guaranteed financing.

"That's when John got involved. He was still in high school but he was already doing all this Free Energy Tesla stuff. He wanted to set up a Web site in his father's memory and collect donations for the work we were doing. He also thought it was a way to bring like-minded people into our research without drawing attention to the cold fusion aspect. He was right, as it turned out. But that's when I started to look at our data a little closer. One of the problems with fusion is that it's so hard to measure if it has actually taken place. You need elevated temperatures but you also need tritium and helium-4 isotopes. We kept getting one or two of the markers of fusion but not all three. For a long time, I didn't think that was significant, and then I started to think maybe the reason we couldn't achieve fusion predictably was because we weren't achieving it at all, that it was just a random chemical reaction taking place. I knew we had more problems than Roland wanted to admit. There were too many factors we couldn't explain. It had never made sense that a nuclear event had occurred without producing any radiation. No one ever questioned that enough. The cold fusion people said that's the beauty of this process—no radiation was produced. But the beauty of it was also the problem: It was too controlled. It created enough heat to bubble politely in a beaker but it was never explosive, never out of control. Roland wouldn't hear any of this. He was more convinced than ever. He was even going to tell you about it."

That was the summer Trish wanted to work for Roland, which Marianne said was fine as long as Trish never saw the lab. They'd told their kids a little bit about their work but never about the lab in the basement, a hard-and-fast rule they always agreed on. Kids were unpredictable, teenagers even worse. If they knew, they'd get curious and sneak down at night to get a closer look, poke a finger in a beaker and skew six months of work. No, they never knew it was there, never even suspected, with the access hidden as it was behind a bookshelf on invisible rolling wheels. They'd done that much right, but beyond that, they agreed on less and less. Roland wanted John brought in as a financial partner. He was all of eighteen, good at Web site design but not ready for the weight of responsibility. It was a terrible time for Marianne. She saw much too clearly how fractured her family was, how damaged by work that she was now certain would never prove itself.

She tried talking in veiled terms to Trish, but telling her the truth: that it was a decades-old dream that might not come true. Marianne thought it might help at a time when Trish was growing up so fast, becoming a teenager overnight, far smarter than the peers she humiliated herself trying to win the approval of. She knew Trish needed something from her and thought talking to her like an adult might be an answer. It wasn't. It's all a jumble in Marianne's mind. A lot of things started happening at once. Trish stopped working with Roland around the time they started seeing a new and measurable difference in their results, more significant than anything they'd seen in years—higher temperatures, beakers boiling over. And then one night—magical, she still thinks, though she wasn't there to witness it—five of them burst. It meant they had a reason to keep going, enough information to get back to work, which they did. They focused intensely, both of them downstairs at night—they could work only at night—and stopped worrying about Trish for how long? A week? Maybe two? By which point it was too late. One night Marianne went upstairs, peeked into Trish's room, and realized she wasn't there at all.

It can't be a coincidence that she started Neighborhood Watch during this time, just as her work was coming to fruition. When I ask, she says, "I had to start that group. The last time we got close to achieving real fusion my husband was killed. I knew people would go to great lengths to stop our work."

I study her face. "But it wasn't outsiders you were really worried about, was it?"

For a long time, she doesn't speak. "You have to understand, no one has ever been issued a patent for cold fusion. The potential is too enormous. The impact it would have on the world is unprecedented. Its value can't be measured in dollars."

"Who did you think was trying to steal your work?"

She looks at me for a long time. "She lived in an empty house with no furniture, no talk of where her money came from or when it would run out. She must have been working for *someone*. What was she *doing* here?"

The telephone rings but before she goes to answer it, she hands me an envelope—plain white with my name typed across the front. "Here. This came for you this morning." There's no address, no postmark, no stamp.

It looks exactly like the letter I got three years ago, with the cat note inside.

My heart speeds up. I open it and find a sheet of white paper with a single line, typed: *I need to talk to you. Please meet me at the library.* I read it again and study the envelope. Could it be from Trish, hiding somewhere, looking for help?

If it is, I need to get to her as quickly as possible. I know enough of the story now to fill in some of the gaps. Yes, this had a great deal to do with the work Marianne and Roland kept far too secret for too long, but there's another piece that both of them have forgotten. Trish had a baby that was taken away from her.

I've been thinking about this ever since Trish disappeared.

It's hard for any woman who has longed for and been unable to have a child of her own to imagine what surrendering a real one would be like. Does she think about him at night? Does she hear his voice in her head? I know this much: She may have given him up, but he's never left her thoughts.

I also know how to help her. There were women in prison who'd lost their children to courts and the foster system. They just wanted an address to write to, they'd tell me, and I'd get to work typing names into data banks. I can help Trish find her baby. If she's at the library now, waiting for me, we can start there; I know how to search for birth records. I can help her find him and take her there.

I slip out the back door before Marianne can ask where I'm going. Outside the library, I feel a chill pass through me opening the old familiar door. I wonder what would have happened if I'd lived out my life working here every day, going home at night, pretending to be fine except for the times when I so obviously wasn't. Would that have been better than what I've been through?

I know the answer before I even finish asking it: No.

I open the door and breathe in the heady, familiar scent of old books and carpet cleaner. Heather is there at the front desk, looking older and thinner with gray hair now, the same as my own. I wait for someone to distract her at the desk so I can slip by unrecognized. I need to find Trish as quickly as possible. If she's not here, I need to look outside. I scan the bent heads, the usual collection of library waifs and old people napping with newspapers open on their laps. It's such a familiar scene it almost feels as if I never left at all. Then I look up and my heart stops.

I see who wrote the letter and it's not Trish at all.

Sitting at a table, with a book open in front of him, is Leo.

CHAPTER 32

"What are you doing here?" I sit down across from Leo an arm's length away, close enough to touch him, my heart beating crazily. Up close like this, I see all the details I remember. His hair is blond, streaked with silver; his hands are spotted with freckles and golden hair. He looks thinner than I remember and I feel my chest tighten. All those months of writing to him every night was the closest I ever came to losing myself entirely in the fantasy of happiness.

"I got released," he says, though he doesn't sound happy or relieved. He's too mad, I can tell. "Six weeks ago. I tried to tell you, but you sent back all my letters."

"No, I didn't. I never sent any back."

We sit for a minute with this—his anger, my confusion. Why didn't we remember where we were living, how anyone around us could have sabotaged our letter exchange, out of jealousy or spite? "I'm sorry, Leo. You stopped writing and I didn't understand. I assumed you'd moved on."

"No," he says, shaking his head. "No. I didn't move on."

I want to reach out, take his hand, do something, and I can't. I think about the dreamy promises we once made to each other. *If I get out first, I'll come every Saturday and bring you cookies. When we're both out, I'll take you for the spiciest enchiladas you've ever eaten.*

Once, after we'd been writing for a few months and letting our letters get racier, he asked if I liked having sex with the lights on or off. *Off, of course,* I wrote back. *Maybe you've forgotten, but I'm a librarian.*

He responded: *Ah, then, you're in for a treat. I'm a lights-on, loud-music type. Jefferson Airplane, Jethro Tull, anything really. Your choice. But the lights, my dear. On.*

Now here we are, sitting so close to each other and crippled by our shyness. Maybe we're both thinking of those letters, how easy they were to write compared to this.

He says the hardest part of being released was leaving without knowing what happened to me. "I thought maybe your husband came back into the picture. I knew there was talk about your DNA testing and I assumed that's what happened." After he got out he kept seeing things we talked about doing, which made him depressed at first, then angry. "You don't know this yet, but I don't give myself away like that. I meant all of it with you."

I meant it, too.

He's been following the drama since my release. When he read about Trish's disappearance and saw my name in the paper, he decided to try to get in touch. He drove here last night, slept in his car, and this morning left a note in Marianne's mailbox.

It's too much to look at his face and try to take this all in. He leans across the table between us, close enough that I can smell his breath: coffee and cough drops. "Can we go for a walk?" he says.

His gait is a little funny, legs bowed like a cowboy who has just dismounted. It's strange. Up close he looks smaller than I remember from watching him through the window. I want to break this nervous impasse by touching him, but clearly, even outside and alone, this isn't in the cards. He points us away from the garden toward a line of trees and undergrowth left to grow untended. A suburban wildness, too swampy for development. As we walk, I tell him about Trish disappearing in the middle of the night. I tell him it's possible she ran away and it's also possible her parents have done something with her, sent her away, silenced her somehow in the interest of preserving their work. I keep thinking of Marianne's words: *The timing was just terrible.*

I don't know what Marianne was about to tell me when the telephone rang and stopped her story. If she did more than suspect Linda Sue of stealing their work secrets—if she killed her to save them. If she had stepped inside Linda Sue's house she would have seen that there was nothing there. No computer, no files, no nefarious motives. It wasn't Marianne and Roland's work she wanted. It was Trish's baby.

Was any of this enough to spark a murderous rage in Marianne? Had she been on the brink of making a confession when she got interrupted?

"And this is *Cat Ashker* we're talking about—the author?" Leo says. "I've read some of her books. The first one came out while I was still teaching. I had one student who was a big fan."

"Did you like them?"

"Oh, sure. Suburban menace and magic. They're great. Amazing that someone so young wrote them."

"She started young. She always talked about becoming a writer. I was her librarian." I blush a little, afraid I sound silly. I wish I could tell him what she said at her reading—that I mattered to her, that I made a difference. "That's who I came here expecting to find."

"Huh." He nods and jams his hands in his pockets. "Were you disappointed?"

"No." I try to sound perfectly clear. "No. I'm not."

"So no one has any idea where she is?"

I tell him she has a history of disappearing, especially from pressured situations. "The police are still looking but I get the sense they're not thinking of it as a crime anymore." I don't tell him, *If they were, I wouldn't be here right now. I'd be down at the station, undergoing my forty-eighth hour of questioning. I'd be so hungry and tired, prison would look like a hotel room.* "I do have one idea about where she might be."

He looks at me, curious, waiting to hear my hunch. I tell him about Marianne and Roland's secret laboratory. "Right before Linda Sue was killed, Marianne started taking Trish into her confidence, telling her about the work they were doing." I think about her getting closer to the secret that lurked all her life in the basement, and I remember the story she told us. The plan for her final book and the ultimate threat to suburbia: slow-acting, toxic poisoning of the environment.

"What if the reason no one's seen Trish outside the house is because she never *left*?"

"You think she might be hiding there, still inside the house?"

I think about it—the drawings and notes on Roland's desk, Marianne's meeting to arm her neighbors with Taser guns, their terrible resistance to seeing Trish again. Marianne and Roland's fears are alive. Is it possible they see danger everywhere because they're still working on cold fusion? Finn saw the beakers of water, and Roland up late, working at night. I remember Marianne's talk about bad timing. Does that mean they're on the brink of another breakthrough? Does Trish recognize the danger of her parents' work? Is she hiding down there trying to draw people's attention to it?

I am grateful to Leo for saying he'll come with me. "I don't know how we'll get in or if they'll let us look, but I need to try." We walk back through the woods and the cornfield so we can approach the house from the backyard and not be seen by whoever is there now. Along the way, he tells me his reading program hasn't been going as quickly as he'd hoped. He's been on *Sister Carrie* for a while. "Good book," he says. "Depressing but good." I remember loving *Sister Carrie,* the decent woman's slide into destitution and crime because so many stabs at love haven't worked out. "I keep thinking, My God, if she just found the right man, she'd be okay."

"She doesn't," I warn him.

"Yeah, I figured."

"We criminal types probably shouldn't look to men for our salvation."

"Hmm . . ."

"It's bound to get us into trouble."

"Right."

We come out of the woods and into the bright light to see the serpentine line of houses on Juniper Lane. From this distance, they look so out of place. What was meant to happen with this development—the influx of new houses and streets; a community beyond this single winding street—hasn't. For whatever reason—our soil composition, our water table issues, the chemicals that killed our plants and our babies—Juniper Lane is a mistake no one wants to duplicate.

"You could always do that thing where you use a man for money and sex."

I don't know if he is making a suggestion or trying to acknowledge what feels like something that will never happen between us.

"Ah." I smile, shaking my head. "Okay."

"I'm just kidding about that."

"Okay."

"I think for right now we should get this over with." He points toward the house. "We should find this girl and then go back to our premature talk about living together and getting married. Then we can have the conversation about how we should obviously get to know each other first."

I turn and look at him, my heart pounding so furiously I fear he must hear it. "Okay," I say, wishing I could kiss him. If I was more practiced at these things I would. I remember standing at the window, watching him work, waiting forever for him to look up. It's almost too much to have him so close.

"Are you ready?" I notice something odd. It's hard to tell from here, but it looks like the crowd that's been gathered at Marianne and Roland's house for most of the day is gone. From this vantage point, I can't see any cars at all.

"Yes, but can I just say this first?"

"Go ahead." I keep watching the house for signs of movement.

"I haven't had a drink since I've gotten out. I've thought about it a lot. I've come very close, but I haven't. That's all I wanted to say. Yes, I'm ready. What are we thinking, we just break in downstairs and start looking for the access to the secret room?"

Crossing a cornfield littered with fallen stalks is harder than it looks. I stumble and catch myself once. A minute later, he falls. "Are you okay?" I call.

"There's something else I want to say," he says from the ground below the line of broken stalks. "I'm just waiting for the shooting pains in my knee to subside."

I stop walking and wait. Eventually, he gets on all fours, and stands.

He looks over at me across the brown-green line of corn plants between us. "When I think about how much I've wanted to drink since I got out, it makes me scared that I might be a bad bet for you."

"Ah," I say, raising my eyebrows. "How much do you think about it?"

"Once an hour maybe."

I shrug. *Okay,* I think.

"And then all night when I can't fall asleep."

"That's about how much I think of my children. The ones that I've imagined." I don't know why I'm telling him this. It's as if I want to test him.

"Your children?" he says.

"The ones I would have had."

"Ah."

"Sometimes I pretend they're all here and alive. That we live together in our old house. Not with Paul, though. Just with me."

He looks away. "Do they have names?"

"Yes."

"And personalities?"

He seems to be prodding this, like a tongue in the hole a tooth once occupied. *How deep does this go?* "Yes," I say, and think: *This is it. He knows the truth now. I'm crazy with loneliness, comforted by the fantasy of being needed.* I wish I could tell him: In my mind, my kids are funny and disrespectful. They call me Blah Blah Ma. I deliver speeches they listen to, and afterward they say, *Get a life, Ma.* They think I'm equal parts funny and embarrassing. They love me, even though I have my shortcomings. I'm a terrible shopper, and every Christmas in our house (in my mind) is fraught with tears and disappointment. Once Shannon asked for Gap straight-leg jeans and I got her Lee bell-bottoms. Another time, Ben, my oldest and sweetest, privately returned what he'd gotten and kept the money. These are the children I've given myself—

real ones who haven't aged in the strict sense that other children do. I have kept little Charlotte perpetually six because she loves first grade and has a teacher who studies pioneer life by turning the classroom into a log cabin, like mine once did. I want to defend myself, tell Leo I don't harm anyone or insist that these fantasies are real. They are private, a small pleasure I keep to myself. One could certainly do worse, but looking at his face, I suspect this doesn't matter. I've made a mistake. Revealed too much. I seem sad to him, I fear. "Recently I've been starting to think I should help real children instead of putting so much mental energy into imaginary ones."

"Good idea, probably."

We start walking again. "In my own defense, I don't think inventing imaginary children is a terrible way to pass time in prison. Especially when it turns out you didn't do anything wrong."

"Good point." We've started walking again, him with a limp and me slightly ahead. "Imaginary love affairs are good, too," he says.

"Is that what ours was?"

"I don't know. You tell me. I was all ready to dive in and then we did such a good job at that picnic taking it to another level."

"I don't think that was all my fault."

"No, given the choice I would have spent my time talking to Wes as well. He's an attractive man. Except for the four-teeth thing, I'd call him a catch."

"At least he talked to me."

"And he stayed solid in school, right through the sixth grade."

"Why are we talking about this?"

He stops walking for a minute, forcing me to as well. "Because I don't want to be here if there are other people in the picture."

He studies me carefully—as if he knows about the one night I spent in the basement, sleeping alone in Roland's bed. As if he's been outside watching me. "There's no one else, Leo," I say simply. He narrows his eyes as if he's not sure whether to believe me. I don't know if we can manage this—get past all our fears and every defense we've put up. "Can we just get this over with, please?"

He holds out a hand. "After you."

No one is home. By the look of things through the window, wherever they've gone, they left in a hurry. Lights are still on, the radio is playing. Though the basement door is locked, the sliding-glass side door in the back is not. We slip downstairs and find the lab door that is indeed located behind a rolling bookshelf against a far wall. Even as I push the door open, my heart sinks. "Trish?" I say.

Nothing. She's not here.

It's a dark room piled with equipment and evidence of old work that hasn't been used in a long time. There are beakers in cardboard boxes along with their stands, and cathodes that look like thermometers with curly phone cords attached to one end. It's all a disappointment. Not only have we not found Trish, but what happened to Marianne's story? What about the breakthrough they were just on the cusp of? Leo runs a finger along the dust-covered metal counter.

He remembers cold fusion, and the hoopla around it. "God, it was so exciting when they first announced it. I remember my high school teacher saying everyone should remember where they were the first time they heard about it because our lives were never going to be the same."

By the look of it, this equipment hasn't been touched in months, possibly years. As if they gave up a long time ago, when Trish left their lives. Leo digs through a box, studies a sheet of paper attached to a mini-fridge still running in the corner. "I'm just surprised they did this with a family upstairs. It seems so dangerous. There was a guy in Santa Clara who died doing this."

"Really?"

"Yeah. The whole apparatus blew up in his face and he died from injuries. Afterward there were articles about this underground cold fusion network that had existed for years, funded by private companies without any oversight. It turned out they were investing because everyone wanted a piece of it if it ever got a patent."

I think about the way Marianne told the story. How the explosions were a good thing. A sign of life. She'd lost faith until they happened.

"Were there other explosions?"

As he asks this, I think of Barbara's words, *It all started with that accident.*

CHAPTER 33

I t's a glimmer on the periphery of my vision. Standing on the street again, as night falls, I see a movement in the corner of my eye. A shadow. Someone watching me. I know it's not dangerous. It's not going to hurt me. But it could. It's both things at once, like my father once was.

I remember this now.

How my father came into my room at night and lay down on the bed across from me. How he would talk to himself, assuming I was asleep. The first time it happened I held my breath and pretended to sleep. Some nights he came and said nothing at all. He simply wept, a keening sound that went on for hours. Only once, when I feared something terrible might happen, did I speak. "Dad?" I asked.

He stopped himself.

When my mother met my father he was head of the grounds crew at Cal State Northridge, where she worked as an administrator in the personnel department. She loved to tell the story—how he was planting a flower bed outside her office during a June heat wave; the students were gone and work was light. She handed him Dixie cups of water through her window and asked him the names of the flowers he was putting in. He told her each one in a voice so soft she had to lean out the window to hear. He was older than she was, from a conservative Catholic family. On their early dates, he brought her fresh flowers laid in shoe boxes lined with damp paper towels. They were lovely—tiny blue bonnets and pink bleeding hearts—too delicate for vases of flower arrangements, so she'd float them loose in a bowl of water and marvel at their unexpected, jeweled beauty.

He was quiet and a gentleman, she once told me, a man who worked with dirt and spoke with flowers.

With his daughters, he was shy and easily embarrassed by any talk he thought of as female. We knew him by his silences and the stories our mother told, full of sweetness.

I never saw him cry until his night wandering brought him into my bedroom, where he'd weep until the first bars of light streaked the sky and brought relief to us both.

Over time his episodes got worse. He started talking during them. "You girls need another father," he once said. "I can't do it anymore."

I tried to tune him out. I bought spongy earplugs that just made his words more distorted and frightening. Sometimes he'd blame my mother and say if she would just let him kill himself we'd all be better off. Other times he passed the blame around, to the doctors, his parents, the assholes on TV who thought the world owed them. He made no sense, though I understood in those terrible, endless nights that he spoke a truth. He couldn't go on like this.

I have other memories from my childhood: My father, smiling sweetly from our lawn, waving at the neighborhood blind boy. My father watching women's shows for hours: cooking, home decorating, soap operas. My father throwing a plate of birthday cake at my mother. Though the plate shattered spectacularly against the wall, the cake fell whole onto the counter.

The only time I ever saw my father cry during the day was on the phone with his brother, talking about the driving trips they once took with their father, a violent man they both worshipped inexplicably. "I just don't want to do that," he wept.

I didn't understand any of it. How could I hear him at night and turn back to my own life? Eventually I learned that cough syrup helped. When I gave it to him, he stayed quiet and fell back asleep quickly. Doing that I learned the world wasn't entirely out of my control. If adolescence is a time of constructing one's character, I built my own on absences and omissions.

Every night I waited for his arrival, and every night I pretended to sleep through it. By morning he'd be gone and never once did anyone in my family ever mention the unmade bed across from mine, the tear-stained pillow, what I did instead of sleeping for most of my adolescence.

Now I understand my father better. In the weeks before my trial, as we pieced my past together to build a defense, I realized he'd been sleepwalking that whole time, unaware of anything he was doing to me. It took my breath away to think about what *I* might have done, what *my* unconscious might have said to Paul.

When Paul was asked on the witness stand if he'd ever seen me sleepwalk, I honestly didn't know what his answer would be. It was something we'd never spoken of directly—*Have you seen me at night? Have I done or said things I shouldn't have?* I held my breath because I

wanted to hear, in front of all those people, about the ways I had revealed myself.

And then he surprised me. "No," he finally said. "I haven't."

At the time, I was enormously relieved. Though it weakened my
case, it meant I hadn't unconsciously terrorized him the way my father
had terrorized me. Now I remember more and I think I understand.
We were both looking at each other, and lying.

CHAPTER 34

That night Leo takes me for my first restaurant meal, burritos, which have gotten more complicated in our absence, and full of choices. It's possible to have bacon and eggs in a burrito now, or Caesar salad. "Oh, my," I say, staring at the menu, panicking for a moment. He almost touches my hand and stops. It feels as if we are trying to pass somehow, pretend like we are part of the world that moves much faster and is louder than either of us remembers. Like very old people, we ask too many questions at the counter until finally, food in hand, we move to a table where a girl next to us talks on a cell phone the whole time, loud enough that it's hard not to listen and try to figure out what the other person is saying.

Leo fills me in on what he's been doing in the six weeks since his release. His old job isn't an option anymore, nor is teaching in a public school with his record. The advice he's gotten is to establish himself in a new community and work slowly to build trusting relationships with people who might one day be in a position to hire. For now he's volunteering twice a week for ESL tutoring with newly immigrated adults.

In the five hours we've been together, except for him falling in the cornfield and me helping him back up, we haven't touched at all. I haven't blamed him for holding back. After my admission about my imaginary children, why should I hope for anything to happen? We both come with baggage and have futures that look, from where we're standing now, dim and uncertain. Touching, after what we've said to each other and everything we know, would be a lot. I told myself this when he asked if I'd like to go out for dinner. *Don't read anything into this. It's nice being friends.* It is nice having someone I can talk about my last twelve years with. We laugh about the coffee, the powdered toothpaste, the surprise of eating real vegetables again. "I'd forgotten that lettuce comes in other colors besides white," I say.

After we finish eating, he asks if I'm planning to live indefinitely with Finn and Bill. "More like a night or two probably," I say.

When we get outside, he turns, takes my hand, and says, "Good."

Before I can react, he pulls me toward him. Our bodies don't touch but hover inches apart. "Let's just get something clear," he says, touching my face with hands still rough with the calluses from work I spent six months in prison watching him do. "It's nice to see you again."

His breath in my ear, so close to my face, leaves me a little breathless. "It's good to see you, too."

"If you don't have anywhere to go after that, I have this place. It's not very comfortable and it's above a doughnut shop, so it smells like grease."

"*Yes,*" I whisper, and we move from anticipating the kiss to the kissing itself, slow and careful. He doesn't bury his tongue in my mouth or grind his hips against mine. There's no sense of rushing into the next part, no urgent reminders of how long it's been. He seems to feel the same way I always have about kissing: *Let's enjoy this part.* He touches my face, my shoulders. He slides his hands down so they're holding mine.

We stop kissing and start walking again. "Nice hair, by the way. Interesting choice."

"What, you hate it?"

"On the contrary. It's got a kind of Annie Lennox appeal."

When we get back to the block, a half dozen cars are parked in front of Marianne and Roland's. The house is lit up, the front door open, and music is playing.

They've found Trish.

She's home, safe and sound, and there's a celebratory chaos, neighbors stopping by. "She's fine! She's here!" Roland says when we walk in, and then, a little sheepishly, he has to explain. She's been in a Buddhist monastery forty miles away. As this news travels around the neighbors gathered in the room, an awkward uncertainty settles over the group. No one is quite sure what to say. Women I recognize from the Taser gun party clutch their purses and give Marianne a hug. *Better if they hadn't called the dogs,* people are thinking. *Would that the paper had waited a day or two to run it as a front-page missing-person story.* But in the end everyone is happy. "Just happy and relieved," one woman tells Leo, who stands by my side, letting the backs of our hands brush periodically.

Happy as they might be, I can sense what they're thinking. *Trish isn't well; she never has been. The family has problems.*

For her part, Trish seems quiet but fine, unaware of the commotion she caused. At one point, she tells everyone that she left so early in the morning because she was trying to get there by seven, before morning meditation started. "That's my favorite part and I didn't want to miss it. After that is chanting, which I don't like as much."

The police fiddle with their belts, Roland scratches his knee, and then, as if a rash were spreading, his ankle. Trish explains the blood in the bathroom with a shrug, saying she cut her leg a few days earlier and the scab opened up again when she was standing in the dark. She didn't think she was leaving that much of a mess, but she also hadn't turned on the light to look. Everyone nods uncomfortably and looks at the door. Before we leave, Trish asks if she can talk to me alone for a second.

"Of course," I say, following her up to her room.

When the door is closed, she turns around. "The blood wasn't just from a scab."

"I guessed that."

"I tried to kill myself that night. It was terrible. Like the walls were pressing in on me. All the secrets my parents kept."

I try to think of the most reassuring thing I can tell her. "They aren't doing it anymore. Keeping secrets, at least."

She looks up, surprised. "Do you know what my parents do?"

I nod.

"Did you know they're still at it? They've moved the lab but they're still doing it."

"They *are*?"

"That night I spent here, after you'd woken everyone up, my mom left the house. She went into the woods beyond the cornfield, and I followed her to this place that looks like a metal storage facility. It's hidden away. You can't see it from here. But that's where they've moved their lab." She tells me she knew about their cold fusion work for years before Marianne told her. It wasn't that hard to figure out. She knew it had to be something important because of the people who drove out to the house and talked to her parents in the basement. She listened in on a few conversations, went to the library and looked up some words. "You helped me once, I remember."

I did?

"I was looking for the difference between *fusion* and *fission*. You found it."

I shake my head in wonder. I remember the impossibly difficult reading she did as an eight-year-old. How we all assumed she was an odd child, a little troubled maybe, but no one considered this: Maybe she understood everything. Maybe she saw it all better than we did.

"My mother didn't talk to me about it until I was fifteen, and by then she'd decided it was never going to work. That the reaction they were getting was chemical, not nuclear, because they'd never found any measurable radiation. Low levels of radiation are almost impossible to measure, and are usually inaccurate when you do. She said if they'd really been achieving fusion all along, their own bodies would be a barometer. They would have had side effects and they didn't."

"What would the side effects have been?"

She looks away from me. "Cancer, infertility."

What is she trying to say?

"But it wouldn't necessarily affect everybody. It just increases your chances. What my mom never knew is that John and I found the lab when we were kids and we used to steal beakers and pour them on people's lawns. We thought it was funny, coloring the world brown in the middle of the night. Killing all the gardens, one plant at a time. I laughed about it until I was thirteen, and then I realized it wasn't funny. Our parents had no idea how powerful this stuff was."

When her mother finally told Trish about her work, she was convinced that her detractors were right all along. "She kept insisting that they hadn't created any significant energy. They'd stumbled on nothing more than a chemical reaction that wasn't nuclear. She said they could *drink* the stuff and be *fine*. I wanted her to know that there must have been low levels of radiation because we'd seen the evidence in everyone's gardens. But before he moved away, John made me promise I'd never tell anyone what we'd done. Then I read about the explosion in Santa Clara. A year later, there was another explosion, two people doing cold fusion in Japan. Everyone was trying to push the bar, get bigger reactions and higher temperatures. I was scared that my parents were going to kill themselves. That's when I poured out all of their work and called the Hazmat people. I wanted my parents to see what this stuff did. There were eighty beakers and I dumped all of them. In four hours, every blade of grass was dead."

I think about our gardens, and the mysterious battles we all waged to defend our lawns and save our plants. Were we all out there digging in dirt that was killing our babies? Or us? I put together the pieces of the timeline in my mind. This must have all happened after my last miscarriage, when I was told to stop trying. When I was here but I wasn't, sitting alone in my darkened house oblivious to any crisis beyond my own. This was also when Marianne arranged our final meeting and brought Gary in. That must have been Trish's last night at home. After that, she moved out.

Then something else occurs to me.

"What happened to the cat?"

"He came over while I was dumping the stuff out and drank some of the water. I knew I should push him away and I didn't. My mom liked the cat and I wanted her to *see*. She'd said it wasn't harmful, that it wasn't even working, and I wanted her to see . . ." Trish is crying now. "I wanted the cat to get sick so I could say, Look, Mom. *Look*. It *does* work."

"Did you?"

"No. I ran away that night and when I saw them again I was pretty messed up. They put me in the hospital and I didn't come home again until after I'd had my baby."

How could I forget? She was pregnant during all this. "What happened with your baby?"

"He was okay. I've seen him a couple of times."

It's impossible to imagine. "How is he?"

"He's twelve now. His mother writes me letters on his birthday. I could see him more if I wanted to but I don't." She shakes her head. "It's hard."

Henry, my youngest, would be twelve, too, though I've kept him five years old in my mind because I want someone who still needs uncomplicated comforts: hot dog dinners and sleeping in my bed with me. It's frightening to imagine meeting a twelve-year-old boy who is five in my mind.

I've always tried not to idealize my imaginary children too much. The key to parenting, I believe, isn't avoiding problems but handling them when they arise. I try to be as matter-of-fact as possible. I tell them the truth, even the parts that are hard for me to talk about: *I was never in love with your father the way parents are meant to be, though I always liked and respected him very much. He is a good and decent man,* I tell them, *but love is harder to define. I've learned this much: Love has more to do with the person you become in its presence than it does with anything else. You must always be yourself, honest and true. I was never that with your father, which isn't his fault. I didn't understand what it meant until I felt the other, the relief of being wholly straightforward.*

I go over to the bed where Trish is sitting, shoulders slumped, hair hanging down over her face as if her body has lost its ability to hold itself up. "You were brave about a lot of things, Trish. Braver than the rest of us."

"I don't think my parents see it that way."

I fear she might be right that her single act of validation and defi-ance has probably been misread all these years. I suspect she meant to say, *Look, Mom, it works. Now stop.* I don't think she meant to destroy a lifetime of work. Nor did she mean to hurt anyone or their pets. And yet that's what happened.

CHAPTER 35

Leo and I sit on two folding chairs he's set up in Finn and Bill's backyard, drinking iced teas. It's evening but the sky is still purple, bright with the reflected glow of distant city lights. I've explained as much as I can to him, what I've learned about my past over the last three days. All of us carried secrets inside of us, ticking like bombs waiting to detonate. We isolated ourselves, retreated too much, everyone terrified of getting caught in lies.

"So who did it? Who killed Linda Sue?" He takes my hand and holds it flat, between his.

When I called Jeremy to tell him that Trish was back, he updated me on the status of the testing. So far, three more names had been cleared: Marianne, Roland, and Trish Rashke. "They may know more than they're telling us, but their hair wasn't in her blood, nor was their skin under her fingernails."

I'm not surprised. Now I understand that Trish would never have gone back to Linda Sue's that night. If Marianne or Roland had, Linda Sue wouldn't have opened her door and offered them tea.

This is the piece that has never made sense: She invited the person in. She was happy to see him or her, which wouldn't have been true of the other women on the block—Helen or Barbara or Kim. "They try too hard," she once told me. "Have you ever noticed how they always want to make suggestions?"

It was true, they did do that because we all did: *You should try seltzer and salt on red wine stains. Have you heard about putting eggshells on rosebushes?* Just trying to help, we thought.

This was a few weeks before her death, when I'd started to see our world differently and seek out Linda Sue more. During that time, I began noticing things about her. She talked to the mailman, Walt, who the rest of us had never acknowledged beyond the Christmas cards we gave him every year. Sometimes he stood on her porch for ten minutes, their laughter so loud I could hear it across the street. She also had a roofing crew there once and I watched them eat lunch, gathered in a circle on her porch while she joined them to smoke. She enjoyed men's company, she told me. "It doesn't mean I want to sleep with them. It means they're less complicated than women."

I remember something else she said: "These neighborhoods are built for women, because all of us like looking in mirrors."

I laughed and then saw she wasn't joking. She started to say more—to explain, perhaps—and then stopped herself. For years I wondered what she was about to tell me. *This is why I own no mirrors at all, why I broke them all and glued the pieces to my clothes.* Was this why we all hovered near her and then stood back? Because we wanted to see ourselves, to catch a reflection of different possibilities? Linda Sue couldn't have been killed by a woman. We were too scared of her to get close enough.

No—it was a man who knocked that night. One she saw as harmless, maybe Walt the mailman, or one of her roofer friends. She'd had a long day full of fights she didn't resolve and dramas she probably didn't understand. First Trish, then me, then Roland and Marianne, and somewhere in there Geoffrey came over, bearing his necklace. Whoever knocked late must have seemed innocuous and simple—someone who wanted nothing from her but to pass a bit of time.

"We should go inside," Leo says.

We are spending tonight here in Finn and Bill's guest room and tomorrow we will go to Leo's apartment in West Hartford. I have told him I am not going to move in with him yet. That we need to take our time with this, which he understands. Standing here, though, the night alive with the cicadas' song, I see something, as if it's been there all along—in some corner of my brain: Our garden with no pet fence, no toys, nothing but the patchy grass and a person standing on it.

It's just a flash, a splinter of memory, but I know in that instant who I'm seeing.

CHAPTER 36

"Paul," I say when he answers the door. I've asked Leo to wait in the car but keep an eye on us and come in if it looks like I'm in trouble. "I need you to tell me what happened."

He nods and steps aside, looking over my shoulder at Leo in the car. "I think I remember more," I say, which is only partially true. My memories are images, shadowy and indistinct. "You followed me outside that night, didn't you?"

"I didn't follow you," he says. "I woke up and you weren't there. I went out to find you. I thought maybe you'd gone back to Linda Sue's house. I saw her lights on so I went over and knocked on her door."

This must have been earlier in the evening when I was over at Roland's. "Linda Sue said she hadn't seen you but she asked if I'd mind coming in and sitting up with her for a while. She said she'd just had a terrible evening and needed some company."

I can picture all of this. Paul was always amenable. He liked being needed, craved it even. "What happened when you went inside?"

"She was upset about Geoffrey. He'd been over to her house, proposing marriage and she wasn't sure what to do. She didn't think she was in love with him."

I think about the time when Paul and I stood on her lawn and watched Geoffrey standing behind her, that moment of intimacy that took our breath away. How could she not have loved him? Neither of us can imagine it.

"She called him a fake. She said she was sick of people pretending to be something they weren't."

But we all did that. I think about Helen with her faux finishing business, painting new chairs to look old. About Marianne hiding a career—and her brain and intelligence—for twenty years, believing that if it showed, people would come after her. Did Linda Sue die because she wouldn't let us all keep up our illusions?

"Did that make you mad?"

"No. I felt bad for Geoffrey. I knew he was in love with her—"

Not once in our marriage did I ever see Paul raise a hand in anger. Yes, I saw him be surprisingly sarcastic about people at work. I saw him retreat at times, into his own world. I saw flashes of what I suppose now was anger though I used to think of it as something else: an impulse to express what could never be said aloud. When he stood beside me peering in through Linda Sue's window, when he drove, mute with grief, home from the doctor. I married him because I understood those silences. Or I thought I did, anyway.

"Linda Sue invited me upstairs to show me something. I don't know why I followed her. I wanted to see what her secret was, why everyone was so fascinated by her." His voice cracks and it's hard to understand him though I think I know what he's not saying: *I wanted to see why*

Geoffrey picked her. "I wanted—" It's happening again, his words breaking off, his eyes focused on something within. "Then she turned on the light and I saw the nursery."

All this time, I thought I understood him but why didn't I see this? A man can feel this loss as much as a woman.

"I assumed she was pregnant, but then she told me no, Trish was. That they'd made all the arrangements for her to adopt it. She said she'd been on the phone that morning with a lawyer and it was all set." He shakes his head as if, after all this time, he still can't fathom the injustice of Trish picking such a woman to mother her child. "I didn't mean to hurt her. It was an accident."

Beating her with a lock? Crushing her skull? "Tell the truth, Paul. It's better."

"I just kept thinking it wasn't *fair.* When we were right here and so ready for it."

I remember during our one pregnancy that made it past the first trimester, we once let ourselves spend a Saturday afternoon shopping for cribs. I can still see Paul: how serious he was the whole time, pressing each mattress with his hand, testing the railings. He spent three hours in the store and two more at home, reading *Consumer Reports.* "It's our most important purchase," he said when I tried to make a joke, something about it being *just a crib.* Somewhere deep inside of me I must have understood then what this said about Paul and about our marriage. In picking me, he'd made a choice. He'd denied one part of himself because he wanted this other thing even more: to be a father. Maybe I shouldn't have been so surprised. He'd been parented in a confusing mixture of good intentions and self-absorption by a mother who gave and withdrew her love. He wanted what I did: the chance to do it over, right this time.

He shakes his head now. "I just envied her. That's all."

I don't tell him we all did. Nor do I tell him it's going to be all right. I know too well it won't be. And then something else occurs to me: Is it possible I've known this all along? That I cleaned up twelve years ago not for one friend but for another?

"When I got home that night you still weren't there, so I showered and waited. When you finally got home, I told you what happened."

He did?

"You thought of the idea. You said, let me do this. Let me do this my way."

I don't remember saying this but I think about my father and the nights when he put me through one unwelcome revelation after another. I never told anyone because this was what I learned from my parents—that love meant keeping such silences.

"I never believed you'd get convicted," Paul says. "Everyone said there was no way. Geoffrey promised me it wouldn't happen."

"And you believed him?"

He nods. I shouldn't blame him, I know. We all believed Geoffrey. "Did he know the truth?"

"He might have suspected it. I don't know. He moved away so soon after that I wondered sometimes."

How has he done this? How has he lived with himself all these years? Maybe this is the answer: He hasn't. "Did you write the cat letter?"

He nods. "For so long I looked for an explanation that wouldn't implicate either one of us. I wanted to be here, to take care of you when you got out."

Absurd logic, though I recognize it.

"Then I finally realized, maybe you weren't consciously making this decision anymore. I thought you should have a choice. That if you could get out, you should be able to."

"But why the cat?"

He looks up, surprised, as if I should know this. "That's what made me so mad. When I followed Linda Sue upstairs, she came out of the bedroom holding this cat. That's what she wanted to show me. She said it was about to die and she asked me to take it over to Trish before it did because she didn't want a dead cat on her hands. My seeing the nursery, hearing about the baby, all that was an afterthought."

"What did you do?"

"I told her she should take the cat to the vet. She said she didn't have the money and it wasn't hers so why should she pay for it. I couldn't believe it. Here she was, about to get a baby, but she wouldn't take care of an animal that was *dying* . . ."

No wonder he blew up. I try to imagine all of this. The roar behind the silence on our street that night.

"What happened?"

"I lunged at her. I thought I was getting the cat, but I knocked her over. I didn't think we were fighting but then she started kicking me."

I don't know if it's better to hear this or not. I see the look on his face, rage buried under a vacant expression.

"I wasn't thinking about anything but I fought back. I grabbed her neck. Somewhere in there, I pushed her and she fell down the stairs."

I think about the blood spatter. How she must have still been alive after she fell, coughing up evidence onto the wall. He must remember this part, but he doesn't speak of it. It's too much, even now, to remember all of it.

"After it was over, I took the cat over to Trish," he says. "It was still alive at that point and I went in through the basement, walked up the stairs while Marianne and Roland sat in the living room, arguing about something. I didn't want to deal with them or talk to anyone, I just wanted to do the right thing by this cat. Linda Sue told me to bring it to Trish, and I did."

I can hardly believe what this suggests: He left a dying woman to help a dying cat?

"I wanted to see her. Ask about the baby."

In the confusion of that night did he really think that it was possible to eliminate Linda Sue and have us step in? "What did she say?"

"She was asleep." He is weeping now, his head bent, his shoulders heaving. He makes no sound beyond a wheezy breathing. I realize, after all these years, I've never seen Paul cry before. "I didn't wake her up. I put the cat in her bed and I left."

I don't know exactly what's making him cry. Whether it's his confession or his belief that if he'd done things differently, we might still have gotten Trish's baby.

I understand this much: I need to get out of here as quickly as possible. I know enough now. I know that Paul will have to go on trial and I'll have to testify about my collusion. I'll have to explain how I once looked at my mother and thought *I never want to live this way,* then realized, as an adult, *my God, I do*. For fifteen years, my mother lived in the prison of my father's unhappiness. *This is what we do,* my mother's life said. *We find ourselves in the sacrifices we make.*

I think about *Middlemarch*, the book I loved so much that I made Geoffrey read it, too, a testimonial to the sacrifice a wife can make pointlessly for an undeserving husband. Did I weep when I read it because I saw my life and my future in that story?

No, I think, it's more complicated than that. Paul was not undeserving just as I am not innocent. We both needed the reassurance of having another person wholly dependant on us. I had played that role for him in my bad spells and then, for a time, we switched.

I don't remember consciously confessing to a crime I knew Paul had committed but I do remember the feeling, through all those babies lost, of waiting to be needed like this by somebody else. I remember thinking—and this hardly makes sense—*At last, here's my chance.*

How do I say this? Paul is right.

We both wanted a child and he'd become mine. When I get back out to the car Leo takes my hand. "Everything okay?"

"Not exactly," I say. "But it will be." I squeeze his hand as he drives slowly out of the condominium complex where all the exteriors are painted the same earth color, tan with the same maroon doors, like open mouths issuing the same silent scream, all with the same rhododendron bush to the side, growing upward as if reaching for the window to cover what they don't want anyone to see.

"Let's go," Leo says softly.

And we do.

ACKNOWLEDGMENTS

If *Neighborhood Watch* is a book about looking below the surfaces we all construct, I am especially grateful to the friends and early readers who helped me do just that with this story: Melinda Reid, Diane WoodBrown, Mike Paterniti, Katie and Bill McGovern, Liz Van Hoose, Jessica Almon, and Laura Tisdel. And for his enthusiastic interest in reading multiple drafts, my dear brother, Monty, deserves a special nod, as does Mike Floquet, who also read many versions and came up with some of the best ideas in here.

Huge thanks to Eric Simonoff for his grace and good cheer through all matters literary and financial and Molly Stern who remains so very smart and funny as she shepherded this book to its strongest incarnation. Thanks to all at Viking for feedback and support: Hal Fessenden, Nancy Sheppard, Clare Ferraro, and Louise Braverman.

And last but not least, all my love to the threesome who keep me going: Ethan, Charlie, and Henry!